Stare At The Sea

Baylea A. Osborn

Illustrations Copyright © 2017 Rebecca Ladish, Kaylee Abele, Jayme Osborn
Cover design Copyright © 2016 Phillip Ortiz

Printed in the United States of America

First Printing, 2017

ISBN-13: 978-1541047075
ISBN-10: 1541047079

Dedicated to Talia,
You are like the sea- beautiful and strong.

Acknowledgments

Thank you to everyone who read, edited and supported this book!

To Faith and Boze; my dream team. Hopefully one day I'll find a way to repay you guys for all you have done for me, because words are insufficient and I have no children to give you.

To my sistie; I dedicate this book to you in honor of all the stories and dreams we have shared in the past. Thank you for being a forever in my life.

To Janessa, Anna, and mom; you've been there since book one and I can't imagine better people to have on my writing team for the rest of my life.

To Demetrius and dad; thanks for proving that my books aren't just for girls. Bonus points that I sometimes make you cry.

To Leanne and Sydney; the love and support I have received from you both is unbelievable. Never stop telling stories. *"If I could dance//here forever..."*

To Kris; who has done nothing but support and promote every single book I share!

To Monica, Erin, Benny, Sarah, Kalina, and **Emily** for answering my questions and giving me feedback on everything from ballet, to commas, to the UK, to how to set up a preorder. You made research delightful and sweet!

To Phillip, Kaylee, Rebecca, and **Jayme** for your artistic talent. I'm so happy that I get to share your work with the world. Thank you for helping me tell this story!

Also:

To my Alex, Peter, and Chloes; you're my family and my home, my favorite characters in my favorite stories. I [will always] love you with all of my heart.
Dima entouma f'9elbi.

To my Sarah and Martins; my MacSweeney family, the Davids, those cool kids I used to hangout with on the playground at night, Bus #5. Each of you has a piece of my heart and I am forever thankful to have you in my life.

To my trio: you keep me grounded, you keep me reaching, you keep me steady.
all my love.

To the dancers in my life; Thank you for bringing beauty into the world and sharing it with us. I hope this story honors you and dancers everywhere.

To The One who created the sea, holds it in His hands, and is bigger than all my pain; Let this story be what You dreamed it would be when You put it on my heart.
I love You.

Table of Contents

-Chapter 1-

A Good Start

The train rumbled down the track. Fog shrouded the scenery on the other side of the window as it rushed past in a blur of gray and green. The sound of the tracks slipping steadily under the wheels vibrated in the air. A lone passenger sat with her eyes closed and forehead pressed against the window.

"How do you spell your name?"

A memory tugged on the young woman's thoughts, begging for attention. She could see her second grade teacher at the blackboard, a crease in her forehead as she tried, and failed, several times to pronounce her name correctly. The little girl in the memory tried to hide her flaming red cheeks, embarrassed and on the verge of tears.

"It's okay! I just want to say it right!" Mrs. Johnson waved the chalk in her direction again. *"Do you know how to spell it?"*

The little girl dragged her feet as she walked slowly from her seat to the large, dusty blackboard. She could hear every cough and whisper of her classmates behind her. They would make fun of her, she knew; everyone did. They had already started when the teacher called her "Eva" three times in a row and she shook her head no at each attempt. Maybe she should have just pretended...

"Go ahead, dear."

Chalk in hand, the little girl pressed it uncertainly against the smooth surface. It was deafeningly loud in her ears as she pressed the white stick against the black wall. Slowly the letters lined up in a row, a shaky assembly of four vowels and one consonant.

A-O-I-F-E.

"How do you say your name?" asked Mrs. Johnson.

"EE-fa," the girl whispered.

The teacher smiled at her and gave the name on the board a second glance, a furrow of consternation growing between her eyebrows. Little Aoife's eyes darted down to her feet; her new school shoes looked unfamiliar and strange on the wooden floor. She had asked for the blue ones, but the purple ones with the cats on them had been on sale. They were just as good, she had been told.

"I think that's a beautiful name," said Mrs. Johnson. *"Do you know where your name comes from?"*

Of course she did. Her mom had named her after her grandma, a woman the young child would never meet. The stories she was told about her late grandmother were exciting and grand, but Aoife never felt grand or exciting in moments like these. She felt small. Embarrassed. Stupid.

"It's not you who's stupid, Aoife," said her father with a pipe between his teeth. *"It's them for being so narrow-minded and thinking that everyone should have American names."*

She never corrected him to tell him that there were two Juans, one Amina and even a boy named Ishmael in her class. It was just that all of those names were spelled the way they sounded and hers was not. When they were lined up alphabetically, people would snicker as she stood with the A's.

Aoife opened her eyes and stared out the train window. Her hands lay motionless on her lap, her palms slanted up towards the ceiling and her fingers curved gracefully. It was a habit that accompanied her everywhere. The window reflected her weary face back to her, showing her the way exhaustion had painted its dark circles under her grey-blue eyes. Her mother had always said that her eyes were the same color as the sea on a cloudy day.

"How do you say your name?" Once again, the question echoed through her mind and Aoife shifted in her seat.

Maybe in the UK people would find her name a bit more common. She knew her name was Irish, but surely the close proximity of England to Ireland would make it easier. If not, she could always say her name was Eva and forget about the whole name thing entirely. She didn't want to, though. Her name was her only connection to her mother these days.

The man sitting a few rows ahead of Aoife drummed his fingers loudly against the surface of his shiny, black briefcase. She licked her chapped lips and kept herself from sighing loudly. For the last twenty-four hours she had been surrounded by people and noise, engines and wheels, but she was almost to her destination, almost to a place where she could stand still and just breathe. Her hands smoothed the frizzy braid that hung over her shoulder before she leaned back against the seat. Her eyes slipped shut and she dozed off.

The feeling of falling woke Aoife with a gasp. She caught herself from tumbling out of her seat as the train pulled to a stop. Her brain was clouded as she struggled to remember where she was and where she was going. She saw the station roll into view through the window and saw the sign for *Brighton.* Then she remembered.

The wheels shuddered to a stop and the doors opened, letting off the crowds of people. Aoife blinked her sleepy eyes before she grabbed her worn-out suitcase. She kept her backpack on one shoulder with one hand while she pulled her suitcase with the other. Her feet hit the platform and she paused, only for a second, before a man behind her shouted and a woman babbling into her cellphone brushed past her on the right. Aoife didn't have a chance to find her bearings before she was pushed along with the crowd. Three teenage girls paused in front of her to take a selfie. Aoife rolled her eyes before she walked around them.

Exiting the train station put Aoife in the full strength of the sun. Its rays picked up the golden highlights of her hair and made the dirty blonde color almost glow. She squinted up at the cloudless blue expanse above her, wishing she had her sunglasses on the top of her head instead of in her backpack. Someone stepped on her foot and she stumbled back, knocking into a trashcan that was just out of sight to her left. Irritation bubbled up inside of her. Why couldn't people just watch where they were going? She looked down to find a smear of white dust on her black leggings. She hugged her cream-colored sweater around her more tightly and struggled to maintain her balance. Brighton wasn't a big city, but it was a popular destination.

Like the people in New York were any better than this, Aoife said to herself as she narrowly missed being smashed into by a group of rowdy young men coming into town for a party, probably. All she wanted was a cold glass of water and to lie down on a bed, any bed, and sleep for hours. She took in a deep breath to calm herself and...

There it was; the smell of the sea. She could smell the salt and the fresh breeze. Her heart pounded happily in her chest; it was so close. She felt her mouth turning up into a smile as everything around her disappeared except for that smell. She pictured it in her mind; big and wild and glistening in the sun, there to remind her that she was going to be okay.

"Whoops! Watch out!" A young woman with chewing gum between her teeth startled Aoife from her thoughts when she tripped over Aoife's suitcase. The stranger looked to be about Aoife's age and her accent proved her a local of Great Britain. "Sorry."

"Oh, no, I'm sorry." Aoife bent over to move her case closer to her feet. "I shouldn't have left it in the middle of everything."

"You're not from around here!" The girl sounded surprised. "You here for holiday?"

"No, uh, I'm, uh." Aoife cleared her throat. "I'm moving here."

"That's cool!" The stranger studied her face, intrigued.

"Actually, uh, do you know where this is?" Aoife reached into the pocket of her sweater and pulled out the piece of paper that had been touched, smoothed and stared at over a hundred times in the past three days. "I was told it was easy to find."

"Yeah, right down near my mum's. Little place near the beach. We can share a taxi if you'd like."

"Sure." Aoife swallowed hard and gratefully took the paper back into her hand. She had the address memorized, just in case, but it felt like her ticket into her new life. Like if she lost it, she would be denied access into everything she was desperately hoping for.

"I'm Hattie, by the way." She held out her hand with another smile.

"Aoife." Hattie's hand was smooth in her own. She had kind eyes and a faint smell of roses and cigarettes on her Nirvana t-shirt.

"Irish name." Hattie's grin grew. "Welcome, Aoife. You'll love Brighton."

"Thank you." Aoife breathed easily. Her first introduction was more than she could have ever hoped for.

Hattie chatted amiably as they made the twenty-minute drive through traffic to the neighborhood where Aoife's new apartment was waiting for her. Hattie offered to help her up to the place, but Aoife declined. All she had was her suitcase and backpack, nothing she hadn't been able to handle in the twenty-four hours since she started her travels.

"Thanks for sharing a ride with me." Aoife smiled before shutting the door of the taxi and stepping back from the vehicle. She waved until they turned the corner and she was left standing on the sidewalk. With a glint of determination in her eye, the girl gathered her bags and walked up to the building.

It was maybe four or five stories tall, each level with windows facing the sea. Aoife paused to listen. The waves on the rocky beach were like music to her ears and she wanted to drop everything and dance along with the rhythm. She didn't, though. Not yet.

Donna Brixton was the landlady and she smiled widely at Aoife when she answered the buzz at the door. She ushered her all the way up to the top floor where the air was musty and the heat crowded against you like an overbearing instructor. Aoife waited for Donna to unlock the door and let them into the one-roomed flat with a window facing the beach.

That window was all Aoife cared about. She left her bags by the bed and walked over to see the full view. There it was; the sea. Her heart pounded inside of her chest and she smiled softly, her fingertips reaching for the window to brush against the glass. The waves crashed over a patch of beach and Aoife could almost feel the salty spray against her face.

9

"...strictly forbidden, or the entire building will be at risk of catching on fire." Donna's voice finally broke through to Aoife. The girl looked over her shoulder and saw the landlady staring at her expectantly. She hadn't even realized Ms. Brixton was speaking. "Is everything all right? You fancy the view?"

"Oh yes, very much." Aoife turned then. "It's perfect."

"Well, like I said, that corner of the roof leaks and the chair there can't hold more than someone your size, and we're not sure if the new pipe under the sink leaks or not, but at least you'll be warm in the summer and you have the sea."

"Thank you, Ms. Brixton."

"Just give me a ring if you need anything. My number is there on the table."

The door shut behind Donna and Aoife finally looked around. It wasn't much. In fact, besides the bed against the far wall and the little table and chair by the corner kitchenette, there was nothing else in the room. The floors were wooden and dusty. Aoife spotted a door near the bed that she assumed was either a closet or the bathroom. Maybe both? she thought as she realized there were no other doors.

Aoife didn't have a lot of clothes, but she would need a dresser of some sort to hold her things. She opened the door and saw a toilet, a sink, and a shower head without a curtain around it. At least there was a drain. As long as that worked, it wouldn't be too bad. She would have to keep her toilet paper someplace else when she was showering, though.

There was a beep from Aoife's pocket and she pulled out her phone in time to see the screen go black. It had lasted her entire trip, it deserved a break after all the traveling. She tossed it lightly onto the bed and noticed the patchwork quilt and white sheets that made it up. There was only one pillow on the double bed. It was fine, though; she only needed one.

Aoife hesitated before slipping off her shoes. This was her home now, but she still felt like she was in a strange place that required her to maintain her appearance. She shook her head at herself and left her shoes by the end of the bed. She could hear her feet as they brushed against the floor while she made her way over to the kitchenette in the corner. The faucet squeaked when she struggled to turn on the tap. She let it run for thirty seconds, but there was still no hot water when she gave up and twisted it off again. The fridge was empty, just like her stomach.

Well, this is it. This is my new home. Aoife turned in a complete circle. That was when she saw it; a rusty old bicycle leaning against the wall behind the door. She hoped it was in good enough condition to get her to and from the shops and her job.

That was when Aoife let herself entertain the idea of what her job as a caretaker of an elderly woman would look like. She didn't know Bonnie Wilcox, but she knew Genny Wilcox. That was how she had this apartment, the bicycle, the job... everything was because of Genny.

"It will be a good start for you, Eef," Genny had said with conviction when Aoife had mumbled and shrugged.

A good start. Aoife went back to the window and let the words roll around in her mind. They sounded good. They felt good.

The sea met the blue of the sky and stretched on forever as Aoife stared, her eyes growing tired and her body beginning to feel weighed down. She needed sleep. She needed food and a shower and furniture in her new home, but sleep won. She turned and tripped over her shoes at the end of the bed before falling on top of the covers. She forced herself to stand up and pull the covers back before allowing herself to drift off. Slipping her sweater from her shoulders, she draped it over the back of the rickety chair in the middle of the room. She pulled the hair-tie from the end of her braid and combed her fingers through, letting her hair fall down around her face.

A good start, she thought one more time as she slid under the covers and pulled the pillow down to reach her head. *This is a good start.*

The moon was high in the sky when Aoife woke up thirsty and hungry. She rubbed at her eyes, flopping onto her back and hearing the bed frame squeak with her weight. It took a minute before she could remember where she was and what had happened. She stretched her arms over her head and pointed her toes as she yawned, her mouth opening as wide as it could. She exhaled deeply, still tired and groggy, but too uncomfortable to fall back asleep instantly. Maybe she should get up and get a drink. Her hands patted the bed for her phone before she remembered it had died. There was no way to tell time apart from the moonlight reflecting on the sea.

Everything was quiet. She could hear the faint crashing of water against the rocks through the window. Aoife focused on the sound and let her breathing slow again. The heaviness of her eyelids pulled them down until she was sleeping once more.

The sky was bright and blue when Aoife next opened her eyes. Her body was telling her it was still time to sleep, but there was nothing between her and the sun except a single pane of glass. Hunger drove her from her bed and she placed her feet on the floor. The first thing she did was find her phone charger and plug it into the wall with the outlet adapter. The screen was still black when she decided to finish getting ready for the day. After a slow shower and digging through her suitcase for something to wear, she put her sunglasses on and stared at the bicycle in the corner.

Aoife knew how funny it would look to anyone who saw her struggling down the stairs with the bike, the strap of her purse crossed over her chest. She wasn't considered tall, barely even reaching the average height of five feet and five inches, but her body was filled with muscles and strength built from years and years of dance. Two decades, really. Still, she was relieved when she saw the last flight of stairs and knew she was almost to the bottom.

With her phone in her hand chirping out directions to a nearby grocery store, Aoife settled herself on the seat and put her feet on the pedals. For a second, she thought maybe it wouldn't work, but the chain groaned into action and the wheels began to turn.

A good start. Aoife smiled as she rode down the street.

There were people walking down the sidewalk, cars driving past, windows open to let out the murmur of television and radio talk shows. Little by little, the sound of the sea was swallowed up, and Aoife had to continue away from the beach. The sun was beating against her shoulders through her white, long-sleeved shirt, drying her ponytail and warming her through her skin until she was sweating. She parked her bike with cheeks red from exertion. It wasn't until that moment that she realized she didn't have a bike lock.

Oh well. Not like anyone would want to steal a rusted-out old bike anyway.

And she was right. For two days, Aoife traveled the streets of Brighton, leaving her bike outside of stores, cafes and shopping centers. Every time, it was right where she had left it. Her fridge filled up and her body's clock made the switch to the new time zone, helping her feel more at home. The only thing left to do to settle in was to find something to hold her clothes. As it was, she had spread them across the tiny table in the middle of the apartment, stringing her hanging clothes along the empty curtain rod. It wasn't a good solution as the sunlight would fade the colors if she kept them there for long.

She stood by the window and stared at the sea as she ate a strawberry jam sandwich. The window was open and she could hear the sound of the water mixed with the noise of traffic and seagulls. Her eyes followed the motion of the waves as she chewed and savored the taste of sweetness against her tongue. It was better than her breakfast of scrambled eggs without any salt or pepper from that morning. That reminded her...

Aoife finished her sandwich and left her apartment, locking it behind her. Ms. Brixton said she could keep her bike at the bottom of the stairs, as long as the other tenants didn't complain. So far no one had said anything about it, or about anything, actually. She saw one family go into the third-level apartment, but they were too busy to notice her and introduce themselves. The two sisters on the first level were old and apparently deaf as Aoife had practically shouted hello to them when they were on the stairs the first morning and neither of them turned around to acknowledge her greeting.

There was a shop up the street Aoife had noticed the day before, so she decided to walk. That way, if she did buy something, she wouldn't have to balance it on the handlebars. The cute little store was called *Pop's Shop* and based on what she could see through the window, Aoife assumed it sold furniture and knick-knacks. Perhaps they would have something she could use as a dresser or a closet.

A bell tinkled over her head when she pushed the door open and stepped inside. It was cool in there, the air conditioning still blasting into the establishment despite the fact that summer was practically over. There was a man with the longest arms and legs Aoife had ever seen perched on the edge of the counter. His head was bent over a newspaper, his eyes quickly scanning a row of words before he flicked the page over. He glanced up at the sound of the bell and flashed Aoife a tired smile.

"Welcome, hey." His thick accent made Aoife smile.

"Thanks," said Aoife in return, crossing her arms across her chest to keep herself from touching anything that could break.

Just as Aoife had suspected, *Pop's Shop* was filled with knick-knacks and odd bits of furniture. She saw cupboards, bedside tables, ceramics, antique silverware sets and cushions. Quilts lined one whole wall and Aoife eyed them with interest. She wasn't sure how long she would last during a winter by the sea with only one quilt on her bed.

"Hello!" a cheery voice called out from behind her.

"Hi." Aoife turned to see a young woman about her age come out of the back room, a huge smile on her face that made her blue eyes dance and sparkle. "Just looking."

"What are you looking for? We just got in a load of the most cozy cushions ever!" The girl led Aoife back to a corner she hadn't reached yet. "They are so soft! Here, try one. Aren't they the most cozy thing you've ever felt in your whole life?"

Her enthusiasm was contagious and Aoife rubbed the cushion. The girl wasn't lying; it was soft and inviting.

"I have about three of them back at mine now, I keep buying them because they are just so cozy." A high, glittering laugh came from the young woman's mouth as she spoke. "We have some in green in the back if you want that color."

"Oh, thank you." Aoife smiled and handed the cushion back to the shop lady. "I'm not here for pillows or cushions, though, unless you can store your clothes in them."

"Wouldn't that be a great invention!" Again, the laughter rang out and brightened the entire store. "But no, these ones are only good for cozying up with on the sofa or in bed."

"Maybe after I have the rest of my apartment furnished I'll buy one."

"Yeah! I'll set a couple aside for you!"

"Oh, no, you..." Aoife was about to tell the woman she didn't need that when the tall man from the counter appeared in view.

"Sarah, are you trying to sell more cushions? Leave the poor people alone!" The exasperated tone in his voice was cushioned with fondness as he shook his head. Apparently Aoife wasn't the only person to fall prey to Sarah's sales tactics.

"But everyone needs cozy cushions, Martin! Even you have them at your house! You love them!" Sarah protested as she picked out one blue cushion and one cream-colored one and tucked them under her arm.

"I do love them, but not everyone who comes in are here to buy cushions."

"Only because they've not seen them, yet. I'm determined to get at least one in every single home here before Christmas." Sarah's smile was still warming the entire shop as she disappeared into the back with the two cushions that Aoife could only imagine were for her.

"Sorry about that," apologized Martin. "When she gets obsessed with something, that's all she can think about."

"They are very cozy." Aoife felt like she hadn't properly spoken to people in days.

"I'm Martin, by the way." The young man held out his hand, his long fingers gripping Aoife's firmly as they greeted one another.

"Aoife." There was a curl of nervousness in her stomach as she said her name.

"Oh! What a lovely name!" The green in Martin's eyes lit up. "I've always loved that name!"

"What name?" asked Sarah, emerging from the back, her eyes wide at the thought of having missed anything.

"Aoife. This is Aoife." Martin let go of Aoife's hand as he pointed at his co-worker. "And this is Sarah."

"It's very nice to meet you both." Warmth spread across Aoife's chest as she took in the friendly faces of the two strangers in front of her.

"Yeah, same!" Sarah's smile burst forth. "Now, you were saying you needed something for your clothes?"

"Like a wardrobe?" asked Martin, his eyes roaming around the store.

It was comical to see Sarah standing next to him, the top of her head not even reaching his shoulder because of the height difference. Aoife tried to see if there was a family resemblance, but beyond the happy expressions on their faces and their dark chocolate-colored hair, their features didn't match. They led her back to the front of the store and stood her in front of a handsome piece of furniture she could barely keep herself from reaching out to touch.

"Isn't it beautiful?" asked Sarah, her tone quiet, but smile still in place.

"It's gorgeous." Aoife glanced at the price tag and swallowed. "I don't think I can afford it, though."

"We have a smaller one, right over here." Martin led the way again, not even batting an eyelash.

The smaller one was what Aoife needed, but the price was still more than she knew she could spend. Her job as a caregiver didn't start for another three days and most of her pay from that was going to her rent. The leftover was supposed to cover food and other amenities she would need. Her savings were low from buying the plane ticket just days before she flew out of the country, and if she didn't take care, she could quickly run out. It was because of those reasons that Aoife frowned and stepped back.

"I will have to think about it."

"Yeah, course, love," said Martin easily. "Just pop 'round whenever you've decided. I'm here every day and Sarah is here most days unless Max convinces her to take the day off."

Aoife quirked her eyebrows at the last comment; a smile pulled up her frown. Sarah blushed and shook her head at Martin, a teasing look in her eye.

"Don't listen to anything he says! I've only done that twice!"

"Ah, but you have done it!" Martin stepped away quickly to keep Sarah out of reach of smacking his shoulder.

Besides Donna and Hattie, these two shop workers were the first people Aoife had really met there in Brighton. She wanted to stay and just chat with them, but that would have been creepy. Right? Creepy? Aoife shook away her thoughts when Sarah laughed again.

"Thanks for everything," said Aoife as she adjusted her purse and took a step towards the door. "I'll have to stop back in sometime."

"Please do!" Sarah nodded. "Even if you just want to have a chinwag sometime. I'm always up for a chat."

"Sarah!" Martin sighed. "You can't just tell people that!"

"I will," said Aoife, looking Sarah in the eye.

There were a lot of thoughts going around Aoife's head as she went a few streets further to buy salt and pepper from the grocery store. She smiled as she thought about Sarah's warm, friendly manner, her dark curls, her slight frame and pretty features. Martin's long legs, easygoing personality, exasperated fondness for his friend and calming voice went through her memory. It had only taken her two days to find herself a couple friends.

"All you have to do is meet one," her father had always said. *"Then they'll introduce you to their friends."*

Aoife wasn't holding her breath that they would invite her into their inner circle, but she was happy enough with the thought that two people knew her name and wanted her to come back and see them. It was a thought that made her smile for the rest of the weekend and even on Monday morning when she woke up for her first day of work.

Aoife dressed herself carefully. She knew Genny and had heard stories of this old relation of her friend's, but not enough to know how the elderly woman felt about most things. She finally settled on a casual look of skinny jeans without any rips, a plain gray t-shirt and a maroon scarf that she didn't put on for the bike ride across town. Her backpack was flush against her back, causing her to sweat only three blocks into the ride.

The sweat stain didn't matter as Miss Wilcox was mostly blind and needed little more than for Aoife to help her from her room to the bathroom, into the living room where the television was turned on for reasons Aoife didn't quite understand, and then back to her bedroom after lunch for a nap. A nurse lived with Miss Wilcox when Aoife wasn't there, so Aoife didn't have to worry about bathing or dressing or taking her out to doctor's appointments.

"Would you like to go outside for some fresh air?" she asked after watching the same infomercial for a spray that would eliminate dog odor from anything for the fifth time.

"Oh, no, dearie," the frail voice shook as the woman spoke kindly. "I like my chair and my sitting room just fine, thank you."

While Aoife sat and struggled to find ways to keep herself from going crazy with boredom, her charge would knit. The needles flashed and clicked against each other so quickly that Aoife was amazed. The woman couldn't even see, yet she was knitting with such accuracy that Aoife could only imagine how many out of her eighty-seven years she had been doing it.

Miss Wilcox's house was big, not especially opulent, but well-tended and expensively furnished. The curtains were thick and silky, the carpets lavish and patterned while the paintings on the wall spoke of the artistic taste the woman had before her eyesight left. There was a housekeeper who arrived while Aoife was there. She smiled once, then scurried off to do her job, leaving Aoife to sit and watch Miss Wilcox knit.

"What would you like me to do?" Aoife tried again, hoping for a task.

"Oh, just sit, my love," the voice still spoke kindly. "I like having someone near me. Gives my heart a bit of joy in my old age."

"But I could be doing something," she insisted, hoping her tone came off as encouraging, not complaining.

"Sit, dearie," she hummed. "Just sit."

As she sat, Aoife let her toes flex against the carpet, her feet remembering the steps to dances she had learned years ago, worked so indelibly into her muscle memory she could do them still. Her hands twitched as they lay in her lap, palms slanted towards the ceiling and fingers curved gracefully. She wondered if the people who lived below her would hear her if she used the small, empty space in her apartment to practice dancing. Genny had told her of a dance studio in Brighton, but studios cost money. She couldn't afford it, at least not yet.

After she tucked Miss Wilcox into her bed and made sure everything was where the old woman could reach it if she woke up, Aoife left quietly. She passed the nurse in the hallway and mentioned how all she had done was sit in the living room with her.

"Is that what I should be doing? Are there exercises? Activities? I don't know, anything?"

"Oh, no!" The nurse laughed. "You just get to sit with her. Poor old lady is so lonely. Bring a book if you feel the need to do something else, but really, I just need you there to help her move about when it's time for lunch."

It seemed silly to be upset over a job not being challenging enough. A break from hard work, emotionally draining work, was needed. Necessary, according to Genny. Aoife climbed on her bike and began her journey back towards the sea.

Aoife left her bicycle at her building and continued on foot to cross the one street that separated her from the beach. She let her hair down, allowing it to blow around her face in the salty breeze. Her sunglasses shielded her eyes as she stepped closer to the water. Everything felt calm and right. This was why she was here; it wasn't for Genny, or her dad, or the job, or anything she had left behind. It was this: to stare at the sea.

-Chapter 2-

The Coziest Cushions in all of Brighton

Aoife heard the bell go off above her as she opened the door to *Pop's Shop* for the second time. Her smile appeared when she noticed Sarah organizing some clocks on a shelf at the back and Martin sitting on the edge of the counter with a newspaper like he had been the first time she walked in. Martin looked up first, his eyes flicking above the article he was reading.

"Well, hello!" He immediately put the paper down and stood to his feet. "Sarah, look who's come back to see us!"

"Aoife!" Sarah's squeal reached the girl's ears as she abandoned the unsorted clocks and rushed to greet her. "How are you? Good to see you!"

"It's nice to see you, too." Aoife wasn't expecting the delighted greeting. It was a pleasant surprise.

"We've seen you riding past on your bike the last three days and we kept thinking you'd stop by, but you never did."

"I've been going to work." Aoife stepped closer to the counter and leaned a hip against it. "I started on Monday."

"What's your job?" asked Sarah. Her eyes were just as bright as they had been the first time Aoife met her.

"I take care of an elderly lady until after lunch. Well, not really take care of..." Aoife's cheeks pinked up as she thought about how little she actually did. "I just keep her company."

"That's a lovely job!" gushed Sarah. "Don't you think, Martin? To just sit with someone and keep them company when they're old and frail?"

"I hope that's my next job!" said Martin.

"As if you'd ever get rid of the family shop!" Sarah rolled her eyes at him. "You'll be passing it down to little Tansy one day."

"Oh, don't even say that!" Martin was smiling as his hands flew to his mouth. "She's such a tiny babe, I can't think of her old enough to tend the shop!"

"Tansy is his niece," said Sarah, remembering Aoife. "She was just born on Sunday night. I'm going to see her for the first time after work this evening."

"Aw!" Aoife saw tears welling up in Martin's eyes.

"She's the tiniest thing you've ever seen, and her nose is just like this tiny little button!" Martin tried to blink the tears away.

18

"Martin! Pull yourself together, mate!" Sarah was glowing. "I can't wait to hold her! I love babies!"

"Well, don't tell me that, tell Max! He's your fiancé!" Martin seemed to have recovered from his emotional moment.

"I have told him! He said not until after the wedding!" Sarah pouted. "What about you, Aoife? Do you want babies?"

"Yeah, of course." She nodded and ignored the tug at the back of her heart.

"I bet Max is thrilled that you're going to see Tansy today," laughed Martin.

"He told me I'm not allowed to take any pictures to show him as blackmail." Sarah's laughter rang out.

"Too bad he's out of the country and can't stop you from coming to see her."

"I know," said Sarah with a cheeky smile that dissolved into a frown. "He's gone for so long this trip, though. He doesn't get back until Friday."

"That's good, that means I'll have you for sure at work for the rest of the week."

"Shove off!" Sarah laughed again. "I miss him! It's not fair that he's spending the week with my brother and I've had to stay here and work!"

Aoife was watching the two friends with a smile. It was nice to just be around people, even if she didn't have anything to contribute to the conversation.

"So, have you decided about the wardrobe?" asked Martin, changing the subject.

"Oh, yeah." Aoife glanced over at the piece of furniture she really would love to own. "I just can't afford something like that right now. Not so soon after the move."

"Aw! Bless!" Sarah frowned again. "I think you need a housewarming present. Stay right here."

Martin rolled his eyes as Sarah scurried away. He clicked his tongue as if he knew what she was going to grab when she appeared again from the back carrying the two cushions she had set aside for Aoife the week before.

"You don't need to!" Aoife smiled as Sarah tried to put the cushions in her arms. "Honestly, Sarah! I'm good, I'll buy them once I've been paid."

"No! Aoife, I insist!"

"Thank you." Aoife finally took the cushions, noting Martin's grin out of the corner of her eye. There were probably very few people who could resist Sarah's wishes.

"Do you want me to wrap them up for you?" asked Martin politely.

19

"No, I only have to walk a couple blocks."

"You'll come back and see us, right?" Sarah's face lit up with another smile.

"I'm sure." Aoife shifted the cushions under her arms. Her clothes were going to have to continue to live on the table, but at least she had the coziest cushions in all of Brighton. "Thank you so much, Sarah."

"It's all right!"

Aoife didn't want to avoid Sarah and Martin, but she also didn't want them to think that she was taking advantage of them in any way. The cushions were a nice gift, but she wasn't sure if she should go back. If Sarah tried to give her anything else, she would have to refuse. Or, she could just not go back. Not often, at least.

After work the next day, she decided to eat at a little cafe she had seen during one of her rides back and forth from Miss Wilcox's house. She parked her bike and walked into the brightly lit establishment, settling her sunglasses on the top of her head as she looked around. It had a rustic feel, with cozy chairs at the tables. Aoife smiled. She loved places like that. She was about to order when she heard her name being called.

"Aoife!"

"Hello, Sarah!" Aoife turned and saw Martin sitting behind her. "Hi, Martin."

"Come sit with us!" Sarah motioned to an empty chair next to her. "We can't stay much longer because we have to get back to the shop, but you can sit with us until it is time if you'd like."

"Sure." Aoife moved to sit at the table where her friends were. "Nice to see you two here."

"It's one of our favorite spots because Martin can get the fish pie and I can get sweet potato fries."

"Ah." The menu lay open in front of her, waiting to be read. "What do you suggest for a first time visitor?"

"They're ace at burgers," said Martin, leaning over the table a little to look at the menu upside-down. "Their shepherd's pie is really tasty, too."

"You want to know who does a good shepherd's pie?" asked Sarah, turning to Martin. "Max's mum."

"Karen Burgeon?" Martin made a low whistling sound through his front teeth. "Never would have guessed that."

"Max the fiancé?" Aoife looked from Sarah to Martin.

"That's the one." Martin pointed at Sarah's ring finger on her left hand. "Only going to get hitched in December, isn't she?"

"Congratulations!" Aoife's eyes took in the sparkling diamond.

"Thanks!" Sarah looked down at her ring, a smile tugging at her lips. "We're really happy."

"You should see them." Martin shook his head as he spoke. "Just a couple of lovebirds."

Aoife said nothing, but watched Sarah blush.

"What about you?" Sarah changed the subject. "No ring?"

"Nope." Aoife held out her hands and shrugged. "No ring. No man. I'm one of those single ladies Beyoncé sings about."

"All the single ladies, all the single ladies," sang Martin before Sarah turned to him and burst out laughing. "Hey!"

"You just can't help yourself, can you?" Sarah giggled.

"Are you a single lady, too, Martin?" Aoife asked the question in jest.

"I am, but I'm a bit busy to be putting any rings on anything."

Aoife laughed easily and listened to Sarah and Martin banter back and forth about the girls Sarah had tried to set Martin up with in the recent past.

"Honestly, Sarah," said Aoife in mock seriousness. "I feel like matchmaking isn't really your strong suit."

"Well, it's not my fault he's single!" Sarah held up her hands in a show of innocence. "I've tried my hardest and I'm all out of ideas!"

Martin mouthed the word "finally" and clasped his hands in front of him as he looked heavenward. Sarah smacked his shoulder and narrowed her eyes at him. There was a moment where Martin smiled innocently at Sarah and batted his eyes at her, causing Aoife to choke on a laugh she was trying to hold in.

"He thinks he can be like this because he's going to be giving a toast at my wedding and if I'm mean to him, he'll say the embarrassing story about Michael Penser from year four."

"Sounds like a great story. Michael Penser from year four? Definitely a winner."

"That's what I said!" Martin agreed. "But Sarah said no."

"It is her wedding, though." Aoife looked over at Sarah.

"Thank you!" said Sarah.

"Wait! Whose side are you on?" Martin pointed a finger at Aoife and watched her shrug with a smile.

"I like Aoife! Let's keep her around!" Sarah grinned. "You always look so serious with your shoulders back and standing up straight, but you're actually really funny."

"Sarah!" Martin put a hand over his eyes. "You can't just say that to people! I told you, she just has good posture!"

"It's okay," said Aoife lightly. "My mom was a big stickler about posture, so I've had it ingrained into me since I was little."

"I think it's great." Martin made a face at Sarah to tell her to agree with him.

"I wish my mum made me do it when I was little so it wasn't so hard now that I'm an adult." Sarah's bright eyes studied the way Aoife sat straight and proper in her chair. "You look so graceful and grown up sitting like that."

"Thank you." Aoife laughed.

The server came over to ask Aoife her order. Martin glanced at his phone to find out the time. The young man nodded at Sarah and she sighed.

"Time to head back to the shop?" asked Aoife once the nice young woman had left with her order.

"Afraid so." Sarah stood to her feet. "But stop by on your way back home. I have cute baby pictures from last night I need to show someone!"

"Okay!" she found herself agreeing, despite her resolve to not visit the shop.

The sun was still high in the sky when she finished her chicken Caesar salad and her cup of coffee. She always had tea when she was with Miss Wilcox and she didn't have a coffee maker in her place yet, so her drink that afternoon was like liquid gold. She walked her bicycle slowly down the crowded sidewalk, allowing herself to take in details that were too hard to catch when she was riding quickly to and from work. She smiled at a little girl wearing a princess dress and knelt down to pet a friendly dog that was wearing a sweater. She didn't think she could feel any happier with life when she walked into *Pop's Shop*.

"Sarah, she's here!" Martin barely looked up from his newspaper. "She's been waiting since we left you at the cafe."

Aoife's heart went warm with the thought. His eyes were friendly as Aoife looked up into them. He folded his newspaper and set it down on the counter beside the cash register.

"Is she always this friendly with everyone?" asked Aoife with a chuckle.

"She's always trying to make people feel welcome, yeah, that's Sarah," said Martin. "Her parents owned a bed and breakfast for a bit when she was younger and she loved meeting the guests who stayed there."

"She's very sweet. It's nice to have an acquaintance in town."

"It's nice for us, as well. It can get a bit boring in here some days."

"I like it here. You have some beautiful things." Aoife looked around for the first time since the first day. "One day I'll buy something, I promise."

"Oh, hush!" Martin shushed her. "We don't mind at all. We enjoy the company."

"Coming! Coming!" Sarah's voice preceded her as she came from the back.

"I'm going to do the inventory," said Martin, stretching out his long legs and standing up. "If she gets to be too much, just give a shout."

Sarah didn't even respond, her smile stretching across her face while her phone rested in her hand.

"Are you ready to see the cutest baby in the world?"

"Absolutely!"

The picture glowing on Sarah's phone was a close up of a tiny face, and Aoife could definitely see why Martin had teared up thinking about his niece. She was perfect and pink with wisps of blond on the top of her head.

"I wish I could tell you just how sweet of a baby she was, but I honestly have no words!" Sarah was saying as she swiped across her phone screen to show another picture.

"She's beautiful." Aoife didn't— couldn't— say anything else. She was as familiar with the sweet baby smell as any mother. She knew how soft the skin and silky the hair could be. She knew how kissable little cheeks were, and how precious tiny baby coos were to wake up to, even in the dead of night after no sleep. It had been years, but the memories sprang to the surface faster than a gas burner reacts to a lit match.

"I wish you could have met her, she is just so precious." Sarah was pouting down at her phone, her finger pressed against the baby's cheek. "Tansy is such a cute name, as well. Don't you think?"

"It is." Aoife found a smile and put it on. She glanced at the clock on the wall and pretended to be surprised by the time. "Oh, I have to go!"

"Really?"

"I'll come by on another day." Aoife hoped her voice was steady as she backed out of the store on shaky legs. Her stomach was burning and Aoife knew she needed some fresh air before she was plunged irrevocably into a swirl of memories she wanted to forget.

And it wasn't like Aoife couldn't look at a baby without breaking down, but then again, it had been years since she had properly looked into the face of one and remembered. Her legs took her down to the beach, the familiar sound of the waves like a lullaby to her ears. She sat down on the pebbles and hugged her legs against her chest.

It hadn't been her baby— not biologically— but her heart, oh how it had ached when the infant was snatched from her life. She wanted to say it was because of her youthful innocence, but there was so much more wrapped up in that tiny child than that. A few tears worked their way down Aoife's cheeks and she sniffed before taking a deep breath. This was her good start, her fresh start. She had to let it all go and keep going.

She didn't bump into either of her friends again until Friday evening when she was at Tesco doing some shopping. She was out of everything, again, and she knew that simply buying a loaf of bread and a jar of strawberry jam wouldn't cover it. Her cart squeaked as she made her way down the canned goods aisle. There was a special on breakfast beans and she wanted to stock up. She hoped she liked breakfast beans.

"Aoife! Hello, love!" Martin's voice caused her to look up from the bottom shelf, her arms full of cans. "Buying some beans?"

There was laughter touching the edges of his question, as he crouched down beside her to offer a helping hand. She smiled at him, allowing herself to chuckle at the thought of what she must look like. Martin took a few of the cans in his large hands and placed them in Aoife's cart while she simply dumped hers, holding too many to put them in gently.

"Well, that's a lot of beans." Martin's comment made Aoife's lips push up into another smile.

"I figured I would buy a lot since they will last and they are on special."

"Are they really?"

Aoife nodded and went back to the handle of her cart. Martin stooped down and plucked two cans from the shelf and put them in his basket.

"How is Tansy?" asked Aoife as they strolled slowly down the aisle. She noticed the canned olives and nearly stopped to grab one before telling herself she didn't *need* them and kept walking.

"Beautiful as ever. I'm actually here to buy her more formula." Martin smiled as he spoke.

"Get a little distracted?" Aoife eyed his basket that was partially filled with chocolate bars, a bottle of coke, two different kinds of cereal, and now, some cans of breakfast beans.

"Well, Shannon needed some food, too. She's my sister."

"Ah. Do you guys live together?"

"Yeah, it's just best that way," Martin stated matter-of-factly. "I'm able to take care of most things and Shannon takes care of the baby."

"Is she your younger sister?"

"Oh, no. She's well past thirty. I'm still only twenty-four."

"I'm twenty-four, too!" Aoife jumped at the similarity between them.

"Aw! Then you're the same age as Sarah as well! Max just had his birthday so he's twenty-seven now, but we're all about the same."

"That's nice." Aoife smiled. "Didn't Max come back today?"

"Not yet, Sarah last sent me a text saying she was still tidying his house." Martin pulled his phone out and looked at the screen. There was a new message from Sarah waiting for him. "Oh, she said his train has arrived."

She wondered what Max looked like, if he was tall and thin like Martin, or if he was more slight and wiry like Sarah. Or if he was like neither of them. They passed an aisle filled with chips and other snack foods Aoife was craving but knew she shouldn't buy. Martin turned down the aisle, though, and Aoife decided to stay with him.

"Do you like crisps?" he asked, pulling a few bags off the shelf and piling them into his now full basket.

"Yeah, but, I don't need any." Aoife smiled and looked down at her cart. All she had was about twelve cans of beans.

"Love, your food is depressing me, please let me buy you a bag of crisps!" Martin was laughing as he looked into the cart.

"No, Martin! Thank you, though. I'm going to buy some pasta and rice and sauces. I just... I haven't found them yet."

"I'll show you!"

Martin helped her find all that she felt she could afford and piled it into her cart. They then found the formula and went to the checkout. Martin waited patiently as Aoife counted out her money and paid. She then waited for him as he quickly swiped his card and grabbed all of his bags easily.

"Don't tell me you've ridden your bike here!" Martin exclaimed when Aoife started towards the rack. Her face flushed, but she smiled. "How are you going to do it with all these groceries?"

"Well, I usually don't buy this much..." Aoife frowned pensively.

"Come on, I'll give you a ride. I even have a rope in my boot, I can tie your bike to the roof."

It didn't take long for Martin to get her bicycle and her groceries loaded into and onto his little black car. She slid into the front seat, feeling weird that it was on the opposite side of the vehicle than she was used to. Martin chattered away, commenting on traffic and the weather and how his little niece was the cutest thing ever.

"You should meet her someday!" he said suddenly, as if the idea had only just come to him.

"Sure," Aoife agreed. She had already gotten her tears out of her system. She could hold the baby and be neutral now.

"Really? You'd like that?"

"Of course!" She laughed lightly at the surprise in his voice.

"Brilliant! I'll invite you over for dinner someday."

Once they arrived outside of Aoife's apartment, Martin tried to insist he carry the groceries up. Thankfully Aoife was able to convince him she would be fine. No one needed to know just how small and empty her home was. She smiled, though, when she set her bags on the floor in the corner by the kitchen and she saw a bag of crisps shoved into the top of one.

Chapter 3

Pretty Blue Eyes

Saturday was a free day for Aoife. She woke up to the sun shining in her window and her toes warm under the quilt. She stretched and reached for her phone. It was nice to take her time getting ready for the day, dancing around to her music as she made breakfast and took a shower. She put on a dress since she wasn't going to have to ride her bike anywhere. It was close to lunchtime when she left her apartment and walked across the street to the beach.

There were families and groups of friends and people on their own all enjoying the beautiful weather. Aoife smiled at puppies being chased, little kids throwing rocks into the water and a young couple holding hands as they walked to the water's edge. She stood away from most of the people and hugged her arms around herself, the skirt of her dress fluttering against her legs in the wind. The waves whispered to her and she smiled into the sun's rays. She stayed on the beach until she was too hungry to stare at the sea any longer.

Aoife wasn't going to go to *Pop's Shop* that day, but her saucepan broke and she knew they had a display of saucepans by the window. She realized she wasn't even sure if they were open on Saturdays as she skipped down the stairs and out onto the sidewalk. She hoped they were, as she would rather give her business to Martin than a corporation. The sign on the door said it was open, and Aoife listened to the bells as she stepped in.

"Hello? Martin?" she called. "It's Aoife."

"Aoife!" a muffled voice came from the corner. "Just hang on a minute! I have to tell you something!"

Aoife finally spotted the lanky young man on his hands and knees attempting to assemble a set of shelves. She tried to keep a straight face, but the way he had his legs folded underneath him was too comical for her to ignore. It took him a whole minute to stand up to his full height and he was chuckling when he finally rose to his feet.

"Usually I have Sarah do stuff like that, but she's taken the day off since her brother is in town for the weekend." Martin wiped his hands on his jeans.

"Do you need help? I'm pretty good with a screwdriver," said Aoife, gesturing at the tools and parts still on the floor.

"Nah!" Martin waved away her offer. "But, hey! I was supposed to invite you round to a do this afternoon. At four o'clock a group of us are meeting down at the pier for drinks and a meal. Sarah asked me to tell you if I saw you."

"A do?"

"A party! It's 'cause Sam's in town, and everybody wanted an excuse to get drinks anyway."

"Aw, that's very nice of you guys, but I'm okay, thanks."

"Are you sure?" Martin frowned. "This isn't a pity invite, you know."

"Well." Aoife gave a shy laugh and looked down.

"Come on! Don't be nervous about it. It's just drinks down at the pier. Max will be there and you need to meet him."

"If you're sure no one will mind a random American girl tagging along."

"Of course not!" Martin waved away her concern with a sweep of his long arm. "It's just drinks, yeah?"

"I mean," joked Aoife with a casual shrug. Her heart was pounding a bit heavier than normal at the thought of being invited out, but she hid it with a smile. "Thanks for thinking of me. I feel welcomed."

"Good! Sarah would have my head if you said no, she really wants you to meet Max."

"I don't know how to get to the pier, though."

"Don't worry! We can go together! I close up shop at half-past three, then I just need to stop by home for a minute to change my top. You could come with me and we'll leave from there."

"Okay." Aoife nodded. "As long as you're not worried that I'm a dangerous criminal."

Martin laughed so hard that tears ran down his face. Even Aoife was giggling as Martin caught his breath to talk again.

"Definitely not worried about that!" he managed to say between spurts of laughter.

"Glad to know I don't look like an evil villain," she said as Martin finally calmed down.

"Anything but! Anyway, come back to the shop at half-three and we can start off for the party."

She remembered as she was heading for the door that she needed a pan. She laughed and told Martin she had actually come in as a customer. There was a light feeling in her chest as she left, the saucepan in hand. She could see the sea as she walked from the shop to her building. There had been moments in the past week where Aoife would pinch herself to make sure this was really happening; she was really staring at the sea.

Once Aoife was back home, she began to worry about all the little details she hadn't thought to ask Martin when she was with him. What should she wear? Should she bring a jacket? What about her hair? Her makeup? Aoife had an hour before she was supposed to meet Martin back at the shop. She left five minutes early, but only because she knew if she stayed she would change her outfit again, and she was out of options.

"You look quite lovely!" Martin's eyes lifted from his usual newspaper when she walked in.

"Is this okay? I wasn't sure how to dress for a do down at the pier." Aoife pulled at her long black shirt nervously. Her white jeans had a rip in one knee, but she had accessorized with a necklace Genny had given her for her last birthday. It was a simple gold chain with a bird pendant hanging low across her chest.

"This is perfect!" Martin glanced at the clock on the wall and folded up the paper. "Should we leave, then?"

"Yes." Aoife smiled and waited for Martin to close up the shop.

They chatted about nothing important as they walked the three blocks to Martin's house that he shared with his sister and niece. She found out he had been on the swim team when he was in high school, and for his twentieth birthday he went on a trip to southern Spain where apparently he bought the coolest cactus shirt in the world. Aoife was smiling as Martin unlocked the door and let them in, but the smile soon disappeared when she heard the wailing of a baby coming from somewhere in the house.

"Oh, goodness." Martin swore softly as he walked quickly down the dark hallway. He stopped and knocked on a door. "Shan! Shan! Shannon! Wake up! The babe's crying! Shannon!"

The door finally opened and the crying grew louder. It was clear that the mother was not happy with being disturbed from her nap. Aoife tiptoed closer, her chest physically aching at the sound of the tiny baby's anger and discomfort.

"No, Shan! I haven't time to feed Tansy! I'm about to leave for a party. N-No! Shannon! I've made plans for the evening! She's *your* baby!"

Aoife swallowed the words that were bubbling up inside of her. Her fingers pulled at her shirt and she sucked in her cheeks to keep from pushing past the two siblings and scooping the child in her arms.

"Who's this, Martin?" Shannon eyed her, noticing her creeping closer.

"It's my friend Aoife. Please, Shan, just pick up the baby! She needs you!"

"I'm so tired, Martin. You need to feed her for me." Shannon's expression was blank and her tone flat. How could she hear her baby and just stand there?

29

Martin swore under his breath again before pinching the bridge of his nose. Aoife quickly stepped closer and spoke up.

"I can. Martin, if you want to get ready, I-I can... I can feed her. If you're okay with it." Aoife turned to the mother with wide eager eyes.

"You could feed her from yourself if you had milk and I wouldn't care. Just as long as I get to sleep."

That was all the permission Aoife needed to barrel through the doorway into the dark, messy bedroom and locate the neglected child. She could feel the way Tansy's arms and legs were rigid from her fit. Her little face was red as she wailed.

"Sh." Aoife tucked the child against her chest and stared down at the baby. It felt so natural all over again. "Sh, baby, it's okay."

The cries ended until Tansy realized she wasn't being fed yet. Her cries revived, but Martin was ready with a bottle. Aoife followed him into the kitchen and watched as he started to put the bottle in the microwave to heat it.

"No!" Aoife stopped him. "Don't use the microwave!"

"What?" Martin froze.

"The microwave can heat unevenly. Here, do this." Aoife took the bottle from Martin and walked over to the sink. "Run hot water over it."

"Our hot water takes forever and she's screaming, shouldn't we just warm it up quickly?" Martin stuck one finger into the flow of water coming out at the kitchen sink.

"No." Aoife shook her head. "This is the best way."

"Finally," said Martin when the water turned warm. Tansy was crying so hard she was having trouble breathing. "Are you sure this is necessary?"

Aoife said nothing, but kept her eyes on the bottle. Finally, she nodded at Martin, telling him it had been long enough. She didn't actually know if the formula had warmed to the desired temperature, but she didn't think she could listen to Tansy any longer.

"Here we go, sh." Aoife put the bottle by Tansy's mouth, waiting for her to latch on. "Come on, baby. Here's your food. Come on."

"Are you sure you know what..." Martin didn't finish his question as Tansy clamped her mouth around the rubber tip of the bottle and began to suck vigorously.

"Okay. Good. Good," Aoife was saying the words more to herself than to anyone else.

"You okay with her while I change quick?" Martin seemed reluctant to leave her alone.

"I'm fine. She's probably just hungry and needs a new diaper."

"Ah, the nappies are there, by the sofa." Martin pointed before leaving the room. "Just shout if you need me."

Tansy was still sucking away as Martin walked quickly out of the room to get ready for the party. Aoife stared at her, remembering a million different moments, but keeping her mind on the present, not allowing it to go back to where the hurt was.

"Sh, now." Aoife swayed as she stood in the kitchen, her eyes never leaving the pale blue of the child's. Tansy sucked noisily until she let go with another wail. "Sh. It's okay."

After a moment of patting her back, Tansy burped and was ready for the rest of her bottle. Aoife hummed "Jesu, Joy of Man's desiring" as she paced with the baby in her arms. The baby was about to fall asleep when Aoife lay her down on the sofa to change her diaper. Of course, Tansy was upset, but Aoife shushed and cooed over her until she had changed the dirty diaper for a new one. Aoife cringed when she saw how red the baby's bottom was.

She cuddled Tansy against herself and rocked back and forth. The baby fell asleep quickly, her mouth still sucking at nothing as her eyes closed and her breathing slowed. Aoife was so busy staring at Tansy she didn't notice Martin watching her.

"Is she asleep?" he asked quietly.

"Yeah." Aoife glanced up. "She was just a hungry little baby."

"I keep telling Shannon she has to feed her when she cries, but she doesn't always want to get out of bed."

The words scared Aoife and she nearly didn't let go of the baby when Martin came to take his niece from her. She bit her lip as she followed him into his car and they started off down the road to the party. They were fifteen minutes late, but that was the last thing on Aoife's mind.

"Is Shannon just having a hard time recovering from the birth? Is that why she's sleeping so much?" Aoife hoped her questions were innocent enough.

"No, she's always been like that. She's always slept to cope with life. She has depression, you know, and uh, bi-polar disorder. She has medication, but she doesn't like to take it."

"Probably can't take it if she's nursing," said Aoife mostly to herself.

"Oh, she's not nursing. Shan's too tired for that."

"Does she have postpartum depression?" asked Aoife before she could stop herself. "Sorry. I'm sorry, I shouldn't have asked that."

"I don't know what that is," said Martin quietly.

"Oh, it's just... When a mom feels... bad, you know, after having her baby." Aoife wanted to kick herself. "But I'm sure the doctors have talked to

31

Shannon about it, considering, you know, that she's dealt with depression in the past?"

"I don't know." Martin was chewing on his lip. "I'll have to ask."

"Sorry, Martin. I didn't mean to ruin your mood for the party." Aoife's heart sank.

"No, no, I-I need to know. I need to make sure Shannon's okay. Does she act like a normal mother, you think?"

"What?"

"When you saw her? Is that what other mums look like?"

"I'm not... I've never been a, uh, a mom before..." *but even I wanted to hold her the second I heard her crying. I didn't want to put her down. I wanted to stay with her and make sure she was never hungry, cold or lonely ever again.*

"Right, right!" Martin forced a laugh. "I should really just wait until I talk to Shan's doctor."

"Yeah." Aoife nodded.

"Ah, here we are! Oo, looks busy." Martin pulled into the parking lot and put the car in park. "There's Sarah's car. She's probably going crazy texting me and wondering where we are. Are you nervous?"

"What? Oh, I'm not..." Aoife shrugged and tried to act casual.

"Don't worry, I'll sit next to you at dinner if you'd like."

"Thanks. I would love that."

Aoife was glad it was a long walk down to the pub where everyone was gathered. It gave her a chance to take a few deep breaths and get rid of the tight feeling in her chest. She was propelled towards Sarah and a tall young man with black hair and broad shoulders as soon as she walked through the door. The man was shorter than Martin by a couple inches, but his frame was sturdier, and more muscular. He was laughing loudly at something Sarah had said when Martin caught their attention with a wave of his hand.

"Ah! Aoife! You're here!" Sarah's smile was as big as it ever had been as she rushed towards the newcomer, her fiancé trailing along behind her. "This is Max; Max, this is Aoife."

"Hello! It's good to meet you! All day Sarah's been going on about you. I kept asking her questions about where you were from and what you used to do in America, but she didn't know." Max was laughing as he spoke.

"I suppose we haven't talked about that yet." Aoife felt instantly at ease with Max's deep brown eyes, big smile, big laugh and happy manners. "I'm from New York City."

"See! I guessed that!" Sarah shot up a finger in Max's direction. "I told you, 'Oh, I think she's probably from the east coast somewhere. Probably New York.' I said that!"

"Yes, you did." Max smiled and rolled his eyes affectionately, a hand on Sarah's back.

"What did you do in New York?" asked Martin.

"I was a, uh... dance teacher." It wasn't a whole lie, just like it wasn't the whole truth.

"You're a dancer?" Sarah's eyes were wide with awe. "What kind of dancing? I want to see you dance!"

"Ballroom. Contemporary. Jazz. A few other types." Aoife wished she had a drink to sip on and hide her face. She couldn't tell if her cheeks were heating up because of the amount of people packed into the bar, or if it was because she was afraid they were going to call her on her bluff.

"That's cool!" Max grinned. "Well, it's very lovely to meet you, Aoife."

"You as well." Aoife forced herself to stop pulling nervously at her clothes. Her fingers closed over the pendent on her necklace and she calmed down. "What do you do? Sarah said you were traveling."

"Yeah, I help manage football teams. We had a workshop we were putting on for charity up in Scotland this last week. That's why Sam's here this weekend with us, since we were together in Scotland."

Aoife didn't understand the connection, but she nodded anyway.

"I want you to meet Sam, but I can't seem to find him." Sarah grabbed Aoife's hand and pulled her along behind her. "Do you want a drink? Let's get you a drink!"

"Thanks." Aoife took another deep breath to steady herself. She leaned against the bar next to Sarah, looking down the line of faces when suddenly she stopped. She stopped moving her eyes, stopped breathing, stopped noticing anything else except for a pair of pretty blue eyes that were staring right back at her. Then, the eyes disappeared and Aoife was too dazed to see where they had gone. A drink was pressed into her hands and Aoife smiled automatically. "Thanks."

"It's all right." Sarah had her own drink. "Now, where's Sam?"

"Looking for me?" a deep voice asked from behind them.

"There you are!" Sarah whirled around to face the young man who was a head taller than she was. "Aoife, this is..."

Pretty Blue Eyes.

"Hello, I don't believe we've met," Sam was saying as he stuck out his hand. He had a crooked grin on his face as he used his free hand to push his mess of brown hair back from his high forehead. "I'm Sam."

33

"H-hi." Aoife wished she wasn't shaking on the inside.

"What was your name?" He pressed closer to hear her better.

"Aoife."

"Are you Irish?" Sam's eyes were sparkling as he spoke. It must be a family thing.

"My mom." It was all Aoife could manage to say.

"Cor, that's cool!" Sam was staring at her face.

Aoife glanced away and took a sip of her drink. It didn't help.

"Well, this is a good start," said Sarah, glancing between them. "Sam, Aoife used to teach dance back in New York, and Sam plays football on a team."

"Or, as you would call it, soccer," said Sam, mimicking an American accent. It wasn't terrible, actually.

"Are you good?" Aoife didn't know why she asked that. Why? Why had she asked that?

"Guess I'm pretty decent at it." The young man chuckled and turned to look at his sister. "They put me on the team."

"I'll have to take you to one of his games! You'll love it!" Sarah's face lit up with the idea.

"Yeah, absolutely." Sam held her gaze.

"Oh. Perfect. Yeah." Aoife's stomach swirled and she swallowed hard, her drink forgotten in her hand.

"Do you like football?" asked Sam.

"Playing, or watching?"

"Do you play?" Sam's eyes lit up in the dim light.

"Oh, no, not really, but..."

"Sarah! Aoife!" Max's voice rose above everything in the pub and Sarah quickly turned to see her fiancé waving her back over to where he was. "Come and look at this!"

"Sam!" Someone put a hand on Sam's shoulder before he could take a step to follow the girls. "Did you hear what William was saying about..."

"Sorry..." Aoife tried to say over her shoulder as Sarah pulled her away to where Max and Martin were laughing together at a booth.

"There she is!" Martin welcomed her with a smile. "I was hoping Sarah hadn't lost you."

Aoife glanced back over her shoulder and saw Sam staring at her, a young man with shaggy blonde hair whispering something in his ear. He looked like he was only half listening as he nodded, but didn't look away from Aoife. She gave him a small smile and lifted her glass before slipping into the booth.

She didn't see Sam again until they moved to a different location to eat and he claimed the seat beside her before Martin even knew what was happening. Aoife was mostly quiet during the meal, except for when Sam would lean his head closer to her and ask questions in a low voice. Where was she from? What was her job? How long was she going to stay in Brighton? Did she hang out with Sarah much?

Along with the questions, Aoife was introduced to Sam's friend Conor, a young man with a blonde fringe that hung down almost to his gray eyes. She assumed Conor was his best friend as the two of them seemed to have more inside jokes and laughs than anyone else. Conor was taller than Sam, but the two fought over which one of them was the fastest. Aoife only smiled and continued to eat her burger.

After dinner, they went down the road to a club where Max knew the man at the door. Aoife felt someone grabbing her hand as they walked through the dark crowded room and saw Sam out of the corner of her eye. Sarah grabbed her other hand and the siblings kept her close between them until they reached a corner that was emptier than the rest of the place. Clubs and bars weren't Aoife's normal scene, but with Sarah there to dance with her at every song, she didn't mind. It wasn't until Max claimed a dance with his fiancé that Sam also asked Aoife if she wanted a dance.

The lights skittered across the walls, changing colors and playing tricks with Aoife's mind as she tried to focus. Everything felt like it was moving; the light, the bodies, the sound of the music. But with Sam's hands holding onto hers, she felt anchored to the moment. Then...

"Aoife, do you mind if we leave? I've been thinking about Shan and Tansy. I should check on them." Martin's apologetic face appeared in front of her.

"Yes! Oh my goodness, yeah, of course." Aoife glanced at her own watch. She should have suggested they leave hours ago. The poor baby.

"I can bring you home later," offered Sam, putting a hand on Aoife's arm, reminding her he was there.

"Thanks, but I should go with Martin. I'll see you around, though, right?" She hesitated, pulling Martin to a stop as she waited for Sam to answer before she left.

"Yeah, probably." With an easy smile, Sam waved and nodded.

Aoife followed Martin out through the crowd of people and into the cool night. She jogged behind him to keep up with his long, quick strides. He was obviously worried as he barely said a word between pulling on his bottom lip and sighing.

"If you need any help," Aoife said quietly. "Let me know."

"Yes! Oh, yes, thank you, Aoife. Can I have your number?" Martin was stopped at a red light. He pulled his phone out of his pocket and unlocked it before handing it to Aoife so she could put in her contact information. "I don't know a thing about babies, not really anyway. I've been feeding her if I hear her crying when Shan won't wake up, but like, I don't... Shan said it was normal for babies to cry like that."

The ache in Aoife's heart pushed her supper that she had just eaten to the back of her throat and she had to swallow several times to keep from vomiting at the thought. She knew it wasn't really Shannon's fault, she didn't choose a mental illness, but Tansy...

"Call any time. Day or night. I'll come."

"Do you have a lot of experience with babies?" asked Martin. He was sniffling and Aoife realized he was crying.

"Not..." *three months, two weeks and five days...* "Not a lot. No."

"Well, you seemed to know what you were doing when you were feeding her."

"I have a little experience. And some of it is just... natural instinct."

"How come Shannon doesn't have that?"

"I don't know, Martin. But I'm sure she's doing the best she can. She probably doesn't even realize."

They pulled up outside of Aoife's apartment and Martin stopped the car.

"Seriously, Martin, call me if you need anything."

"Thanks, love." Martin gave her a wobbly smile and an awkward hand on the shoulder before Aoife climbed out of the car.

Aoife went up to her apartment and watched the sea until she was too tired to stand anymore. She tried to see the waves, but the moon was hidden behind the clouds, leaving the beach dark. She left the volume up on her phone when she went to sleep, careful to make sure it was plugged in so that it was charging. Just in case.

There were no calls, though. Aoife heard the people who lived below her leave for the day so she decided to take her chance and put on her pointe shoes. Her feet slipped into the familiar shape of them as she remembered the hours and hours of practice she had done just to get her first pair. She didn't do it often, just often enough to keep the calluses on her feet. Her current pair of shoes that she had would have to be replaced soon.

She stared down at her feet for a long moment, pretending she was fifteen and about to perform her first big role as Odette in *Swan Lake*. Everything about that night had seemed magical. The way the lights caught the surface of the rhinestones on her costume, the swirl in her stomach as her best friend clasped her hand backstage and grinned at her, the ebb and flow of the music that reminded her very much of the way the sea would swell and still. The feather crown was set on her head as another friend gave her a nod; he knew she was going to be brilliant. Then it was time to take her spot on the stage. She flexed her feet and went up onto the tips of her toes. Her pointe shoes squeaked, shiny and new. By the end of the performance, they would be so worn in she would have to wear a new pair in the next performance. Each night brought a new pair of shoes that fit her as perfectly as the first. Each night she would stand on their tips and take a deep breath, stilling the flutter of nerves in her stomach.

Everyone said she would do great and that she was made for the stage, and she had believed them, thinking it would always be magical every time. The ache in her heart reminded her that she couldn't have been more wrong. Aoife stood to her feet and picked up her phone. She pulled up the music for an old recital piece and stretched as Beethoven's "Für Elise" poured out of the phone speaker.

A grimace crossed her face as her feet remembered their positions and her arms swept up and around her head, keeping her balance and maintaining their beautiful, graceful shape. She slid across the floor as she did simple warmup exercises for her feet and shoes. Dancing all alone in a tiny apartment was her penance.

See, it wasn't a lie when she told them she was a dance teacher; she had indeed taught dance classes. Hundreds of them, in fact, but on her resume she was a professional ballet dancer. For years it had been her life. From dawn until late after midnight, she had trained, practiced, stretched and worked until she was part of the best ballet company in New York City. She had been in *The Nutcracker, Swan Lake, Coppélia* and countless others. She was trained in ballroom dancing, contemporary, jazz and almost any other type of dance you wanted, but ballet was her heart.

The music dimmed as the faint sound of an incoming message pinged on her phone. Aoife sighed and stopped dancing. Her lungs were heaving and skin glistening with sweat, but she felt better than she had in days. The phone pinged again, and Aoife walked over quickly, wondering if it was Martin. She was relieved when she saw it was only from Genny.

checking up on u

how is aunt bonnie?

For all the hours she had spent with Genny, the girl had never mentioned her family in England. Perhaps that was why she was so quick to push the job that was handed to her off to Aoife. Of course Genny's parents had wanted Genny to put her family first and go live in Brighton to take care of Miss Wilcox, but that wasn't part of Genny's five-year plan. It wasn't part of her two-month plan, either. Aoife, on the other hand, didn't have any plans, and she was struggling.

"*You know it has been years, right?*" asked Genny the night she proposed that Aoife take the job offer. "*It's never going to go back to how it was. You have to move on.*"

Aoife knew it would never go back, but sometimes, if she pretended like it had never happened, it was easier. That was why she left the company, started teaching dance and only went to the studio when everyone else was gone. That was why she gave away all of her recital costumes and donated the DVDs of her performances to a junior ballet company to use. If she looked in the mirror just right, she could ignore the scar on her left shoulder that she got during a rehearsal in Milan. It had been a long time since there was any magic involved in her love for ballet.

Three months, two weeks and five days...

Aoife turned off the music and ignored the texts from Genny. She showered, massaging her fingers through her hair and trying to push away the ache that was there. The shampoo got into her eyes, but she let it sting, embracing the pain as if they were tears. Once she was dried off and dressed, she made herself a sandwich and ate it by the window. She stared at the sea, wishing the water could wash over her and wipe away memories that were almost too heavy to carry at times.

It was growing dark outside when her phone rang. This time it was Martin, and when Aoife answered, his panicked voice came through the line, gripping her heart.

"You have to come! Shan won't feed the baby and I, I, I don't... I don't know what to do! Sarah doesn't know what to do! Please, please come!" Martin was babbling. "Please, Aoife, I need you to come..."

"I'm on my way!" Aoife promised as she ended the call.

Her feet ached a bit from her dancing earlier, but she didn't let it slow her down. She pulled on her sweater and ran down the stairs, sticking the key to her apartment into her jeans pocket as she nearly tripped and fell headlong to the bottom of the staircase. It wasn't far from her place to Martin's, and she remembered the way from the day before. She knocked on the door, noting a blue car parked out front. Maybe it was Sarah's car? Martin had mentioned her. The sound of a crying baby grew closer from down the long, narrow hall before the door was opened and Tansy was deposited into her arms. Instinctively, Aoife's arms wrapped around the warm, squirming bundle and pulled her close.

"Sh, baby. Oh, it's okay. It's okay." Aoife forgot she was standing on the front step of Martin's house as she stared down at the squalling infant. She swayed back and forth, her hand covering the back of Tansy's head protectively. "Sh, it's okay. I'm right here."

"Is she calming down?" Sarah's worried voice sounded from the doorway and Aoife glanced up. "She's calming down! Oh, thank God! Aoife, you're a lifesaver!"

"How long was she crying?" Aoife asked, then immediately wished she hadn't. She didn't need to know. "Have you fed her?"

"Tried to, but she just won't take the bottle from me!" Martin rubbed his hands together anxiously. "I have a bottle all prepared."

"Let me try." Aoife stepped into the house. "She's calm enough, she may take it now."

"Here." Sarah reached the bottle first. "We've changed her nappy and her clothes probably ten times, but she just wouldn't stop crying."

"She may be feeling gassy or something." Aoife touched the nipple of the bottle to the baby's lips and she opened, still whimpering as she took the food that was offered her.

"This is the first moment's peace I've had in hours." Martin leaned heavily against the kitchen counter, his shoulders sagging.

"You could have called me when she started crying," Aoife said softly. "It's okay, Martin. I know you did everything you could."

"I'm going to take Shan to see the doctor tomorrow. And Tansy. Just to make sure everything's all right." Martin took a deep breath. "I can't bear to have her crying like that all the time. I can feel my heart breaking for her."

"Come sit, Martin. You've done so much today." Sarah put a hand on her friend's arm and pulled him towards the sofa.

Aoife followed, the baby eating happily in her arms. She settled in the recliner and crossed her legs to make her lap cozier for Tansy. The baby's pale eyes were open, staring up at Aoife. Aoife's heart pounded with a mixture of pain and affection as she put her finger in the weak grasp of the child and smiled down at her. When was the last time she was just cuddled and gazed upon? Tansy's eyes drooped closed and Aoife pulled the empty bottle out of her mouth. The baby jerked, searching for the nipple to fill her mouth again, but Aoife pulled her closer, shushing her gently and rocking her. Tansy's arms settled back down to her belly and Aoife continued to rock.

"How do you do it? Baby magic?" whispered Sarah in awe. "You're going to be my nanny whenever I have my own children."

Aoife glanced back up at her friends with a little smile. Tansy's dead weight in her arms felt good, and the muffled suckling sound she was making soothed her.

"You look perfect like this." Martin's exhaustion clearly showed on his face. "Happy and serene with a little babe in your arms."

"She's precious," was all Aoife allowed herself to say.

"I need to head back home, Conor and Sam are going to be leaving for London soon," said Sarah with a yawn. "Aoife, can I give you a ride back home?"

"Oh, I... you don't need me to stay?" Aoife looked at Martin.

"No, love. She's sleeping now. Thank you for coming over." Martin motioned to the bassinet in the corner.

"Any time, Martin." Aoife hoped he knew just how much she meant those words.

It didn't feel right to let go of Tansy and leave her, but Aoife did it anyway. Tansy wasn't her baby. She was Shannon's, and in just a few hours, the doctor would be meeting with Shannon and Martin to make sure everything was okay. She didn't need to worry about the baby. It was okay. It was going to be okay.

"Bye, Martin. I've got the shop covered tomorrow. Don't worry about a thing."

With a silent wave, Aoife left with Sarah. Sure enough, Sarah climbed into the blue car that was parked out front. Aoife thought about telling Sarah she would just walk, but Sarah was already smiling at her expectantly.

"I just live a few blocks that way," said Aoife as she pointed to the left.

"I know, but I have to see Conor and Sam off to the train station. You don't mind, do you?"

"Oh, I don't want to be in the way..." but Aoife had a sneaking suspicion Sarah had planned it that way on purpose. "I don't mind. Whatever is easiest for you."

"Thanks!" Sarah sighed happily, as if she had been holding her breath in case Aoife refused. "And thanks for coming over to help Martin. I've never seen him so worked up about anything before, and I was with him the day his mum was in her car accident."

"Car accident?" Aoife turned to look at Sarah.

The driver just shook her head and waved the question away.

"Him being so worried about Tansy is probably my fault." Aoife bit her bottom lip and stared straight ahead. She didn't recognize this part of town. "I shouldn't have mentioned anything."

"No! I'm so glad you did! If you hadn't, maybe Martin wouldn't have ever known! It's better to know, right? This way we can fix it." Sarah put a hand on Aoife's shoulder for a moment. "It's brave to say something like that to someone you don't know very well. I'm really glad you did."

"I'm glad they're going to be able to get help." Aoife nodded. "And honestly, it was no trouble to come over."

"I told him to call you earlier, but he was determined to get Shannon to do it." Sarah shook her head.

"Do you know Shannon well?" Aoife turned to watch Sarah's expression. It became pinched, careful, like she didn't want to say the wrong thing. "It's okay, you don't have to answer."

"I don't know her well. Like Martin probably told you, he and I were in school together. That's why I work with him at *Pop's*, because we've been like brother and sister for forever."

"It's good to have friends like that."

"Yeah, especially since Sam is off traveling and being famous most of the time these days." There was a fondness in Sarah's tone to cushion her words. "So proud of him. Don't tell him I said that, though."

Aoife grinned as Sarah winked at her. The conversation became lighter as Sarah pointed out her favorite sandwich shop, the best cinema in town, the boutique where she bought all of her favorite clothes and the road that led to the bookstore. Aoife took in all the details she could. She would need to know more about Brighton to carry on living there and not go crazy with boredom.

"And there's the dance studio! I can drive you there sometime if you wanted to check it out."

"Oh, no, I don't want to dance." Aoife shook her head.

"Well, it's there. You might change your mind." Her tone was hopeful and Aoife took a deep breath. "I'd love to see you dance someday."

"Maybe someday."

Then Sarah turned down a road into a nice neighborhood with nicer houses. They reminded Aoife of the house where Miss Wilcox lived, except these houses were newer. She took in their details with wide eyes, seeing the trees and gardens, beautiful windows and tasteful architecture. Even so, none of the houses had a view of the sea. Aoife was satisfied with her little apartment and table dresser.

"Here we are!" Sarah sang out as they pulled up to a three-story house with a brick exterior. "Sam said they were all packed and ready to go, but I doubt it!"

Aoife was unsure if she should get out of the car as well, or stay. Her questioning look was answered with a laugh as Sarah motioned for her to follow her inside. She could hear Max's loud voice through the door as Sarah opened it and welcomed her into a well-lit entryway. There was a spot for shoes and a staircase to the right, carpeted, unlike the wooden floor Aoife was standing on.

"Leave your shoes on," said Sarah as she walked past and turned to the left. "Boys! Come on, then! We've got a train to catch!"

"Not you, just us!" Conor's playful tone reached Aoife's ears as she crept towards the corner, following Sarah shyly. "Stop trying to include yourself in our lives!"

"Yeah, Sarah!" Sam's teasing came to an end when Max grabbed him from behind and lifted him from his feet. "Hey! Put me down! Sarah! Max is being mean to me!"

"Yeah right, I'm not saving you now!" Sarah rolled her eyes and turned back to find her guest. "I've brought Aoife, now behave like civilized people."

Instant quiet filled the house as all eyes turned to her. Aoife waved shyly and came fully out of the entryway.

"Hey!" Max dropped Sam onto his feet and walked over to shake her hand. "Good to see you! Sorry you had to leave so early last night. Sarah and I could have brought you home if you had wanted to stay later."

"No, it's fine." Aoife chanced a glance in Sam's direction. A smile played at the corners of his mouth as he watched her. She knew her face was red. "I am glad I went home with Martin. He needed someone to talk to."

"Yeah, he's a right mess at the mo'." Sarah sighed as she leaned into her fiancé. "Taking Shan and Tansy to the doctor's tomorrow."

"Are they okay?" asked Max and Sam at the same time.

"Aoife knows more than I do."

"Oh, no, I..." Aoife was flustered as once again all eyes were on her. "I just... I was worried that Shannon was sleeping, you know... when Tansy was..."

"She won't wake up when the baby cries," Sarah finished for Aoife.

"That's not good." Conor's forehead furrowed. "Mums are supposed to know when their babies need them."

"That's why he's taking them tomorrow. So, I've got to be at the shop all day."

"Sounds good. I've got meetings all day, anyway." Max rubbed a hand up and down Sarah's back and placed a little kiss on the top of her head.

"What about you, Aoife?" asked Sam. "What are you doing tomorrow?"

"Special knitting date with Miss Wilcox, I guess." Aoife shrugged and let a smile tug at her mouth. "Nothing exciting."

"Please say you'll come keep me company in the shop tomorrow after you're done!" Sarah turned to Aoife. "It's so lonely without anyone there to talk to."

"Yeah, but Sarah, this way no one will catch you talking to yourself." Sam dodged the back of Sarah's hand with a laugh.

"All right, I've had enough of you!" Sarah's fake stern voice made her brother only laugh harder. "To the car! I'm sending you back to London right now!"

"Well, good!" Conor grabbed his backpack and swung it over his shoulder. "Because I was getting bored of your house anyway."

"Hey!" Max protested.

"It's not even my house, Conor!" Sarah stuck out her tongue and narrowed her eyes at him. "It's Max's!"

"All right, children. Let's go." Max took on the tone of a patient parent and tried to usher them all out of the house.

"I can sit in the back," said Aoife, quickly ducking into the backseat before someone insisted she take the front.

"Well, hello!" Sam's voice sounded close as he clambered in behind her. "Fancy meeting you here!"

"Funny, huh?" Aoife laughed lightly.

"Sam, scoot over, your bum is too big for this seat!" Conor squished into the back with them, forcing Sam to move over until he was pressed alongside Aoife.

"Sorry," he apologized to her quietly, a little smile on his face.

"It's okay. We all know Conor is the big one."

Sam chuckled and nodded. "True."

Max took the wheel and turned up the song on the radio. Apparently it was a favorite, because the passengers in the car instantly erupted into singing. Aoife laughed, wishing she knew the song so she could join in.

"Do you like to sing?" asked Sam, leaning close to hear her over the sound of the radio.

"Not very good at it," she said. "Was always better at dancing."

"Did you dance to this type of music?" The pop song was still ringing loudly around them.

"Not often."

"You should come to London sometime," Sam said with a smile. "I have a friend there that's a hip-hop dancer. He could teach you."

"Is it Conor?" Aoife's grin gave her away.

"He wishes!" Sam poked his friend in the side. "This one here is all arms and legs, falls over every time."

"What?" Conor shouted over the music.

"Aoife said you were handsome!" said Sam.

"Aw, cheers! You're handsome, too!" Conor tried to reach Aoife for a friendly pat on the shoulder, but Sam blocked him.

"But you will come to London someday, right?" Sam lowered his voice again. "You're welcome to come around mine anytime you want."

"Thanks." Aoife didn't have plans to visit London. "Maybe one day."

"Good."

And that was the last thing Sam said to her before they arrived at the train station and the two young men were rushed out of the car and on their way. Aoife was glad no one mentioned anything about her and Sam after he was gone. The couple in the front gave Aoife a small tour of their favorite part of town, showing her places to eat and coffee shops to hang out in if she was bored.

"Brighton really is a great place to live. I love it here." Max had one hand on the steering wheel and the other hand resting on Sarah's knee. "Also, Sarah told me you take care of Miss Wilcox. I know the Wilcox family. I used to play tennis with Sophie Wilcox when they lived here."

"Oh, I only know Genny. And now Miss Wilcox, of course," said Aoife. "I think Sophie is Genny's cousin."

"Miss Wilcox is a sweet lady, isn't she? Used to love going to her house around the holidays. She always had the best sweets and the coolest decorations. I'm sad she's so far gone that she can't even see anymore."

"Is she fully blind?" asked Sarah.

"Not quite. She can tell when the curtains are closed." Aoife liked hearing Max talk about Miss Wilcox. "I'll mention you to her tomorrow."

"Yeah, tell her I say hello. She'll remember if you tell her I'm Geoff Burgeon's son."

The name meant nothing to Aoife; she simply assumed that Max's parents were better acquainted with the elderly woman than the young man was, which made perfect sense.

"See you tomorrow at the shop when you get off from work!" said Sarah with a wink.

"Okay." Aoife waved before walking up to the door of her building.

It was dark in her apartment, but she didn't switch on the lights as she toed off her shoes and walked quietly over to the window. She pushed it open an inch, enough to hear the waves more clearly. The familiar sound reminded her of her mom and the time she went with her to the sea. She remembered how the waves had sounded and how it was so cold all she wanted was for her mom to hold her. She didn't remember anything other than the fact that she was wearing her favorite yellow shirt, and that was mostly because of the picture she had from that day.

"*Oh, careful, wee one.*" Her mother's lilting Irish voice echoed through her mind. It wasn't from the day at the beach, but from a home video she used to watch daily. "*Point your toes, Aoife.*"

Aoife pointed her toes as reflex, then stopped as another voice crowded into her head.

"*Point your toes! Shoulders back! Aoife, head up! Faster! Más rápidos! Vamonos! Stronger! Soften your hands, Aoife!*"

That was before Genny was her bossy friend, before she had been in *Swan Lake*, before she went to Milan and before...

Three months, two weeks and five days...

Aoife quickly left the window and changed into her pajamas. She pulled the quilt up over her shoulders and tried to shut her eyes. She wanted to think of Sam, of his pretty blue eyes and the way his leg had pressed up against hers in the back of the car, but all she could think of was Tansy. Her heart squeezed tightly at the thought of the baby crying without anyone to pick her up.

-Chapter 4-
Three months, two weeks, and five days...

Miss Wilcox smiled and nodded when Aoife mentioned Max. She wasn't sure if the elderly woman knew who she was talking about, but she definitely recognized the father's name. She made a humming sound as she smiled, and Aoife didn't know what that meant, either. Their morning passed pleasantly with Miss Wilcox continuing to knit the afghan she said she was going to give to Genny's parents for Christmas.

"I heard you don't do ballet anymore."

Aoife was about to ask how she knew that, until she remembered Genny.

"Taking a break." Aoife hoped her voice sounded neutral, even though her mouth turned down with the bitter taste on her tongue.

"Don't lose it forever. Someone like you has to keep a passion like that alive."

"Did you ever see Genny perform?"

"You mean, did I ever see you perform?" asked Miss Wilcox with a small smile, the knitting needles never pausing for a second. "I did. Your final performance."

Christmas 2011. *The Nutcracker.* The last performance Aoife had done before...

"You were a beautiful Clara."

"Thank you. I wish I had met you there."

"Well, I've met you now, love."

"Yeah. True." Aoife fell quiet.

She couldn't sit still after that, not with all the memories triggered by their conversation. With Miss Wilcox settled in her spot, Aoife stood up and walked around the room, looking at the old family pictures that lined the walls. She didn't recognize anyone, but she loved watching the figures grow up until there were spouses and grandchildren included in the portraits. There was some family resemblance that she could see from knowing Genny's face, but otherwise everyone was a stranger.

The rest of the morning went by quickly and Aoife was surprised that it was raining when she went to leave. Miss Wilcox smiled as she loaned her a rain jacket and told her to be careful on her bike. Aoife was soaked through when she finally made it back home. She left her wet clothes in the shower to dry while her hair dripped down her back. She put on a pair of loose-fitting black pants and a zip-up hoodie with the name of her old dance school on it. Goosebumps stood up on her arms before she rubbed them away, standing in front of her counter-top stove warming up a pot of water as a source of heat. Her stomach rumbled, and she pulled her loaf of bread off the shelf to make a sandwich. She found herself making two; an extra one for Sarah, just in case the girl hadn't been able to get away to eat anything yet. Once the sandwiches were done and she had warmed up as much as she could, she pulled her hood over her ponytail and went back out into the rain. The awnings provided a little shelter as she attempted to stay dry on her way to *Pop's*.

"Finally! I was beginning to think you'd forgotten all about me!" Sarah sprang up from a chair behind the counter. "You've brought me food? Aw, Aoife! Thank you!"

"Do you like strawberry jam?"

"I love it!" Sarah came to meet Aoife halfway through the store. She laughed at Aoife's wet hair as she took a sandwich. "Did you ride your bike in the rain?"

"It wasn't raining this morning!" Aoife wiped some drops off her forehead. "I borrowed a rain jacket from Miss Wilcox, but it can only do so much when you have to ride for twenty minutes across town."

"Aw, bless!" Sarah took a bite of the sandwich. "Thanks for this. I was about to phone Max and beg him to bring me some food."

"Isn't he in meetings all day?" asked Aoife, following Sarah back to the counter. She perched herself on the edge where Martin usually sat with his newspaper on his lap. The smell of his cologne was thick in the air and she smiled. Her hood slipped down as she turned to see Sarah back in her chair behind the desk. A novel sat next to her, a bookmark sticking out in the middle.

"Yeah, but he could get out of them if it was an emergency."

"A food emergency?" asked Aoife with a smile.

"It was almost one!" Sarah took another bite. "Until you came and saved the day."

"You're welcome, Max."

"I'll be sure to tell him to thank you!" laughed Sarah. "Tell me about your day! How was Miss Wilcox?"

The conversation about her final ballet performance immediately came to mind.

"Good." Aoife nodded. "I still wish my job was a bit more involved, but I enjoy her. She's a very nice woman."

"Did you tell her hello for Max?"

"Yes, but I'm not sure if she knew who I was talking about."

"Maybe not." Sarah shrugged with a grin. "How do you know her again?"

"My friend Genny, it's her great aunt. Her parents wanted her to come stay in Brighton and look after her, but she was... busy."

"Is Genny your best friend?"

"Uh..." Aoife gave a little laugh at how interested Sarah was in their conversation. "I guess, maybe."

"How did you meet her?"

"Dance. Teaching dance." One truth. One lie.

"I bet she's nice if she's friends with you."

"She is nice. A little bossy sometimes, but nice."

"Like a big sister, innit? Bossy, but nice?"

"I wouldn't know. I never had an older sister."

"Is it just you, then? No brothers and sisters?"

"I have two brothers. They're a lot younger than me." Aoife paused for a moment before adding, "They're my half-brothers."

"Do you get on with them?"

Aoife shrugged. She never really spent time with them.

"Sam said your mum's Irish. Is she pretty like you?"

All of Aoife's old acquaintances acted as if they knew everything about her and it gave them little to talk about. Everything about Aoife's life was brand-new to Sarah, and she looked as if she couldn't get enough. It was refreshing and a little scary. After all, some things were better left unsaid until... well, Aoife didn't know when.

"I guess I do favor her in looks." Aoife remembered a picture that used to hang on the wall before her dad remarried.

"Can I see a picture? Do you have one?"

"I don't have any recent pictures. None of my dad, either, actually."

"What are their names?"

"Carl and Rebecca."

"Carl and Rebecca," Sarah repeated. "Good names. Solid. Intriguing."

Sarah sat back in her chair and smiled as she ate the last of her sandwich. She looked as if she were trying to conjure up what Carl and Rebecca would look like so she could trace them to their daughter and point out the familiarities between them. If Sarah could see Aoife's parents, she would see the gray in her mother's eyes, and the fair skin that freckled in the summer, especially on her shoulders after a day by the sea. Aoife had been told her ears favored the Stewart side of the family, and she picked up more of Carl's mannerisms, as one would expect, but most people didn't say she looked like her dad.

"I'll stop asking you questions about them now, but I'm well interested! I love stories and books and hearing about your parents is like hearing about characters in a book and you have to figure out who they are and what they've done."

"It wouldn't be a very nice book." Aoife didn't know why she said that. Sarah appeared troubled by the statement. "I mean, because, obviously, since I have half siblings, that it didn't work out between them."

"I suppose, but that's just some stories." Sarah brushed the crumbs off her lap.

"What about you?" Aoife changed the subject. "Did you have any customers this morning?"

"Oh my gosh, I had this one lady come in, right? And she's looking at everything, and I realize..." Sarah's eyes were wide as she spoke, drawing Aoife into the story— "that she has been leaving chocolatey fingerprints absolutely everywhere!"

"Are you sure it was chocolate?" Aoife grimaced.

"Aoife! That's disgusting!"

"People can be disgusting sometimes! One time I was on the subway with my friend on our way to class and a man stood up from his spot and there was a brown smudge all up the back of the seat."

"Ew!"

"It smelled so bad!"

"Well, it was definitely chocolate. But she ended up buying everything she touched, so that was good. Martin will be happy."

"Do you get much business here?"

"Not during the fall, really. Mostly during the summer hols or in the winter when we have our Christmas decorations out."

"Is that hard on him? You don't have to answer that if he wouldn't want me to know. I have never been a part of a family business, so I don't know what it is like."

"His father's life insurance set them up pretty well. This helps, of course, but they're able to draw from their savings if they have to."

"Sorry to hear about their father."

"I don't want to speak ill of the dead, but his kids had it pretty rough with him around." Sarah's eyes were no longer sparkling. Her eyebrows were drawn together and she looked at her hands. "I think Shan might have turned out different, you know what I mean?"

Aoife nodded. She understood.

"I really hope things are going well at the doctor's. Martin was so worried about it."

"I'm sure the doctor knows what to do," said Aoife.

The girls had to wait until five o'clock before Martin came to the shop. His face was drawn and pale and Sarah was by his side in an instant. She didn't say anything as she hugged him. He leaned against her, weary of just standing on his feet. Aoife watched the pair with a sympathetic frown on her face, making space on the counter for Martin to sit.

"Oh, Martin! You look awful! What happened?" Sarah kept her friend's hands in her own as she stood in front of him.

"The doctor didn't understand." Martin looked so defeated. "Shan made up some rubbish about taking care of the baby all morning and since I'm at the shop and she doesn't look neglected, they took her side."

Aoife's mouth dropped.

"I explained that she doesn't go to her every time she needs to be taken care of and he just, he just said it was okay because babies are resilient and if Shan is doing more than she used to then it's a good thing. They said to give it a month."

"A month? Did you explain that she's not acting the way most mothers do with their babies? Did he say anything about postpartum depression?" asked Sarah.

"I asked, but Shan was in a mood and made me sound like a horrible person for even suggesting it."

"But you were just trying to help her, love! Surely she knew that!" Sarah rubbed the back of Martin's hand.

"She didn't care. Screamed at me that I was never home to help, that she couldn't trust me because I'm just going to accuse her of being a screw up even when she's trying her hardest." Martin was crying. "I don't know what to do! It was a disaster!"

"Aw, love!" Sarah glanced over her shoulder nervously, as if she was expecting a customer to come in and find them like this. Aoife quickly walked to the door and flipped the sign to say it was closed. "Maybe this means she's going to try with Tansy?"

"She's not." Martin shook his head. "She's just the same, Sarah. She's not going to. She doesn't care."

Sarah's shoulder sagged in a defeated manner. Nothing she said could cheer up her friend. She looked to Aoife, her eyes begging her to say or do something. Aoife felt her stomach sink. They had all been hoping this visit with the doctor would fix everything.

"She can't stay like that, Martin," Aoife said quietly.

"I know." Martin wiped his eyes. "But I don't know what to do. I'm about as useless with babies as Shan is, except I know I'm doing it all wrong."

"You're not," Sarah soothed, shooting Aoife another look, one that asked her to actually say something helpful this time.

"Do you have any relatives? Anyone who could take her, at least until Shannon gets herself together?"

"No. My mum, but I mean, how can a woman paralyzed from her neck down help a baby?"

Of course, their mother would be paralyzed.

"I was trying to think of people on my way over here, and I couldn't think of a single person."

"There must be someone," urged Aoife. "I would hate to see her taken away by social services. Not that they're bad, it's just... for a baby, you know, to have to leave everyone they know. I just don't like the thought."

"I feel like I have no options," said Martin with despair in his expression. "Especially since the doctor is on Shan's side."

"We'll help you, Martin. Right, Aoife?" Sarah squeezed Martin's hand.

Three months, two weeks and five days...

"I can't do this all alone." Martin wiped at his eyes.

"You won't have to," Sarah was saying.

"Sarah, you know I'm useless with babies!"

"No! Martin! You love her! You can bring her with you to work and I'll help you. Aoife knows how to take care of babies, too."

"Yeah." Aoife nodded automatically, her ears ringing.

Three months, two weeks, and five days...

Martin pulled his hand out of Sarah's grip and rubbed his palms over his face. He took several deep breaths, each one a little less shaky than the last. His hands fell slowly into his lap and he looked from Sarah to Aoife, his eyes wet and scared.

"I have to do this, don't I?"

"Shan might turn around in a couple days, love, it's not forever, just until things change, you know?"

"Yeah." Martin nodded, but he slumped his shoulders even more. "Just waiting for Shan to get better."

There was so much more meaning in that sentence than Aoife knew, but she could imagine a younger Martin watching his older sister become a shell, someone filled with darkness and pain and who didn't know how to smile back. How many times had hard things happened in Martin's life and Shan couldn't help? It was clear that he loved his sister and wanted what was best for her, but she knew it couldn't have been easy, especially with both parents gone in one way or another.

"Oh, Martin." Sarah's eyes filled with tears. "I know this is so hard, but we're here for you."

"Yeah." Again, Aoife nodded automatically, unsure of what else to say. Her heart was going out to him, wishing he wasn't in such a difficult place, but her own past was reaching out to choke the life out of her.

"Aoife's going to help, you know, and so will I." Sarah continued to say the same words, over and over, or maybe it was just in her head. "Aoife's going to help..."

Three months, two weeks, and five days...

"Aoife's going to help..."

Three months, two weeks, and five days...

"Aoife's going to help..."

"I need to go." Aoife came back to the present with a gasp, lungs burning for a deep inhale of oxygen. "I-I just..."

"Okay." Sarah barely looked at Aoife as she stumbled backwards to the exit.

"I need to go..." Now she was the one repeating herself. Aoife reached the door and rushed out.

She turned immediately to the sea and kept her eyes on the familiar blue color until she reached the rocky beach. There were groups of people dotted around her, but Aoife paid them no mind as she walked almost to the edge of the water. She had a moment of wanting to plunge headfirst into the waves to wash away the dirty feeling that was coating her from the inside out, but she knew from experience this feeling couldn't be washed away. Here she was, five years later, still struggling to breathe through the tightness that gripped her every time she remembered back to the day when it all came crashing down.

Three months, two weeks, and five days...

Aoife shook her head to clear her mind of the thoughts. This was her fresh start. She focused on the waves, focused on the rocks glistening with water, focused on the salty tang in the air. Seagulls flapped and squawked around her, searching for food. The sun warmed the back of her neck as she turned to walk to her apartment. It was okay, she told herself. It was all going to be okay. This was part of moving forward, just like she wanted. Besides, it wasn't like she was going to be the primary caregiver, she was just going to be helping out from time to time.

Right?

The sun set slowly that night and Aoife watched from the window, her supper of boxed macaroni and cheese cold and forgotten on the counter. It was times like that when she felt the most alone. Sometimes she was glad she didn't have anyone to remind her of what she gave up, but other times it meant that the pain and the broken dreams were hers alone to feel as the stars blinked to life. Once upon a time there had been friends that were more like family to stand with her in moments like this. She didn't think she would ever find friendships like that again, the ones tested by time and trials.

Martin wasn't sitting on the counter at the shop the next day when Aoife rode past after work and she knew she should stop to check in. She fought with herself for a moment, but her strong side won and she parked her bicycle. Tansy was a baby and Martin was her friend; she wanted to help them both.

"Hello!" Aoife called out as she walked in. The bell didn't sound above her and she glanced up to see it had been taken down. "Sarah? Martin?"

"Sh! She's finally calmed down!" Sarah popped her head around the corner from the back of the shop, a finger to her lips.

"Oh." Aoife put her own finger to her mouth and tiptoed closer. "Was this morning hard?"

"You have no idea." Sarah pressed her fingers to her forehead as if there was an ache there. "She needed to be changed and then it got on all of her clothes and, of course, we would have the busiest morning in ages and we ran out of change in the till and every time the bell would go off, Tansy would just scream her little heart out."

"Aw, I'm so sorry." Aoife frowned sympathetically. "Is she sleeping now?"

"No, Martin's trying to get her to sleep, but she's just not having it now, is she?" Sarah huffed out. "Poor little thing can't get comfortable. Martin is about to lose his mind."

"Does he need a break?" Aoife stood up straight and tall. She wasn't going to let her strong side lose now. "I could maybe..."

"Oh yes! Please!" Sarah was already on her way to the back room before she could finish talking. "Martin! Aoife is here to take a turn with Tansy!"

"Thank you, thank you, thank you!" Martin came out with his niece in his arms. His normally smart-looking outfit was wrinkled and disheveled, as was his hair. "I just need her to sleep! She's eaten and been changed, but I can't get her to sleep."

"Do you... I have... I mean, my apartment is just..." Aoife took the child into her arms and settled Tansy against her. It was like two pieces of a puzzle fitting together and Aoife couldn't ignore the way her heart beat a little faster at the feeling. "If you're comfortable with me taking her there to sleep, I can."

"Yeah, can I walk there with you? You've got your bike?" Martin wiped his brow and attempted to smooth out his shirt.

"Yeah, yeah, I have it just outside."

Tansy was quiet as she blinked her eyes against the bright sun and the sounds of people driving past on the road. Aoife didn't know what to say as she walked beside Martin. They were ascending the stairs when she thought about the fact that her apartment was mostly bare and the table was covered with her clothes. Martin didn't say anything when Aoife unlocked the door and let them in.

"I'll just let her nap and then bring her back to the shop when she wakes up, I guess. Do you have a bottle or something for me to feed her if she's hungry?" Aoife glanced around her home a bit self-consciously.

"Yes, I brought her diaper bag. Here." Martin handed a large, black bag over to Aoife and looked down at his niece. "You think she'll sleep for you?"

"I'm sure she just needs a little quiet. If she doesn't fall asleep, I'll bring her back," Aoife promised. "Don't worry."

"Right."

The sound of the sea didn't seem to bother Tansy as she slowly fell into a deep sleep, still cradled in Aoife's arms. Aoife wanted to sit in front of the window and rock the baby as she slept, but she didn't have a rocking chair. After she knew the baby was fully asleep, Aoife laid her gently on the bed and covered her with a blanket she found in the diaper bag. Tansy slept soundly, the little wisps of hair on her head blowing gently in the breeze as it came through the window. Aoife alternated between watching the baby and pacing at the end of her bed.

A smile crossed Aoife's face when Tansy woke up and fussed for someone to hold her. The smile was an automatic reflex and a lump pressed against the sides of her throat at the thought of another baby who used to make her smile by doing the same thing.

Stop it, Aoife thought to herself. *Don't you dare go there right now.*

Aoife reached for Tansy, soaking in all the details of the infant that she could. She desperately needed to see the differences and cling to them.

"Hi, Tansy!" Aoife murmured softly. "I'm here, baby. Hi. I'm right here."

The child calmed instantly and Aoife settled Tansy over her heartbeat. She was so small, so fragile, and Aoife couldn't keep herself from stroking the soft skin of her arms and legs, feeling each finger and toe and kissing the tip of Tansy's button nose. There was a tiny birthmark on Tansy's neck, just to the side. Several minutes had passed before Aoife realized she had thought only of Tansy, not anyone or anything else. Her chest felt loose and she breathed steadily.

"Look at that, Tansy girl." Aoife put Tansy back up to her shoulder and cuddled her. "I did it."

Martin expressed his gratitude numerous times when Aoife took Tansy back down to him. Sarah hugged her and whispered her own words of thanks into Aoife's ear. It was already close to the time when Martin would shut the shop for the day. Then he would take Tansy home to Shannon.

"Are you going with Martin's to help him with supper?" asked Aoife.

"I can't. I wish I could, but I'm meeting up with Max for something for his work this evening. He's said he's going to be okay, though."

"I'll try, anyway. At least the babe is in a good mood now. Aren't you, Tansy?" Martin smiled down at the baby that was still in Aoife's arms.

"She just needed a nap." Aoife followed Martin's gaze and tightened her arms around the child instinctively.

"What should I do for bedtime?" Martin suddenly lifted his eyes to Aoife's face, worry etched in the corners of his expression. "Do I hold her? Give her a bottle? Just lay her down?"

"I-I don't... I don't know." Aoife was taken aback by the questions. "I've always held her, but I guess... I guess she might not have to be held."

"I may have to call you a couple times. Sorry, Aoife." Martin sighed and reached out for the baby.

"Well, I don't have plans for this evening." Aoife felt Tansy's warmth leave her arms. "And I don't really have anything for supper..."

"Aoife, you're an angel!" Martin couldn't hug Aoife with his arms full of baby, but he reached over and patted her head. "Thank you so much!"

Aoife spent her evenings with Martin and Tansy for three days in a row before she allowed herself to even entertain the idea that had been knocking at the door of her mind. It was an idea that scared her, but less so now that Tansy was slowly filling all the places where her memory used to hurt her. As she watched the baby girl nap on her bed every afternoon, Aoife knew she could be doing so much more for Martin and Tansy than she was. She brought up the idea to Sarah first.

"I know you guys barely know me, but I'm willing to keep her for a while, you know, until Shan is better." Aoife twisted her hands together nervously. "I only have Miss Wilcox in the mornings and she could come with me. I know Martin is trying to run the shop and take care of his sister and everything. Do you think it's a good idea?"

"I think it is." Sarah was uncharacteristically somber and thoughtful as Aoife spoke. "You already help put her to bed and spend your evenings at his to help. I know the overnights and especially the mornings are hard for him."

"Yeah. Mornings are hard." Aoife nearly went back in time, but caught herself. It was important she stayed focused.

"Thank you for offering, Aoife." Sarah touched Aoife's arm lightly. "I know we don't know you very well, but the opposite is true, too. You don't owe us anything. This means so much to us."

Martin said nothing to Aoife's idea, because he was too busy crying and trying to not fall to his knees in relief. That evening, all of Tansy's things were moved over to the apartment by the sea. It didn't take long to move over Tansy's clothes, her diapers and bottles, and her bassinet. Sarah gasped when she saw how empty and bare Aoife's apartment was and Aoife quickly explained she enjoyed the open feel and the sea. Sarah and Max dropped off a rocking chair and Martin gave Aoife a wardrobe as a thank you present. Then, the door closed behind them all and Aoife was left with Tansy in her arms, her house transformed into a sort of nursery.

"What have I gotten myself into, eh?" Aoife spoke quietly to ease the tense silence she felt on her own. "We're going to become good friends, aren't we?"

Three months, two weeks and five days...

They weren't going to become good friends, though. Aoife knew it as she snuggled down for the night with the baby beside her and pillows building a wall on the edge of the bed. This was a repeat of what had happened years before and Aoife could almost taste the tears on her tongue as she thought about it.

"Hush, little baby, don't say a word..." Aoife started singing softly, even though Tansy was calm and almost asleep. Her voice broke and Aoife squeezed her eyes shut. "Hush, little baby, don't..."

Don't take him from me! Aoife heard her own cries echoing in her mind. *Please! Don't do this!*

"Shhh." Aoife rolled onto her side and placed a hand on Tansy's back. The baby was already asleep and her arms jerked at Aoife's touch. She began to move her mouth as if she were still sucking on her bottle, but then she was asleep again. A tear slipped down each of Aoife's cheeks and Aoife quickly wiped them away.

Chapter 5

Life With Tansy

Life with Tansy was everything Aoife had been anticipating, and so much more. The soft cuddles made up for the middle of the night feedings; the cooing and eye contact made up for the diaper changes; the sweet smell of lavender soap made up for the crying during bath time; and waking up to Tansy wriggling beside her made up for the lack of sleep.

Miss Wilcox was delighted to have Tansy with them in the mornings. She began knitting her little booties and hats and singing songs that she used to sing to her nieces and nephews before they grew up and had children of their own. The nurse even commented on how nice it was to have the baby about, giving everyone fresh perspective on life.

Because she had Tansy, Martin loaned her his car to drive back and forth to work. He would drive it to the shop and she would get the keys from him there. He would give Tansy a cuddle and a kiss before helping Aoife buckle her into her car seat. When they came back, Sarah would take a turn holding her while Aoife ate some lunch and made the baby a bottle. Then it was nap time; Aoife's favorite part of the day. She would wrap Tansy in a blanket and hold her close as she looked out through the window at the sea.

The beginning of October was Tansy's doctor's appointment. Aoife felt like a piece of her was missing as she went to work without her baby. It struck her just how easy it was to spend two weeks with a child and find yourself so wrapped up in her that even just a few hours apart was hard.

"Sometimes it's hard for me to remember you're not really her mum because you look so happy and natural when you're holding her," said Sarah as they waited for Martin to return. "How long have you had her for?"

Three months, two weeks and five days...

"Just, um... Almost three weeks." Aoife swallowed hard.

"You're doing such a good job taking care of her." Sarah's voice was serious as she spoke. "I was talking about it with Martin, like how well you do with Tansy, and he was close to tears saying how thankful he was that he knew she was safe with you."

"She's worth it," Aoife whispered.

"I know this has been a hard thing." Sarah watched Aoife carefully. "I think there's something that happened to you that makes this harder than just what we see."

Aoife gave her a sad smile. Sarah held her gaze for a moment longer, then turned away. There was a change in Sarah's mood as she switched topics.

"Max wants to have a rematch in Rummy because he cannot believe you beat him. He never loses and he can't handle it."

"I don't know why he would want to go through the humiliation of losing a second time, but okay." Aoife shrugged.

"I told Sam that you beat Max at a card game and he nearly lost his mind, he couldn't believe it. You've definitely impressed us."

"I'm known for my card game abilities back in New York, you know."

"Are you really?" Sarah asked in disbelief.

"No! Of course not!" Aoife laughed. "I'm known for... well, not for cards."

"I saw you trying out that hula hoop Martin ordered for the shop the other day and I was quite in awe at your skills, please tell me you're actually a professional hula-hooper!"

"Oh, rats! You've found me out!" Anything but the truth was good at that point. All of Aoife's energy needed to be focused on Tansy, not spent battling a past that looked like pointe shoes and performances. It was just so much simpler if no one knew.

Aoife let out the breath she knew she had been holding when Martin pulled up in front of the shop in his familiar black car. She ran out and saw the baby in the backseat, tucked under a blanket and sleeping peacefully. Aoife couldn't hide the relief on her face at the sight.

"Don't worry, I brought her back to you." Martin hugged Aoife tightly. "Doctor says she's doing amazing! Thank you for the notes you made so I could answer the questions."

"How was Shannon with it all?"

"Held her for a bit. Looked at her like she couldn't figure out where she came from." Martin tried to laugh at the memory. "But she's not ready."

"Okay." Aoife nodded and took a deep breath. "Okay."

Things began to change in October. Genny texted her out of the blue one day announcing that Peter Orlev and Alex Minsky were moving to London. Anyone who had anything to do with ballet and spent any time in New York City knew who they were. Aoife rolled her eyes at Genny's text demanding that the girl go see them.

I think they r starting a company there.

u could join.

Joining would mean leaving Miss Wilcox and Tansy. It would mean dropping out of the little world she had made that consisted of spending time at *Pop's Shop* reading mystery novels with Sarah, game nights at Max's house and walks along the beach so she could stare at the sea. Joining would mean reliving memories and thinking about people that hurt her more than anyone else in the world. Joining was out of the question.

Just leaving Tansy for an overnight to go to London for one of Sam's football games was hard enough for her. Sarah and Max were driving so she didn't have to take the train, but the trip still felt like it took forever. Maybe it was because she knew that once she arrived at Sam and Conor's apartment she could call Martin and ask him how the baby was doing, or maybe it was because she was nervous about seeing Sam again.

She settled in her mind that she wasn't going to be upset if Sam seemed disinterested or neutral towards her. She had been around enough to know that feelings were fickle, and just because he fancied her in Brighton didn't mean he would fancy her in London. It was the unpredictability of it all that made her stomach turn nervously. Sarah's chatter and singing with the music was a pleasant distraction, but not enough to make Aoife forget.

Sarah turned up a song on the radio and Aoife's ears caught the opening notes being plucked out on a guitar. She turned quickly to Sarah. Her friend noticed the sudden movement from the backseat and turned the volume back down before shooting Aoife an inquisitive glance. It took Aoife's memory a few minutes to catch up with what she was hearing, but then it did and for a second she was twenty years old sharing a stuffy apartment with Genny and crying herself to sleep.

"Do you know this song?" Sarah asked.

"Yeah." Aoife blinked the memories away and drew in a shaky breath.

"Do you like *Jupiter Waits*?" asked Max, checking Aoife's face in the rearview mirror.

"What?" Aoife's eyebrows pulled together in confusion.

"That's who sings this song, *Jupiter Waits*."

"I only know this song." Aoife frowned apologetically and looked down at her hands in her lap. "I forgot that was who sang this."

"I still can't believe they broke up," Sarah said to Max. "I really hope Jamie comes out with some solo stuff eventually."

"That would be so good, wouldn't it?" Max agreed.

It grew quiet in the car aside from the song still playing over the radio. Aoife looked out the window and studied the gray color of the sky. Her muscles ached to move with the melody and the crescendo of the music. That song was one of the first songs she choreographed for her contemporary class. She remembered spending hours in the studio with the lights down low, the music pouring through the speakers and her body twisting and swaying to the voice of a man singing about losing everything he loved the most. It was during one of those nights that Genny had confronted her about ignoring a couple of their mutual friends.

"*The boys said you aren't responding to their calls or texts. You have to talk to them, Eef. You're not going to make anything better by pretending like they don't exist!*"

"*I will respond. Later,*" said Aoife as she started the music again to drown out Genny's voice. She never did respond, and eventually The Boys stopped trying to get ahold of her.

To that day she still wished she had treated them differently. Maybe if she hadn't allowed herself to become wrapped up so tightly in how she felt they would still be friends. She didn't blame them for not reaching out to her anymore. She couldn't blame them; it wasn't their fault.

"Here we are." Max pulled into a car park and parked in a visitor spot. "Have you rung Sam yet to tell him we're here?"

"No, I'll do it now." Sarah put her cellphone up to her ear. She glanced over her shoulder at Aoife and gave her a quick smile. "I know he'll be happy to see at least one of us."

"Me, of course," said Max distractedly. He missed the pink in Aoife's cheeks and the wink from Sarah. "I've always been Sam's favorite."

"Sure, Max." Sarah rolled her eyes. "He's not answering, but he knew we'd be in around this time. Conor should be here even if Sam's not."

The three visitors from Brighton went up the elevator to the fifth level where Conor and Sam's apartment was. There was music coming from the apartment and Sarah smiled at Aoife as she muttered how that was probably why Sam had missed her call. They waited for the door to open.

"You made it! Hello!" Sam was smiling broadly as he flung open the door. "Welcome, welcome!"

Aoife noticed that he didn't make eye contact as she walked in. It was okay, though.

"Come on, I'll show you where to put your bags. Conor! They're here!"

The music stopped and Conor appeared from what Aoife assumed was the living room. He smiled as he walked over to greet them all with hugs. Aoife could smell the faint smell of the aftershave Sam had worn the day she met him as he gave her a quick, tight squeeze around the shoulders.

"Hey, guys! Welcome."

"Conor, you want to take Sarah and Max to their room? I'll show Aoife where hers will be," said Sam, pointing the others down the hall. Once they had turned to head to the other room, Sam gave Aoife a little smile. "It's good to see you again."

"You, too." Aoife hugged her overnight bag against herself as she saw the blue in his eyes shine at her.

"Let me take your bag." Sam held out his hand. "Your room is just over here. Wanted to make sure you were comfortable. I wasn't too worried about Sarah and Max since they're family and all, but this is your first trip to London, right?"

"If you don't count my taxi ride to the train station from Heathrow."

"I don't." Sam shook his head seriously. "It doesn't count."

"Well, then, this would be my first time."

"Perfect. I hope this room suits you well enough." Sam opened the door to what was probably the master bedroom. "It's actually my room, but I'll be sleeping in Conor's room tonight. This way you have your own bathroom and, look here! A balcony with a view over the little park over there."

Aoife smiled as she looked around. The room was spotless and she would never have guessed it was actually Sam's room. Sam opened the door to the balcony for her and she stepped out. She pulled her sweater closer around her neck as the wind nipped at her bare skin, but she smiled.

"Do you like it?" Sam sounded tentative as he asked.

"Of course I do." Aoife gave him a smile. "It's beautiful here."

The expression on Sam's face was one of pure delight as he gazed back out over the little patch of London he could see from his balcony. Just then Aoife's phone beeped, and she suddenly remembered Martin and Tansy. She pulled out her phone without excusing herself and looked at the screen. It was a selfie of Martin and Tansy at the shop. She put a hand over her heart and smiled at the image.

"You, uh, hear from someone you like?" Sam coughed.

"Just Martin." Aoife turned the phone so Sam could see the picture as well. "Sent me this."

"Aw, the little baby." Sam's eyes crinkled as he smiled.

"Yeah. He knows I'm missing her while I'm here."

"You spend a lot of time with her, then?"

"Well..." Aoife didn't know how much others were supposed to know about the situation. "I only have my job with Miss Wilcox and Shan's been having a hard time transitioning, so I do what I can."

"That's great." Sam looked Aoife in the eyes as he spoke. "I'm sure they're very thankful for your help."

"I feel like I'm getting the better end of the deal at the moment, though." Aoife looked back down at the picture. *Until it's over...*

"I can't promise you cute babies, but I will do my best to make today everything you could hope for."

"I'm sure I'll love it." Aoife sent back an emoji with heart eyes and slipped her phone into her pocket. "I love watching sporting events, so I'll have at least that."

"You do?" There was a definite pleased tone to Sam's question.

"Yeah, they're exciting and you're surrounded by people who like at least one thing the same as you. My dad used to take me to baseball games all the time when I was little. It was fun."

"Carl?" Sam opened the door to go back into the bedroom. He waited for Aoife to follow before he shut the glass door and locked it.

"I'm assuming Sarah told you his name." Aoife gave a little laugh. She had spent more than one lazy afternoon in *Pop's Shop* telling Sarah minor details about her parents and watching her soak it all in.

"Are you asking me to reveal my sources?" Sam feigned a shocked expression.

"She's the only person here who knows about my parents, it's not like I had to do a lot of detective work to figure it out." Aoife laughed and Sam ducked his head, a red-faced smile working its way onto his face. "But carry on."

"Well, you're all she talks about most of the time when I call her." Sam's cheeks lost their ruddy tinge and he stood up straight again. "She really enjoys being your friend."

Aoife couldn't think of anything to say in response. There was a knock on the bedroom door and Conor stuck his head into the room.

"Gotta leave. Traffic is already bad today. Don't want to be late." Conor's serious expression lifted when he looked in Aoife's direction. "Do you like your room, Aoife?"

"I do. It's very nice." Aoife glanced around again, taking in all the gray tones and muted colors Sam had used to decorate.

"I hope you enjoy it because Sam always steals the blankets when we have to share a room."

"I shall enjoy it," promised Aoife.

"Good! We'll see you after the game!" Conor waved.

"My jersey is number twenty-two, in case you want to know who to look out for," said Sam in a low voice as he moved to follow Conor to the front door.

"Twenty-two. Got it."

The apartment was quiet once Conor and Sam left. Aoife wondered where Sarah and Max were. She walked down the carpeted hallway, enjoying the comfortable squish of it under her feet as she moved slowly. She ended up in the TV room and stood in front of their impressive DVD collection, reading the titles. There were a few she liked and she wondered if they would let her borrow a couple.

"Not like I have time to watch movies with a baby in the house." Aoife hugged herself tightly at the thought. She missed Tansy.

It was colder without the baby's little body snuggled against her chest, her soft head tucked under Aoife's chin and fingers stuck in her mouth. Aoife wanted to make sure she was fed and happy and sleeping. The worrying was pointless as Aoife knew that Martin was more than capable of taking care of his niece, despite his claims of being clueless with babies.

"There you are!" Sarah walked into the room and came to stand beside Aoife. "Oh my gosh, I love this film!"

Aoife squinted at the title. *10 Things I Hate About You.* She smiled and nodded.

"Me, too."

"If we weren't going out tonight, I'd say we should watch it after the game. Maybe next time."

"Going out?"

"Yeah." Sarah looked at Aoife with a grin. "Sam's gotten us into this really great club. Originally it was only if they won we would go to celebrate, but he decided we could go even if they lost."

"Do you think they'll lose?" Aoife remembered how Sam's jersey number was twenty-two.

"Nah." Sarah shook her head. "They're really good. They've won almost every game this season."

"That's exciting. I'm glad I get to see them play." Aoife felt a curl of anticipation in her belly. "I haven't gone to a game for a long time."

"You're always welcome to come to any of Sam's games when Max and I come. Or even if we don't come, I would suppose, seeing as Sam's got a spare room."

"Wouldn't that be weird? For me to come see his games by myself?"

"It doesn't have to be weird," said Sarah cryptically as she tilted her head sideways to read more titles on the shelf.

"Right."

Even if Sam hadn't told Aoife what his number was, she would have figured it out sooner than later. The entire stadium erupted with cheers the second he stepped out onto the field and Sarah stuck her pointer fingers between her lips to let out a loud whistle. Max leaned over at halftime to ask Aoife if she was enjoying the game. The flush in her cheeks and the way her smile hurt her face was all the answer he needed.

"Martin says you look like you're having the time of your life!" Sarah held her phone in front of Aoife's face, distracting her from the game for a brief moment.

"When did you take that picture?" Aoife saw herself, leaning forward, her hands to her face, her eyes wide and anxious.

"Just now, silly. If I'd known you were so entertaining to watch at footy matches, I would have brought you with me ages ago."

Aoife rolled her eyes fondly, but she was distracted from her friend when the ref blew his whistle. The whole stadium was on its feet for the last two minutes as three goals were scored in quick succession with Sam and Conor's team coming out the victors. Aoife and Sarah hugged as they cheered, yelling for Sam and Conor amid the deafening crowd.

"You won!" Aoife watched Sam hug his sister and spin her around out of excitement. She was surprised when he reached to give her a hug as well. "You were great!"

"Well, I wanted to make your first time in London one to remember," he said with a wink. "Besides, my boy Conor had my back."

"Sick goal, mate!" Max was clapping Conor on the shoulder in congratulations for scoring the winning goal.

"Should we go celebrate?" asked Conor with a grin.

More of Sam's football team joined them at the club. All of them knew Max and most of them knew Sarah. They all shook Aoife's hand and asked her where she was from and why she was in the UK before heading to the dance floor with their drinks.

"You said you were better at dancing." Sam had to shout for Aoife to hear him.

"I did." Aoife glanced at the crowded dance floor. "You want to see if you can keep up with me?"

Sam's grin was all Aoife received as an answer. He grabbed her hand, surprising her by intertwining their fingers to keep them together. They had changed clothes after the game, Aoife borrowing one of Sarah's dresses and a pair of black, knee-high boots. It wasn't her favorite to dance in heels, but she could do it. The two inches added to her height closed more of the height difference between herself and Sam. They pressed their way into the middle of the crowd and stopped.

"You look really lovely tonight."

It was hard to tell if Sam's face was red because of the body heat radiating off the dance floor, or if it was from the words he said. Aoife didn't care, because her face was hot as well. She started dancing along with the song, her body falling effortlessly into the beat. It had taken her time to learn how not to always hold herself tall and straight as she danced, but she had finally reached the point where people couldn't tell that she used to be a ballerina when they saw her.

Aoife forgot about Sarah and Max, and Tansy being an hour away in Brighton as she and Sam danced to song after song in the middle of the dance floor. His buddies joined them with girls on their arms. The DJ would hype them up before dropping a beat that made the entire club jump. Aoife forgot she was on the other side of the world and that she was taking a break from being a dancer. Her heart was beating wildly as she noticed another girl trying to out-dance her. With a smirk, she pulled a move and stepped away from Sam. The girl did the same. Back and forth they went for several minutes, until the song was over. As the DJ played a new tune, the girl reached forward and introduced herself.

"My name is Leanne." Her voice was thick with a Northern accent. Her dark skin and hundreds of tiny braids showed up in the dim light of the club and Aoife smiled at her as they shook hands.

"Aoife. It's nice to meet you."

"Aoife?" The girl stopped. "Aoife Stewart?"

Aoife froze, her stomach dropping to her feet.

"Don't look like that!" Leanne laughed. "I'm friends with Peter and Alex. We've been watching your final performance..."

The rest of Leanne's words became a blur as she realized what the girl was saying. Final performance. *The Nutcracker*. December 2011. She was Clara and her heart was broken.

"They'll be so excited to know you're in town!" Leanne's phone was in her hands. "I'm going to tell them I just danced with you! They talk about you all the time."

"I doubt they talk about me all the time." Aoife swallowed hard. She felt Sam's hand on her shoulder, tugging her to come back to him. She didn't want him to know. "Tell them I say hello. I have to go."

Aoife asked Sam if they could get drinks and rest for a minute. He agreed easily and led them off the floor. Conor was sitting at their table, a few others around him. They were laughing and gesturing as they talked.

"You okay? Did you know that girl?" asked Sam.

"No, she just... She wanted to know if I still taught dance." Aoife took a drink and grimaced. She wasn't used to drinks like this.

"You should. You could make a load of extra cash that way." Sam grinned at her before he turned away, seemingly shy all of a sudden.

"Do you want to stay?" asked Aoife, staring at her drink.

"What?"

"Do you want to stay? Here, at the club."

"Do you want to leave?"

"I'm tired." It was true. And now she was missing Tansy. She would have already finished her night-time bottle by now.

"Yeah, let's get out of here. I'll tell Conor."

Aoife waited for Sam by the door, pulling her jacket on over the dress. She knew she would be cold after she left the warm room. Sam's hand found hers as he joined her. She gave him a quick smile when he gave her a questioning look with his eyes. They were so blue, even in the dark of the room.

The cool night breeze filled Aoife's lungs and she paused for a second, taking a deep breath and looking up at the sky. The lights of the city were too bright to see any stars, but Aoife tried to look for them anyway. Their hands slipped apart and Aoife watched Sam shove his hands into his pockets and walk slowly beside her.

"Thanks for tonight." Aoife crossed her arms over her chest, hoping to preserve some body warmth. "I've really been enjoying myself."

"Really?" Sam's head snapped up and in her direction. A grin spread across his face. "Good. Good, I'm glad. Sorry I couldn't take you around earlier and properly show you all the things."

"It's fine. I'll have other opportunities."

"Of course. Any time you want to come to London, you can always stay round mine and Conor's."

"Thank you." Aoife exhaled and saw her breath for a quick second before it disappeared. "Do you think you'll come up to Brighton again soon?"

"Maybe. I do from time to time. It's nice to go back to see everyone, that's for sure." Sam was quiet for a minute. "You really like it there, don't you?"

Aoife's lips twitched up into a small smile as she imagined the view from her window. She nodded.

"Good. That's good."

Taxis and cars rumbled past them. Lights shone out of stores and restaurants. Some of them were closed, but others were still open and accepting customers. People were walking quickly, some talking loudly, some with their heads down, unsure why they were still out at that time of night. No one else seemed to be taking a leisurely stroll down the sidewalk like herself and Sam.

"Tell me about yourself," she said, feeling shy and brave all at once for making such a request.

"You tell me something about yourself," Sam shot back with a crooked smile.

"I hate mushrooms," said Aoife without skipping a beat. "Your turn."

"Ah. I don't like sunflower seeds."

"I once wore a dress that was neon green."

"Wait, where did you wear it?" Sam stopped her. "I need to know."

"It may have been a dance recital," Aoife hummed and kept walking.

"My mum used to dress Sarah and I in matching clothes because everyone thought we were twins when we were little."

"You're the older one, right?"

"Two whole years older," said Sam, puffing out his chest. "Don't let her tell you any different."

Aoife laughed, but was quiet. She shivered the tiniest bit and glanced back up at the sky. Her eyes were drawn to the street light on the corner and she blinked against the brightness of it.

"Come on, your go." Sam nudged her shoulder gently with his own, his hands still in his pockets.

"My favorite type of candy is Swedish Fish."

"I failed maths in college."

"In college?" Aoife turned to look at him.

"Not like American college. It's like high school for us."

"Ah. I set my science experiment on fire once. People still think it was an accident."

"Aoife!" Sam looked genuinely shocked. "The first time I said a swear word it was during an argument with my dad. I was grounded for a week."

"Hmmm." Aoife went quiet again, but this time she spoke up before Sam could nudge her. "I haven't talked to my dad in almost five years."

"Well, that was proper deep." Sam tried to lighten the mood but failed to. "What happened?"

"He has his new family. We were never close," was all Aoife said, even as the shouts rang through her memory.

"I promised her I would never let you give it up, Aoife! I promised her that no matter what I would make sure you kept at it!"

"Well, I'm quitting anyway! You can't stop me!"

"You can't just give this up! I've been watching you on stage since you were three years old! You come alive doing this! This is what makes you happier than anything else in the world, Aoife!"

"Do I look happy to you, Carl? Huh?" Tears had begun to run down Aoife's face. *"Does it look like I'm enjoying this?"*

"I don't know what happened to you while you were gone." Carl's voice lowered until he was speaking softly. *"I don't know why all of a sudden it's so different, but this... this is what you were made to do. Don't give it up."*

"I don't want to do it anymore."

"Then at least find a new type of dance. Anything. I don't care, just...
don't stop dancing. I promised her."

That was the last time she had spoken to her father. It was only because of him that she became a dance teacher, focusing on contemporary, jazz, ballroom, and even a tap dance class. It wasn't for her father's sake, it was because of his promise.

"Do you talk to your mum?" asked Sam, unaware of the thoughts in Aoife's head.

"I haven't spoken to her in years, either."

"I've made you sad, now." Sam frowned at the way Aoife was staring at her feet as they walked. "Can I tell you about the time I let Sarah get in trouble for the dog having a poo in the house?"

"Please," said Aoife with a hopeful smile.

After three more blocks, Sam brushed his hand against Aoife's. They didn't walk all around London holding hands, but they walked farther than they realized when they finally got a call from Sarah asking them where they were.

"Aoife's probably completely shattered, Sam! Bring her home!" she scolded him.

They found a taxi and Aoife didn't complain when Sam sat close to her, his arm around her shoulders. She was too tired to even say goodnight when they finally made it to his apartment. The king-sized bed was more comfortable than anything Aoife had slept on for a long time, and she didn't remember pulling up the covers before she was asleep, her arms close to her chest, empty of the baby.

Her body woke her up at six, telling her it was time to get up and take care of Tansy. She wanted to pretend like she wasn't going to cry when she remembered Tansy wasn't there. She sent a text to Martin, asking him to tell Tansy she missed her and would come back to her soon. There was no going back to sleep for Aoife, even with the curtains closed to hide the inky-black lingering in the sky. When she finished her long shower there was a touch of pink on the horizon. It was still too early to wake anyone else for the day.

The kitchen was cold and dark when she tip-toed in to find something to eat. She hadn't seen around the house the day before so she wasn't sure where to look for breakfast. She wondered if she could slip out of the house to grab some coffee before anyone else woke up and noticed she was gone. The clock on her phone said it was a quarter to seven and she had seven unread text messages. Three were from Martin and four were from a name she hadn't seen on her phone for a long time.

Aoife! come meet us 4 breakfast!
plz
did u party 2 hard last nite?
Peter says he misses u

Aoife typed out a message and waited for an address. She wrote a note saying she was going out for some coffee and set it on the kitchen counter before she left the apartment. Her jacket and the excitement of seeing old friends kept her warm as she walked the two blocks to the cafe she had typed into the GPS of her phone. The cafe was almost completely empty, aside from some bleary eyed workers behind the counter, but two wide smiles in the corner caught Aoife's attention and she hurried over to them.

"Aoife! My, you're a sight for sore eyes!" Alex Minsky wrapped his arms around Aoife easily. "It's been too long!"

"Alex! You're growing a beard!" Aoife reached up to touch the blonde scruff with her fingers, the smile on her face hurting because she was so happy.

"I know! I'm a man now!" Alex placed a kiss on Aoife's cheek before letting her go to hug the tall young man with dark shoulder-length curls that stood behind him. To the world it was Peter Olev, but to her, it was someone she shared one of her longest-lasting friendships with.

"Peter!" Aoife could cry at how familiar the embrace felt. Peter had hugged her at some of the loneliest, darkest moments of her life. Tears stung her eyes. "Peter!"

"Hey, Eef." Peter pressed a kiss on her forehead. "It's so good to see you."

The two young men brought Aoife to their table and had her sit down. A cup of coffee was already at her spot, along with a donut with chocolate sprinkles. They had eaten breakfast together enough to know her order, even five years between times.

"How did you know I was even here?" asked Aoife, warming her hands on the cup that held her steaming beverage.

"Our friend Leanne texted us last night. We got it this morning," Alex said, pushing the cream and sugar to Aoife's side of the table.

"Can't believe you're actually awake," said Peter, the fond smile still on his face as he watched his friend. "I guess you were out pretty late."

"My internal alarm clock hates me." Aoife felt her heart pound harder at the fact that her friends were right there, sitting across from her. "Genny told me you were in London, but I wasn't sure if your numbers were still good."

"We'll pretend to believe you." Alex's voice was gentle and paired with a smile. They knew why she had left, had held her as she wept when she did leave. "Thanks for agreeing to breakfast. Was half afraid you'd make an excuse, or we'd miss you because of our crazy schedule."

"Why are you eating breakfast so early anyway?"

"We don't really like being photographed while we eat," said Alex with a laugh. "Peter decided to just come out early enough that no one will be awake."

"You guys are a big deal here, huh?"

"It'll pass," said Alex with a shrug. "People are always excited when something new happens. Eventually people won't care if they get our picture or autograph."

"I'm so happy for you. You deserve it." Pride swelled in Aoife's heart. "You're both incredible."

"You could be right there with us," Peter spoke again. "Remember when we started in that baby ballet class together with our moms?"

That was how far back her friendship with Peter went: to before they could barely stand.

"Did everything together." Peter watched her face carefully, gauging her response to his words.

"Not everything," Aoife reminded him. "Or I would still be there."

"That wasn't your fault." Alex shook his head and reached across the table to give her hand a squeeze. "None of us knew that was going to happen."

"Are you doing any dancing at all here in the UK?"

"I dance in my apartment sometimes, when the people who live below me are gone." Aoife shrugged. "I don't really know how to start over."

"You're always welcome to join us." The blue in Alex's eyes was darker than Sam's, but more familiar. Aoife had stared into them for hours. Not for the same reasons she wanted to stare into Sam's, but because they had been dance partners for years. He knew her body's strengths and weaknesses as well as she did.

"I can't." Aoife took a deep breath. She wanted to tell them, even though she knew they would be less than happy about the news. "I'm... I'm taking care of someone's baby."

Peter said nothing, his eyes squinting the tiniest bit. The green in them melted together with flecks of gray. Beside him, Alex was quiet as well. They waited, allowing her to explain herself before they spoke.

"I have a couple friends in Brighton. The shop they work at is close to my flat. The guy, Martin, his sister had a baby but she... she's not right in the head." Aoife cringed as she spoke. "She wouldn't take care of her, and Martin runs a shop and takes care of his sister, so I offered to keep the baby for a while."

"Did you tell them about Roe?" asked Alex quietly.

"No. No, I haven't told them. Didn't feel like I needed to. Tansy needed someone to take care of her and I had the time to do it."

"I'm proud of you, Eef." Peter's voice was sincere. "I know how hard it must have been for you to agree to it. That baby is lucky to have you."

"Yeah, for sure. She's a lucky baby." Alex nodded emphatically. "How long will you have her for?"

Aoife shifted in her chair.

"Well, be careful." Peter reached across the table and held Aoife's hand. "Your heart is tender and I don't want it breaking again."

"Might be too late to warn me..." A tear snaked down her cheek as her voice broke. "Just coming here for one night made me ache on the inside."

"It doesn't have to end the same way." Alex had a furrow between his eyebrows, showing his concern for Aoife. "You know that. It could end completely differently."

Three months, two weeks and five days...

"Don't go back there in your head." Peter squeezed her hand. "And if you ever need us, as friends, we're here for you."

"Thank you." Aoife put her other hand on top of Peter's. "How long are you guys staying in London for?"

"Hopefully at least two years," said Alex. "Maybe longer if everything works out like it is supposed to with the company."

"Back in your homeland." Aoife smiled at Alex.

"Yeah, look who's the foreigner now?" he teased.

"How did you even decide to start your own ballet company in London?"

"My old dance instructor set it up, actually. He wanted to do something different and asked Peter and I if we would be willing to run it."

"I've really enjoyed it, though," said Peter thoughtfully. "It has been a nice change. Starting something of our own... I like it."

"It's growing quickly, though," added Alex. "We're really pleased."

"I'm happy for you guys." Aoife smiled at them.

"You'll come visit us from time to time, right?" Alex asked with a grin.

"You can bring the baby," added Peter.

Aoife wanted to cry again, but she stopped the quivering of her lips with a sip of coffee and another bite of her donut. The boys talked about the company and the different dances they were deciding between. Both subjects Aoife understood and could interact with. Aoife mentioned what Leanne had told her the night before.

"Of course we talk about you, what do you expect?" Alex scoffed with a laugh. "We worked with you for years."

"I'm sure you danced with other excellent dancers after I left, though. It has been five years."

"We've danced with other dancers, naturally," said Peter. "But none like you, Eef."

"You're just saying that because we grew up together." Aoife couldn't disguise the way her voice broke. "You're sweet."

"Aoife, we're professional soloists, we don't tell people they're good at dancing because we want them to feel good about themselves."

Aoife knew Alex was right and it made her miss that part of her life, for just a second. Three customers came into the store in a row and the young men pulled up the collars of their jackets. They nodded towards the exit and gave her a sad smile. She understood. Their time had to end.

"Come see us soon," Peter hugged her goodbye. "You're always welcome."

"I will." Aoife took one last look at their familiar faces as they stood to leave. "I promise, I will."

"Bye, Eef."

And then they were gone, their scarves covering their chins and eyes focused on the ground. Aoife could hardly believe how far they had shot into stardom, but it warmed her heart. They were two of the best dancers she had ever had the privilege of knowing. She finished her coffee and the last few bites of her donut before she left.

Aoife didn't realize she wouldn't have a way to get back into the apartment until she was standing in front of the locked door knowing that everyone inside was still asleep. It was barely eight o'clock; she was sure it would be hours before anyone woke up and heard her knocking.

Another picture of Tansy appeared in the texts on her phone and Aoife immediately called Martin, asking to see her baby. Martin babbled on and on about everything that had happened in the last twenty-four hours since Aoife had left, saying how his niece had fallen asleep on his chest as he watched television and it was the sweetest thing ever.

"I'll be back as soon as I can." Aoife touched the screen where the baby's face was. "Okay, baby? I'll be back soon."

"You miss her, don't you?" Martin moved the phone so Aoife was looking at him. "I'm glad you do. Keeping her whilst you're away is showing me just how much work taking care of her can be, yet you never complain. I know it's because you love her."

"I do." Aoife wasn't sure if she was allowed to say it.

"I know she loves you, too. Look, she's looking for you!" The screen showed Tansy again, her legs kicking and fists flailing as Aoife spoke.

"Hi, baby! Did you have so much fun with Uncle Martin? Were you a good girl for him?"

After the call ended, Aoife was more anxious than ever to get back home to Tansy and the sea. She knew the others were still in bed, but she rang the buzzer anyway. There was no response for two whole minutes and Aoife was about to give up and sit down outside the door to wait when the lock slid and the door opened a crack.

"Aoife?" Conor rubbed his eyes as he tried to see who was at the door. "Why are you out there?"

"I wanted to get coffee and I didn't think about needing to get back in. I'm so sorry!"

"How long were you waiting out there?" Conor shut the door behind her.

"Maybe, twenty minutes?"

"You should have buzzed earlier!" Conor frowned. "Didn't you know Sam and I have a coffee maker?"

"I didn't know where anything was."

"I'm so sorry, we're the worst hosts ever," Conor groaned and rubbed his hands over his face.

"No! No, this was my fault. I woke up too early and didn't know where anything was. You guys were very generous to have us stay here last night. Especially since Sam steals all the covers."

Conor chuckled.

"You can go back to bed, I'll be fine. I'm fed and caffeinated so I'm good until you all wake up."

"Do you want to watch a film?" asked Conor, starting towards the room that held the large screen TV.

"Oh, sure..."

"How do you feel about musicals?"

Aoife felt her face practically glowing at the question. Conor smiled at her silent response and opened the cupboard of DVDs.

"I love musicals, but Sam always wants to watch manly movies whenever we watch a film. What about *Les Mis*?"

"Please!"

The others woke up as the movie was ending, their eyes puffy from staying up too late the night before. Conor was asleep again, a blanket wrapped around him like a tortilla. Aoife was crying, as she always did when she watched the movie, humming along with the songs, a picture of Tansy that Martin texted her an hour earlier still on the screen of her phone.

"You watched it without me?" whined Sarah, one of Max's sweatshirts hanging on her shoulders.

73

"Oh good, you watched it without me." Sam stretched his arms over his head and yawned. "Although Conor's sleeping, so he'll probably want to watch it again."

"I don't understand why you don't like it." Aoife knew she had circles under her eyes as dark as everyone else's.

"It's just so hard to pay attention with all the singing."

"Or, you've decided you don't want to pay attention because you're lame." Aoife turned back to watch the last five minutes. She was surprised when the couch dipped down beside her and Sam was there. "You're ruining the whole thing by starting it here."

"It's too late, I'm determined to finish it out to the end."

"Sam! It's the last five minutes!" Aoife gave him a look of exasperation. "You can't ruin a movie like this."

"What are you on about? Make up your mind! Should I watch it, or should I not?" The grin Sam was trying to hide told Aoife he knew exactly what she meant.

"Fine. Go ahead, ruin the movie by watching the last five minutes."

"Sh, I'm trying to watch the movie." Sam leaned closer to whisper in her ear.

Aoife knew he had done it purposefully so their shoulders would be pressed together. He had almost succeeded in finding an excuse to hold her hand when Sarah joined them, singing along with passion and emotion. Aoife laughed and joined in, singing softly, but gesturing widely.

"This is why I don't watch musicals! Because of loonies like you two!" Sam complained when Aoife nearly smacked him with her elbow. But he finally had his excuse to hold her hand; to keep her from accidentally hitting his face.

Sarah left for the kitchen as the credits rolled, leaving Sam, Aoife and a sleeping Conor. Sam leaned his head on Aoife's shoulder and squeezed her hand. A swoop flooded her stomach at the physical touch and she responded with a quick lean of her head against his.

"Did you sleep well?" he asked.

"I did. Your bed was very comfortable."

"Good." Sam shifted until he could give her shoulder a quick kiss. "I wanted you to like London."

Aoife's words froze in her throat as Sam stood to his feet and offered a hand to help her from the couch. He led them to the kitchen where Max and Sarah were already busy at the coffee maker and stove. Aoife thought about Alex and Peter and smiled. Her early morning out had been more than worth it.

-Chapter 6-

Forevers & Not Forevers

Aoife dressed Tansy in her warmest outfit and kissed the tip of her nose as they got ready for the day. It was raining, and the windows rattled with the chill wind that raced across the sea and through the streets of Brighton. Tansy cooed softly, screwing up her mouth into a gummy smile, drool running down her chin.

"Oh, silly girl!" Aoife took the child's bib and wiped her face and between the folds of her neck. She let Tansy grip her pointer finger and shake it in her tiny baby grasp. "What do you have now? Do you have my finger?"

The baby made a happy sound and Aoife let out a deep breath. She had spent the better part of the night pacing with the little one, patting her back and singing any song she could think of, trying to soothe her. Exhaustion didn't even seem to cover what she was feeling at that moment. She almost wished she could cancel on Miss Wilcox so she could sleep when Tansy went down for her morning nap.

"I'm happy you're all good this morning. We're all good, aren't we? All good now?" Aoife kissed Tansy's cheek, feeling it wet with drool again. "I love you, sweet baby."

The electric kettle switched off, signaling to Aoife that her water was ready to pour over her instant coffee. Until she had a coffee maker, she had to make do with what she had. With Tansy in the crook of her arm, she walked over to the counter and carefully poured the hot water into her cup. The hot smell of coffee reached her nose, and she felt her weary body gather its energy at the scent. It was too hot to drink still, but she knew it was just a matter of minutes before it was inside her. She opened her tiny fridge and pulled out the carton of milk. Tansy moved in Aoife's arm and reached out jerkily for the light coming from inside the fridge.

"You like that light, huh, Tansy girl?" Aoife hummed absentmindedly. "Pretty lights."

Aoife's coffee was barely cool enough to drink before it was time to leave. She pulled on her jacket and slipped the strap of Tansy's bag over her head to settle it across her chest. Tansy's blanket was laid out on the bed and then wrapped around the squirming infant. Aoife talked to her as she held her against her shoulder, watching the stairs carefully and putting down one foot after the other. The wind was blowing from across the sea and every breath had a taste of saltiness.

"Oh, Aoife! You look wet!" Martin was almost to Aoife's building with an umbrella when she met him, the blanket over Tansy's head. "Here, stand under here."

"Thanks! It's going to be a cold, wet day!" Aoife snuggled Tansy closer.

"How's the little babe?" Martin couldn't resist pulling the blanket away for just a moment to see Tansy's face. She squealed up at him and Martin gasped with joy. "Hello then, darling! Hello!"

They buckled her into the car seat and tucked her blanket around her. Martin held the umbrella over Aoife until she was safely behind the wheel and pulling away from the curb. She played music quietly, her ears attentive to any cry Tansy might make. The drive ended quickly and Aoife covered the baby's head with the blanket again.

"Good morning, girls," said Miss Wilcox with a smile. "How is the little one today?"

"Say, 'Very well, Miss Wilcox. I'm wearing the hat you made me!'" Aoife pulled the baby out of her seat and held her close to Miss Wilcox so she could feel Tansy's soft hands.

"Oh, very good!"

Aoife spread Tansy's blanket on the floor and put a few of her favorite toys beside her. She helped Miss Wilcox use the bathroom and then settle into her chair. She handed the worn knitting needles to the elderly woman before Aoife took her spot on the floor next to Tansy. Tansy followed Aoife's movements with her eyes, kicking and waving excitedly. Aoife put a hand on the baby's squishy belly and gave it a rub.

"Now, Aoife, tell me," began Miss Wilcox. "What are you doing for the holidays?"

"Holidays? Like, Christmas and New Years'?"

"Mmm." The woman nodded.

"I guess I'll be here." Aoife hadn't thought about it. It was only the middle of October. There was so much time.

"I was wondering if you would be traveling back to New York."

"There's no need to. I would probably enjoy it more being here."

"I'm asking," she paused, "because I need someone to fly with me to The States."

"You mean, you're leaving for the holidays?"

"No, I mean I'm leaving."

Aoife was stunned. She felt Tansy's foot kick against her leg and she heard the rattle as the child shook it in her fist, but everything else was numb. She stared at Miss Wilcox, her mouth hanging open.

"Why?" It was all Aoife could articulate.

"Because I need to be closer to my family. It makes no sense to be here, having you take care of me, when I could be near my nieces and nephews."

But what about me? Aoife wanted to cry. Miss Wilcox had been the start of the new season that brought Aoife back to life. The elderly woman had become so dear to her.

"H-have I... have I done something wrong? Something y-you don't like?"

"No, dear. No." Miss Wilcox stopped knitting. "Come here."

Aoife went and knelt down by the woman's feet. The bony yet soft old hands found Aoife's face and she felt the tear that was there. She clucked her tongue regretfully and leaned forward until she had kissed the top of Aoife's head.

"I'm getting in your way, child."

"No! No!" Aoife didn't even know what Miss Wilcox meant.

"I am. You need time and room to dance again. Between me and the baby, well... All I can say is that I'm not going to be around much longer and I don't want to stand before the Lord and try to explain why I kept you from dancing when that was what He made you to do."

A sob caught in Aoife's throat.

"If I promise to dance, will you stay?"

"I don't want your promises." Her tone was so kind as she spoke. "I know you would mean it, but you wouldn't be dancing for yourself. You need to find those reasons again."

"Please, don't leave me." Aoife should have been embarrassed by the way she was crying on Miss Wilcox's knee, her hands holding onto her like a small child throwing a fit.

"Hush now." Miss Wilcox freed one of her hands and smoothed Aoife's hair back from her forehead, using her sense of touch to make out what her face looked like. "I'm not leaving you yet, but I know I can't keep you from it much longer. Lord knows how much I'll miss you. You and your baby."

Aoife took a shaky breath and reminded herself that Tansy wasn't really hers. When they were done at Miss Wilcox's, Aoife took a different route home and found herself sitting in front of the dance studio Sarah had pointed out to her over a month ago. She sat for a few minutes before mustering up enough courage to even unbuckle and step out of the car. Tansy didn't seem to mind the blanket over her head again as Aoife carried her inside. A girl with a long blonde ponytail wearing a pink tracksuit sat behind the front desk.

"Hello, can I help you?" she asked. She looked very young.

"Is it okay if I see the rooms? I'm looking into doing dance." Aoife swallowed down the word "again" and breathed steadily. Tansy moved, trying to pull the blanket down from her face.

"There's no classes at the minute," said the girl, standing up from her office chair. "But you can see them."

The hallway went past a changing room and two smaller rooms that held pianos and had floor-length mirrors. Aoife could smell the faint odor of sweat and hair spray in the air.

"Here's our main room where we do all our beginning classes."

"Thank you." Aoife stepped in. The lights came on and she saw a large rectangular room with mirrors all down one wall.

The phone rang and the girl left with a nod. Aoife walked further into the room, shifting Tansy so the baby could see. It seemed like sacrilege to be in the room in her street clothes. Her feet went into first position, then second, then third...

"This is how you do ballet, Tansy," whispered Aoife, watching herself in the mirror. She didn't do any turns or jumps because of the baby in her arms, but she moved across the floor in quick fluid motions. Tansy shrieked excitedly when she was jostled from Aoife's arm going out to help her maintain her balance. "You like it?"

She stopped dancing when the girl came back to the door of the room.

"I'll have to think about it. Thank you." Aoife put the blanket back over Tansy's head, even though the rain had mostly stopped, and ran out to the car. Tears were hot on her cheeks and she muttered over and over to herself that she shouldn't be that afraid of dancing. "Miss Wilcox is right, Tansy; I can't just do this for her."

Aoife burst into the shop, tears still on her face. All she could think of doing was handing Tansy to Martin so she could run home and have a good cry on her bed. She froze, however, when she spotted Sam's smile by the counter. He straightened as soon as he saw her, his eyes lighting up. This was not good.

"Hey, I have to go to my place quick." Aoife could see the confusion on the faces of her friends as she pressed Tansy into Sam's arms, the one who had reached her the quickest.

"Are you all right? Have you been crying?" asked Sam, genuine concern in his voice.

"Aoife, what happened? You okay?" Sarah tried to hug her.

78

"I just… I need to go home…" Aoife's chin was quivering and she turned on her heel, desperate to leave before she dissolved into full-on crying again.

"Aoife, wait!" Sam's voice called after her.

She ran down the sidewalk, the large, fat drops of rain hitting her face and shoulders. She didn't want to create a scene by running, but if she didn't run, she would drop to her knees in the middle of everything and cry like a baby. A hand grabbed her shoulder and pulled her to a stop.

"Aoife, hold on for a second!"

It was Sam.

"Sam, no." Aoife tried to get away from him before he could see her eyes swimming with tears.

"Just wait! Please!"

"I-I need to g-go home." Aoife's words caught on the sob working its way up her throat.

"What happened? Let me help." Sam's expression was soft; he reached for her arm with his hand.

"You can't." Aoife stepped back. Her eyes were burning and she knew her nose was probably red from how hard she had been crying in the car. "I just really want to be alone."

Sam hesitated.

"I need to be alone." The tone of finality in Aoife's voice hurt, almost as much as the look in Sam's eye as he took a step back and gave a tiny nod.

It hadn't felt like a lie when she said it, but the second Aoife was alone in her apartment, she felt crushed by the weight she was trying to manage on her own. She clung to the window frame, pressing her forehead against the pane and watching the rain streak down the glass. Her hand went to her phone.

"Peter," Aoife choked out the name.

"Eef, what's wrong?"

And that was Peter for you; he always knew when Aoife was upset.

"I'm having the worst day!"

"Sit down, Aoife. Tell me what happened."

Didn't he have rehearsals or classes or meetings to be in? Didn't he have other people in his life that he should be with at that moment? But he made it sound like he had all the time in the world for his old friend. His slow, deep tones coming through the phone like they had so many times before.

"I went to the dance studio. The one here, in Brighton." Aoife sagged into the rocking chair. "I can't do it, Peter. The thought of going back to it all scares me to death."

"Hmm."

"And when I got to the shop to drop Tansy off with Martin, Sam was there." Aoife pressed her thumb and forefinger against the corners of her eyes. "He wanted me to tell him why I had been crying, and I told him to leave me alone."

"Who's Sam?"

"My friend who lives here, Sarah, it's her brother. He lives in London and I-I think he might have liked me."

"But you think you've changed his mind because of how you treated him?"

"You should have seen his face, Peter." Aoife chewed on her bottom lip. "He wanted to make sure I was okay, and I... I snapped at him."

"If he changes his mind after one emotional encounter, I don't think he's ready for a relationship, Eef."

"You're probably right." Aoife sighed. "But I feel badly."

"I understand."

"Peter, can I come see you guys tomorrow?" she whispered.

"Of course. We told you that you were always welcome."

"Thanks." Aoife wiped the last of her tears away and inhaled deeply. "I'm glad I can call you again."

"You always could, Eef."

"Sort of." The lump crowded back up in her throat. "But yes, I know."

"See you tomorrow. Bring the baby."

Aoife nodded, despite the fact that she was on the phone. Another deep breath helped her to her feet after she hung up. It took all of her courage to walk back down the stairs and up the two blocks to *Pop's Shop*. It wasn't until she saw the shop that she realized she hadn't eaten lunch like she normally did after she dropped off Tansy. Oh well. Her stomach was hurting anyway.

"Aoife! You had us worried!" Sarah jumped up from her spot when the bell tinkled over Aoife's head.

"I'm sorry. Had a bad morning." Aoife couldn't see Sam.

"Is Miss Wilcox okay?" asked Martin, his long arms holding onto his niece a bit awkwardly. He didn't mean to be, but his arms were so long and Tansy was so small.

"Mentioned she might be moving." That was all Aoife was going to say about the situation.

"Really?" gasped Sarah. "I can't believe it! What will you do?"

Aoife shrugged.

"Aw, love, don't be worried. She might change her mind again. She would miss you and the babe too much, I know she would," said Martin.

Aoife struggled to remain calm, to pretend that everything was normal, as she talked with Sarah and Martin. Sam could be heard from the back room on the phone. Aoife pushed the fact that he was there out of her mind and focused on the light-hearted conversation. The secret stash of chocolates Sarah kept behind the counter helped.

These were the things that were becoming normal and steady for Aoife; Sarah's stash of chocolates, Martin singing any song that came up in conversation, the card games at Max's house where they would play 90s pop songs and laugh at how competitive it became between Max and Aoife. Aoife knew that Sarah's first childhood pet was a Parrot named Chaucer and Martin's favorite song at age ten was "Complicated" by Avril Lavigne. They knew that she loved watching *The Magic School Bus* when she was little and that she couldn't snap her fingers until she was twelve. It was safe and she loved it. She didn't want anything to change.

When Tansy rubbed her eyes, signaling it was time for a nap, Aoife gathered the baby back into her arms and left, Sam still on the phone in the back. She was too emotional and tired to have supper over at Sarah's that night, even though the thought of not having to cook sounded nice. There was just too much going on inside her head to risk it. After sending Sarah a text with some sort of excuse about Tansy not being able to sleep, Aoife went to the kitchen and made herself a sandwich, ignoring her twelve cans of breakfast beans. She still hadn't tried them yet. Her phone buzzed when Sarah texted her back.

sam will miss seeing u

soz that T is having trouble sleepin

Aoife sent a frowning emoji, took her sandwich and went to her rocking chair. Tansy was sleeping peacefully on the bed, the blanket wrapped snugly around her warm body. The blond fuzz on the top of her head was longer and curled up into wisps now. Aoife held her cup of tea in her hands as she rocked back and forth, her eyes watching the sea. The sound was murmuring in her ear, reminding her that she was so small compared to the whole world, and she was going to be okay.

Saturday morning was cold and rainy again, but Aoife decided to keep her plans to visit Alex and Peter in London anyway. She called Martin to ask if she could borrow his car, and was surprised when he said yes without asking her what for. Tansy looked so cozy Aoife couldn't help but give her an extra cuddle when she put a gray sleeper and pink-knitted hat from Miss Wilcox on her.

It took longer than Aoife originally planned as she had to stop twice to hold Tansy and calm her down. The infant didn't like riding in the car for so

81

long and she refused to sleep until Aoife held her in the back. She dropped off almost instantly, her mouth sucking at nothing.

"It's okay. I got you," whispered Aoife. She sat and stared at Tansy for another ten minutes before slipping her back into her car seat and carefully buckling her in. The baby slept until they reached London.

Aoife wasn't sure exactly where to go once she entered the large building where Peter had said they would be, but she didn't have to worry about it for long. The elevator dinged and Peter exited the lift. The friends smiled as they approached each other.

"Here's the baby!" Peter reached for Tansy before he even hugged Aoife. "She's beautiful, Eef."

"Thanks." Aoife's cheeks were pink as she watched the young man hold Tansy close to his face, grinning at her. "Tansy, this is Peter. He's my best friend."

"Don't lie to babies." Peter finally curled an arm around Aoife's shoulders.

"Don't take this the wrong way, but I wish it was a lie." Aoife sighed against Peter's solidness beside her.

"What about Sarah?"

"She is a friend. A good one. I'm not myself around her just yet, though."

"And Sam?"

"We've only seen each other a couple times, Peter. I doubt anything will come from it all. He was probably just looking for a fun time."

Peter nodded thoughtfully.

"She likes you." Aoife pointed at the contented set of Tansy's mouth as she stared up at Peter.

"You want to be friends, Tansy?" Peter gently tickled Tansy's belly and chuckled when she blew drooly raspberries up at him.

"I think that's a yes," said Aoife.

"I hope so."

"Where's Alex?"

"Upstairs, going through some steps with Leanne."

"Has to keep working, huh?"

"Mmm." Peter nodded, his eyes staring at Aoife softly. "I can take you up if you'd like."

Aoife nodded.

The baby grew fussy in the elevator, not liking the way it moved while she stayed still. Aoife took her from Peter and shushed her, telling herself internally to calm down as she swayed. They stepped off the elevator and Aoife stalled for a minute.

"I think I need to change her."

"Bathrooms are here." Peter pointed to a door near them.

With shaking hands, Aoife changed Tansy's diaper. She hadn't seen Alex dance since the last time they danced together. Final performance. *The Nutcracker*. December 2011. Being chosen for solos at such a young age was rare, and she should have been as ecstatic as Alex. Instead, she had a breakdown backstage. Alex had hugged her, whispered fiercely into her ear that he believed in her, and that they were going to finish the dance. She swallowed back her tears and allowed him to lead her across the stage. She had done it for him; he deserved that night.

"Ready?" asked Peter as she stepped out of the bathroom. "He'll be done in an hour if you want to wait."

"I want to see him." She meant it.

"Okay." Peter led the way down the hall and Aoife noticed for the first time that he was still wearing his dance slippers, the toes peeping out from under his baggy sweats she assumed he pulled on when he went to greet her.

Aoife didn't allow herself to stop or blink when she heard the familiar strains of *Swan Lake*. She clasped Tansy against her, kissed the baby's forehead, and walked into the room.

It looked like almost every other room Aoife had ever practiced in with the big mirrors, the barre along the wall, and the lights showing every corner. Alex noticed her right away, a huge grin flashing on his face, even as he continued to dance with Leanne. The girl who had danced with Aoife at the club looked different in her leotard, her shoes laced around her ankles and her hair pinned into a bun on the top of her head. She had her eyes halfway closed, as if doing the movements from memory. Aoife remembered what that was like.

As soon as the song ended, Alex left Leanne and jogged across the open floor to Aoife. He grabbed her into a crushing hug, careful only about the baby. His skin was slick with sweat and she could feel him panting as he held her, but how many times had they known each other like this after dancing their hearts out on stage?

"Aoife! So good to see you!"

"You said that last time," said Aoife with a smile.

"Is this the baby?" Alex poked Tansy's soft sides and smiled when she babbled at him. "What's her name?"

"Tansy." Aoife couldn't help but feel like a proud mother. "She's six weeks old."

"Hello, Tansy! Hello! Hello!"

"I forgot how he can be around babies." Aoife laughed as Alex cooed and spoke gibberish, pulling faces at the little girl.

"Hi, Aoife!" Leanne approached the group of friends in the corner. "Good to see you again."

"Hi."

"Fancy another dance off?" The idea was a joke, but Aoife knew the girl was up for it if she said yes.

"Not today."

"Aoife, do you mind, though," Alex started, then stopped. "Leanne and I were trying to do a Présage lift, and we're having a hard time. We used to do those really well, it might help Leanne if she saw us..."

"Alex, I..." Aoife looked around the room. "I haven't done it in so long."

"We'll start with a fish lift first. Don't want to hurt you."

"I'm not dressed for it..." Which Aoife realized wasn't that big of a deal as she looked down at her black leggings and loose t-shirt under her denim overshirt.

"You don't have to, I understand, honestly, I do." Alex rubbed the back of his neck, trying to keep his eyes from begging her hopefully.

"I'll try."

Aoife handed Tansy to Peter, hearing her gurgle and fuss softly as she left Aoife's arms. She slipped off her shoes and pulled off her socks, feeling the floor against the bottoms of her feet. Her eyes went up slowly, giving Alex a tentative smile. His hand fit around hers as he pulled her to the middle of the room.

"Don't worry, I'm not going to drop you," he whispered quietly, his mouth nearly touching her ear when she turned to catch what he was saying. "And if it's too much, just say so. We'll stop."

"I'm shaking." Aoife held her hand out in front of her. Alex grabbed it and gave it a squeeze. "Okay, I'm ready."

"You know how to do this." The confidence in Alex's voice made Aoife straighten, her shoulders back, her arms long.

There was no music, but Aoife knew how to follow her partner's lead, keeping her eyes on him. He held her gaze when he could, smiling softly at her. The lift came and Alex held her easily off the ground. Leanne and Peter clapped as they stepped apart.

"Are you good?"

Aoife nodded, her cheeks flushed with determination. It was as if she had never stopped. Alex's hands found her waist and they went through the steps. How many times had they practiced that lift? She remembered the night they had stayed hours past dark, practicing it over and over. Finally it had been perfect, but they were too tired to celebrate their own success. Adrenaline rushed through Aoife as her body moved automatically and Alex's strong arms lifted her over his head. Aoife's heart stopped beating for a moment as she tried to keep the tears back. They had done it. It was perfect.

The pride radiating from Peter and Alex was enough to make Aoife's heart burst and she buried her face into Alex's shoulder as he hugged her. He was still smiling when she pulled back and wiped at her blurry vision. Leanne clapped loudly, gushing about how perfect it had looked while the sound of Tansy's unhappy squawk filled the room.

"Think the sound of us shouting scared her," Peter apologized as he let Aoife take Tansy from his arms.

"Hush now." Aoife settled the baby in her arms so Tansy could see her face. "I'm right here. It's okay, Tansy. It's okay."

Tansy's whimpers died down until she was sucking on her fist without a peep.

"Is she tired? Remember when Roe would suck on his fists like that when he was getting ready to fall asleep?" asked Alex.

"Yeah," murmured Aoife softly. Of course she remembered, but she was glad Tansy was creating a new spot in her heart. Roe's spot was still there, still empty, still aching at the wrong times.

"He used to always need that one blanket." Alex stroked Tansy's arm with one finger. "Couldn't sleep without it."

"Tansy will sleep with any blanket." It wasn't their fault that the only baby they had to compare her to was Roe. "She won't use any bottle except her own, though. I left her bottle at Sarah's on accident once so I bought a new one at the store, but she refused to open her mouth to use it."

"That's okay, Tansy." Peter's voice made Tansy look in his direction. "I don't open my mouth for weird bottles, either."

"I should take her someplace more quiet so you two can keep practicing," said Aoife.

"There's a room with a sofa in it across the hall." Peter picked up the diaper bag and Aoife's shoes from the floor. "I'll sit with you."

"I'll be done quick as I can and we can go find someplace to eat. I'm starved!" Alex said over his shoulder as he walked back to the middle of the room, Leanne following him.

The sofa was leather and hard, but Aoife snuggled Tansy into her arms while instructing Peter how to make a bottle. As soon as the rubber tip was in her mouth, the baby's eyes closed and she ate until she was asleep. Aoife and Peter spoke in low voices, talking mostly about how life had been since moving to England. They were still talking when Alex tiptoed in, dressed in his street clothes.

"Can we go or do we have to wait for Tansy to wake up?"

"I brought the baby carrier." Aoife jerked her chin towards the diaper bag sitting by Peter's feet. "She'll stay asleep if she's on me. Are there places to go that are walking distance?"

"Always," said Alex.

Their meal at an Italian restaurant was delicious, if also a bit awkward for Aoife as she tried to eat and not spill on the baby's head. The company was delightful, though, and when Tansy stirred from her nap, Aoife was surprised to see how late it was.

"Time to go, eh?" asked Peter.

"I need to make sure I'm home with her before bedtime. Plus, I'm not sure I would like to drive in the dark if I don't have to. This is my first time driving from London to Brighton."

"We'll see you again soon, though." Alex put a smile on his face. "This is the second time in a month, so I'm not too worried about it."

"Thanks for spending the day with me."

The young men hugged Aoife and her baby before they slipped quietly out of a back exit. Aoife was cold, but Martin's car warmed up nicely for her. Tansy cried twice, and Aoife stopped to talk to and cuddle her. It was almost dark before she arrived in Brighton. She pulled up to Martin's house and texted him to let him know she had dropped the car off.

"Come in!" Martin appeared in the doorway, a smile on his face. "Just made supper! Join us!"

There was no pause for an answer before Martin reached the car, where he unbuckled Tansy from her seat and carried her inside. She still had wet eyes from fussing for the last five minutes of the trip. Martin kissed her face and told the baby how much he had missed her that day. Aoife followed behind him until she saw who she was joining for supper; Max, Sarah and Sam.

"How was your day out?" asked Sarah brightly, her eyes and smile big and welcoming. "Did you have a good time?"

"Yes." Aoife tried to smile at Sam, but she didn't know what to do after he smiled back at her. She looked down at the table awkwardly. "Tansy doesn't like driving for long, though, I've learned."

"You had the baby drive? Pretty sure that's illegal!" joked Sam, looking around the table as everyone laughed.

"How far did you drive?" asked Max, cutting into his steak with his knife, holding the meat steady with his fork.

"Just to London." The spot between Sarah and Martin was open, so Aoife sat there, nervous that it was directly across from Sam. She saw him glance up at her when she said where she had been.

"London? Without telling us?" Max put on an air of fake offense. "I'm only joking. You don't have to tell us where you go."

"What did you do? Shopping? Seeing the sights?" asked Sarah.

Aoife took a drink of water. Everyone was staring at her. Even Tansy was quiet and had her face turned towards where Aoife was sitting. The silence made Aoife almost choke on her drink.

"You okay? You're pale." Martin reached over to place a hand on her forehead, but she leaned away from him.

"I'm okay. Just tired from driving." Aoife gave them all a smile. "I went to this Italian place there. The food was delicious."

"You went to London alone with the baby to eat Italian food?" Max was perplexed. "You know there are Italian restaurants here in Brighton, right?"

"What was the place?" asked Sam.

"I don't remember the name," Aoife said with a frown. "Peter knew..."

"Peter?" Max stopped chewing. "Ah! There we have it! You went to meet a boy!"

"Aoife! You have a secret boyfriend?" Martin gasped.

"N-..." Aoife tried to answer, but was cut off. The blush in her cheeks only encouraged them.

"Whoo! This is exciting!" Max rubbed his hands together. "Tell us about this Peter!"

"Peter is an old friend from school."

"Right! Look at how red your face is!" Max laughed.

"You have a horrible poker face, love." Martin shook his head and took another bite of food.

"He's just a friend! Happens to be in London." Aoife directed her words to Sarah who forced a smile in response. Sarah was trying to glance discreetly at her brother to make sure he was okay. Aoife saw Sam blink in her direction a few times before looking down at his food.

"Aw! You should have invited him here! We would have loved to meet him!" said Martin, completely missing the way Sam had gone blank and silent.

"Maybe one day," said Aoife casually.

"You mean, he's staying here for a while?" Sam looked up.

"Yeah." It took everything inside of her to not sigh at the way Sam looked back down at his plate and focused on his food. He had every right to think she was seeing Peter romantically. If he looked at her phone, he would see pictures on the camera roll of Peter and Alex holding Tansy, goofy grins a mile wide. What would she say to that?

"That's nice that you got to see an old schoolmate!" Sarah seemed to be covering for her brother.

"Is he from New York, too?" asked Max.

"Yeah. He grew up just down the street from me."

The subject of conversation moved onto one of Sarah's old schoolmates, and then Max's first football coach. Sam was asked about his favorite memory from school, but he shrugged it off, excusing himself to use the toilet. Aoife kept her eyes on the food, reminding herself that she and Sam had only seen each other a couple times and he was overreacting to the situation.

Sam asked to leave as soon as supper was done, leaving Aoife and Tansy to help Martin with the cleanup. Tansy lay on her back in the playpen Martin still kept in the corner of the living room, allowing Aoife to use both her hands as she washed the dishes.

"Do you know much about Sam?" she asked. Martin felt like a safe person to talk with.

"Yeah, a bit I reckon." Martin paused from putting the leftover mashed potatoes into a container. "I've always been closer to Sarah, though."

"Does he usually have a lot of girls in his life?" It was blunt, but Aoife needed to know what kind of person he was.

"Sam? Could do, obviously, he's proper fit, but he's never been about the girls, him." Martin shook his head as he answered. "Max has tried to set him up, and Sarah, too, but he's not all that interested in relationships most of the time. Think he knows how crazy his schedule is and knows how much work he would have to put into it."

"But he just walked right up to me at the pub that night I met him!" Aoife spun around, letting little puffs of soapy water drip from her hands. "He seemed so flirtatious, so casual about it."

"I see." Martin nodded knowingly. "He did seem well keen on you."

"But why?"

"Don't know, love. Maybe because you're beautiful and you're interesting and Sarah adores you."

Aoife returned to the dishes in the sink. She sunk her hands into the warm water and took several deep breaths. It was hard to have it all make sense, because it didn't really. She washed a fork and two cups before she turned around again.

"I didn't mean to hurt his feelings."

"I'm sure you didn't, Aoife." Martin's voice was kind as he gently patted her head twice. "It will all get sorted."

There was a rustling in the hallway when Shannon shuffled past to sit on the sofa in the living room and watch television. Aoife stared, her breath hitching in her chest as she watched the woman stare at her baby for a full thirty seconds before flopping onto the sofa. There was an unhappy cry from Tansy and Aoife continued to observe. Shannon didn't move.

"You're probably tired. You can drive my car home." Martin's quiet voice startled Aoife. "Call me if you need to talk."

Aoife nodded before drying her hands. Tansy was still crying when she picked her up, glancing over at Shannon as she straightened. Their eyes met, but Shannon's were blank and dull. The taste of her food coming back up made Aoife turn around and hurry out to the car.

Sarah kept a close eye on Aoife for the next two weeks. She invited her over to eat, watch movies, go shopping, do their nails and anything else she could think of. Aoife agreed to the hangouts, keeping in the back of her head that that would be the day Sarah accused her of breaking Sam's heart, but it never was. She laughed, shared secrets, snuggled Tansy, and straightened Aoife's hair.

"Your hair is so pretty," said Sarah as she held the straightener in her right hand and brushed through Aoife's long tresses with her left. "I hope mine gets to be like this when I grow mine out."

"I love your curly hair!" Aoife smiled, even though Sarah could only see the back of her head. "I used to wish I had curly hair, but straight hair was better for..."

Aoife stopped.

"What?" said Sarah with a little laugh.

"Nothing."

"No! You can't just tell me your hair is better than mine and then not tell me why!"

"I didn't mean it like that!"

"Oh really?"

"I was just going to say for dance. You know, when I was a teacher, it's easier to pull it back when it was straight."

"I guess I'll believe you." Sarah's hands moved through Aoife's hair again, taking a handful and straightening the locks carefully. "Aoife, you always mention how you were a dance teacher before you moved here, and you take care of Miss Wilcox now, but you never mention what you used to do before that. Did you go to uni? Did you have any other jobs?"

"Not really."

Sarah sighed and Aoife tensed.

"Aoife." Sarah's voice was quiet. "I don't want you to feel like there is anything you have to hide from me. I won't judge you."

"I know." Aoife tugged on Sarah's hand to pull her closer. Sarah hooked her chin over Aoife's shoulder and left it there, leaning against Aoife's back comfortably. "But some things aren't nice to remember."

"Mmm." Sarah didn't move from where she knelt. "I had a boyfriend in college once, before Max, of course. Never in a million years did I ever think I had a chance with Max Burgeon! Everyone fancied Max."

"Yeah?"

"Yeah." Sarah's voice was low and close to Aoife's ear as her chin stayed on her shoulder. "I didn't really fancy this other bloke, but he was asking me to date him so I said okay. He turned out to be not very nice."

"Sorry."

"Sam was so angry when he found out this guy had been abusing me. He was angry at me, too, because I had tried to hide it from him."

"How did he find out?"

"The guy punched me and broke my nose. Gave me two black eyes."

"Sarah!" Aoife twisted until she could at least see Sarah's profile.

"I'm okay now, you nutter." Sarah straightened and crawled around Aoife until she was sitting in front of her. "I don't tell many people that, because I don't want them to know how embarrassed I was, and how weak I felt. But I've found that if I tell the right people, I don't feel small and looked down on, I feel happier in my friendship with them."

"Thank you for telling me." Aoife wanted to share, but she couldn't; if she started she would never stop. "And I do trust you. I just... I'm not ready yet."

"I'll be here when you are." Sarah took Aoife's hand in her own for a second before turning to look at Tansy. "And I'll be here for you, too."

"Can't believe she's almost two months old," Aoife said with a smile that instantly turned sour.

Three months, two weeks and five days...

"I can't either! Just look at how grown up she looks! Yes!" Sarah leaned over to nuzzle Tansy's neck. The baby giggled and grabbed onto Sarah's hair. "Oh! Tansy!"

Aoife helped Sarah free herself from Tansy's little fist, holding onto her hand for a moment. The baby made a loud, happy noise and Sarah laughed.

"Are you going to dress her up for Max's Halloween party?" asked Sarah suddenly.

"Oh." Aoife blinked. "I don't know if I can go. It will be late for her."

"But Max always has the best parties!"

"It's not that I don't want to go!" Aoife smiled. "I just have a baby. For now. For a while."

There was quiet as Sarah stared down at Tansy. Then, she leaned over and hugged Aoife tightly.

"I hope she stays with you forever."

It was the thought Aoife never let herself grab onto: forever. Once upon a time things had seemed certain and she could say forever about friendships, and passions, and life goals. Then everything changed and she knew forever wasn't real. Not for her anyway. Sarah smiled at her as their hug broke apart.

"Thanks for being such a good friend."

"Aw, Aoife. You don't know how many times I've thanked my lucky stars you walked into *Pop's Shop* that day."

"Still got those cozy cushions you tried to sell me."

"Good. They're the best in all of Brighton."

Aoife set the cushions around herself and Tansy that night as they lay on Aoife's hard mattress. She stared up at the ceiling, listening to the sea and Tansy's tiny lungs moving in the dark. In two hours it would be time to get up and make Tansy another bottle, but she didn't close her eyes just yet. She leaned over Tansy carefully and picked up her phone to text Peter.

u free 2morrow?

She laid the phone on her chest as she waited for a response, before realizing that he was probably sleeping. She wouldn't have to take Martin's car to London if she didn't want to, she could take the train. That way she could hold Tansy the whole time and not have to stop to comfort her. Sleep finally closed her eyes, taking her into fuzzy dreams and memories until her alarm vibrated and Tansy woke, a soft whine escaping her mouth.

"Time to eat," Aoife said to herself, sitting up and climbing off the bed. Her feet touched the cold floor and she groaned, but she turned on the electric kettle to warm up some water. Tansy was still mostly sleeping when the bottle was ready, but she opened her mouth to suck at the nipple when it pressed against her lips.

There was a response from Peter the next morning when Aoife forced her eyes open. Her throat was dry and she wanted to stay in bed, but the promise of coffee and a cozy morning of sitting in Miss Wilcox's sitting room kept her from falling back asleep.

can't c u 2day.
2 much going on
this wkend?

91

That weekend was Max's party for Halloween. Aoife couldn't skip out and disappear to London on a night that was important to her new friends. She didn't have a costume and she knew she would only be able to stay for a while with Tansy, but that was beside the point.

it's ok. feeling better this AM
was thinking 2 much.

Aoife didn't check her phone again until it was time to leave the house. She saw a text from Alex as well as a response from Peter. Alex just said good morning with the sunshine emoji while Peter told her to call him later if she wanted.

She learned something new about Miss Wilcox when she mentioned Max's party. The elderly woman made Aoife lead her into a bedroom where she had never been before and start going through closets and dressers. After two hours of putting on clothes Miss Wilcox herself used to wear when she was young, Aoife had several costume choices.

"I made something for Tansy. I knew she would need a costume."

The bundle Miss Wilcox pressed into Aoife's hands was a tiny ballerina tutu with pink, knitted booties to act as slippers. Aoife tried not to cry as she drove back across town. She had had a tiny leotard and tutu when she was Tansy's age, something Peter's mom had given to hers after she was born. There was a picture of her wearing it, lying on her mother's lap, her mother's elegant hands holding her safely.

"Hey! It's our girls!" Martin was perched on the counter with the paper. He set it down to reach for Tansy, greeting her with a kiss and a raspberry to her cheek. "Hello, little babe!"

"Aoife!" Sarah came out from the back room, her eyes frantic and phone in her hand. "I need you to help me! Sam and Conor just arrived at the train station, but Max's meeting is running late, which means he can't pick them up and take them to his office. I have to meet with the lady who is catering the party because she can't reschedule, which means I can't pick them up. They can't go to the house because it's being decorated, so I told them to come here, but I have to leave."

"Okay?" Aoife's brow furrowed as she tried to follow what Sarah was saying.

"I just need you to entertain them until I get back! Do you mind?"

"No, not at all." Aoife listened to herself spit out the words and instantly regretted her answer. She knew she couldn't refuse Sarah, but spending time with Sam and Conor sounded like a really bad idea. As soon as Sarah had left, Aoife turned to Martin with an aggravated sigh. "Why?"

"Tell me why! Ain't nothing but a..." sang Martin. He stopped when he saw Aoife's stony expression. "Okay, okay. Sorry."

"I'm being serious."

"Come now, Aoife, they're friendly lads. They'll be good to you." Martin gave her a light pat to the head.

"I'm worried about my conscience."

"Maybe this afternoon will be exactly what you and Sam need to get back on the same page?"

Aoife didn't want to think of that. She wanted to hide herself away and think about the tiny ballerina outfit Miss Wilcox gave Tansy. She wanted to call Peter and tell him how much the word forever bothered her. She wanted to stand by her window and stare at the sea.

"Aoife! Did you buy this for Tansy?" Martin's voice held a note of awe as he dug something out of the diaper bag. "This is so cute!"

"Miss Wilcox gave us some outfits for the party this weekend." Aoife saw the costume in Martin's hand. "She's going to be a ballet dancer."

"That is adorable! Tansy! You're going to be the cutest baby at the party!"

The thought that Tansy would be the only baby at the party crossed Aoife's mind, but she didn't say it out loud.

"Did you say she gave you a costume as well?" Martin was still smiling down at Tansy as he asked.

"Yeah, let me show you." Aoife took out her phone and pulled up the pictures she had taken of the different outfits in the mirror as she tried them on. She stopped when Martin gasped.

"That's the one! That's the one, Aoife! Yes! Have Sarah do your hair and you'll look just like a young Madonna!"

"You think?" Aoife had been partial to the 70s rocker chick outfit she was able to put together with everything except for the shoes. "I do like it."

"Aoife, you're going to be so hot!" Martin was beside himself with excitement. "You and Tansy are definitely going to steal the show at the party."

"Can you believe Miss Wilcox had these clothes?" Aoife flipped through a few more pictures before shutting off the screen. She would wear the rocker chick outfit.

"Oh, I definitely can! She was quite the looker when she was younger! Even into her sixties she was dating younger men." Martin's giggle punctuated his statement. "She even dated Max's dad for a while when he was just out of high school."

"What?! Max, our Max!" Aoife's eyes grew wide.

"Yes!"

"Does Max know that?"

"Oh yeah, everyone does. It was a huge scandal when it happened, but Mr. Burgeon is a pretty easygoing fellow and after he married Karen, they got to be friends again."

"Oh my gosh! I don't think I can look at her the same anymore!" Aoife covered her eyes.

"Have you seen pictures of her when she was younger?"

"Yeah, but not that much younger!" Aoife's cheeks were red. "Did you know Max very well in school?"

"Max? No! Not at all!" Martin laughed again. "He was off at boarding schools and traveling the world with his father and mother. He didn't come back to Brighton to stay with his grandparents until he was about fifteen. He tried to act normal, but none of us were buying it."

"Is that why Sarah said she didn't think she would ever date him?"

"Yeah. Every girl thought that, although some girls tried."

"How did he meet Sarah?"

"That's their story to share," said Martin with a wink. He glanced out the window and saw a customer approach the door. He passed Tansy over to Aoife and went to greet the woman.

Aoife knew she only had about five more minutes before Conor and Sam arrived and she would have to play hostess. She wasn't sure if she should take them back to her place or to a cafe or if they would even want to stay with her. A small wave of relief washed over her when she saw them grinning as they climbed out of the taxi and walked into the store.

"Aoife! Martin! I missed you guys!" Conor was the first to greet them. "Little baby Tansy!"

Sam walked over with a slower stride, still smiling. Aoife looked over at him out of the corner of her eye and saw him staring back at her. With a tiny scrap of courage, Aoife raised a hand to wave at him. He waved back, chuckling before he hugged Martin.

"So, Sarah said you're going to keep us busy until she finishes," Sam addressed Aoife, his arms crossed loosely over his chest. He didn't look upset.

"Yeah, sorry." Aoife pulled her shoulders up around her neck in the way that drove Genny crazy when they were teenagers.

"All I really want to do is go to the beach." Sam looked to Conor. "Haven't been down there in ages because it's not close to Sarah's or Max's."

"Really?" Aoife stared at him, half holding her breath.

"Yeah, if you don't mind," said Sam, hopeful.

With Tansy in the front pack, Aoife walked with Sam and Conor down the sidewalk until they passed her building and were one street away from the sea. Aoife paused and took in the sight of the waves, listening to the seagulls and the water. She took a deep breath and let the salty air loosen her lungs.

"It's beautiful here." Sam's voice was low. "Wild. Free."

"Mmm." Aoife patted Tansy's back through the carrier, thankful for her warmth against her. The day was cloudy and the sea was almost the same color as her eyes.

They crossed the street and walked across the tiny rocks until they were where the rocks turned into sand. The water licked at Conor's toes when he crept too close, but he laughed and ran away, as if it were a game. Sam joined in, grabbing Conor's arm to try to push him over, but Conor was too solid to be moved. The water crashed up by them and they hurried to escape the wet of the sea. Further up on the beach, Aoife found a place to sit. She unbuckled Tansy from the pack and held her on her lap, the blanket still wrapped around the baby. A gust of cold wind made the child suck in her breath with surprise. Aoife kissed the top of her head and pulled the blanket up further around her shoulders.

"What do you think, Tansy girl?" Aoife watched the two young men, too far away to hear what they were shouting to each other.

Sam grabbed a rock and threw it as hard as he could into the waves. Aoife watched, as if she could see the rock sinking to the bottom. The next rock was thrown by Conor, and Aoife watched that one, too. Over and over they tossed the rocks into the sea while Aoife sat, swaying with Tansy on her lap. She closed her eyes for a moment and remembered herself on a different beach with a different set of people. They made her feel loved and safe.

"Listen to the waves, wee one."

"It's so big, mam. It could swallow me all up!"

"No, Aoife. It's here to remind you that there's something bigger than anything you ever face in life. No pain, no mistakes, no emptiness is bigger than the sea. Just like the waves wash the sand and make it fresh, life can be made fresh again."

"What does that mean?"

"It means that sometimes things have to wash us on the inside, wee one. You'll understand when you're older."

Aoife didn't remember what her voice sounded like when she was little, but she remembered bits of what her mother had told her. Her father filled in the blank spots, having heard the same talk long before Aoife had been born.

"Can I join you?" asked Sam, startling Aoife from her daydream.

"Yes, of course." She shifted on the rocks, not sure why as there was an entire beach for him to sit down on. "Are you enjoying the beach?"

"Yes. I am." Sam held her gaze for a moment before he looked down by his legs and picked up a rock to fidget with. "Are you excited for Max's party tomorrow night?"

"I've been told to be," said Aoife honestly. "I haven't been to a Halloween party since I was in high school."

"Really? I figured you'd have gone to loads of do's whilst living in New York City."

"Not really. Didn't have the time for it, I suppose."

"Being a dance teacher was that time-consuming?"

"Well, when you teach five daily classes." Aoife squinted at the sea, her arms tightening around Tansy automatically when the baby moved. "You don't get much time for anything else."

"Geez. That's a lot."

"It was my life." Aoife broke her gaze away from ahead of her. "I did get out some, but my social life was pretty sad the last five years."

"Do you miss New York?"

"No." Aoife didn't hesitate with her answer. "I miss a certain period of time when I lived there, but I don't miss the city."

"What time was that?"

"The end of high school. Things were just going really well." A wave of nostalgia hit Aoife's heart as heavy as the waves hit the rocks by Conor's feet.

"What kinds of things?"

"Okay, then." Aoife gave him a smile. "Someone is nosy."

"Just curious." Sam's cheeks turned red. "Didn't mean to be nosy."

"It's all right. I suppose I'm being a bit vague."

"Just a little." Sam put his hands behind him and leaned back, alternating between staring out at the water and glancing over at Aoife. "You don't really talk about your past I've heard."

"Still getting your information from Sarah?"

"I never reveal my sources."

"Fair enough." Aoife chuckled. "Well, I guess it was a much simpler time. I was able to do what I loved best with my friends. I didn't really grow up with a family in the home, you know, 'cause my parents split up, and it was mostly just me and my dad, but my friends... they were my people."

"Peter?"

"One of them was Peter, yeah." Aoife didn't look at Sam to see his reaction. "Anyway, school ended on a high note and I had really great opportunities for my future. As a graduation present, a couple friends and I traveled around some. We went to places we had always wanted to see."

"Right out of high school? Wow, lucky."

"Says the famous footballer."

"I guess that's true." Sam laughed lightly at the words. "Where did you go?"

"St. Petersburg. Amsterdam. Paris. Milan."

"And you didn't think those were things to mention the night we were telling each other about ourselves?" Sam's eyes were wide. "Sure, I've traveled to bloody St. Petersburg. Casual. As you do."

Aoife laughed and shook her head. That was all she was going to say. It was more of a glimpse into her past than most people were given after what had happened. Her arms twitched as she hugged Tansy. She was still there, smelling like the lavender soap Aoife rubbed on her during her baths.

"Thanks for bringing us to the sea. I'm sure you're tired of seeing it all day."

"Not at all." Aoife couldn't hide the surprise on her face. "I love the sea. I could stare at it forever."

Forever.

There. That was the only exception Aoife would use for that word. She wanted to stare at the sea forever.

Despite the warm conversation between herself and Sam, Aoife said no to a dinner invitation at Sarah's. The party was the next day and she didn't want to keep Tansy out later than normal two days in a row. Martin helped her carry the bags of clothes Miss Wilcox had loaned her for the party and kissed Tansy goodbye.

Aoife called Peter that night and was happy when Alex's voice chimed in. She set her phone on the counter as she cooked, talking to them about the party the next day. They had her text them the picture of her costume. She knew they had seen it on Alex's phone when he let out a low whistle from between his teeth.

"Is Sam going to be there?" asked Peter.

"Yes. He is." Aoife nibbled on the inside of her cheek. "We actually had a good conversation today."

"Good. Happy to hear that, Eef."

"What do you talk about when you're around people who don't know your past?" asked Alex with genuine curiosity in his voice.

"I tell them I was a dance teacher."

"Eef!" Peter sounded like he was choking.

"I *was* a dance teacher! And a good one at that!"

"I know, it's just... You were an internationally known professional ballet dancer. You danced on stages across the world! And you tell them you taught five-year-olds jazz routines?"

"Peter's right, Aoife, it does seem a bit backwards."

"Not if you're trying to get a fresh start."

"We miss dancing with you, Eef." Peter's voice dropped as he became serious. "Still doesn't feel right to not see you on the stage with me."

"I miss that, too." Aoife's mouth pressed down in a frown. She looked over where Tansy was lying on a blanket on the floor. She left her pot of vegetable soup on the burner and walked over to scoop the child into her arms. "But it didn't feel right without all of us."

"We miss her, too." Alex cleared his throat to rid his voice of the gruffness that had settled over it. "Took a long while to get over both of you being gone."

Aoife tucked Tansy under her chin and closed her eyes against the stinging.

"How's Tansy?" Alex knew it was time to change the subject.

"Perfect." She spoke the words against the soft spot of the baby's skull, where she could feel the heartbeat against her lips. "You know what I realized?"

"What?" the two men asked in unison.

The word forever became stuck on her tongue and she shook her head.

"Never mind. Incomplete thought." She remembered her soup and hurried over to stir it and turn off the burner. "I have to go, guys. I need to put a baby to bed."

"Take care, Aoife. Kiss Tansy for us."

"I will." Aoife smiled, even though her friends couldn't see her face. "See you soon."

"Love you, Eef."

Aoife hung up. Leave it to Peter to still say he loved her after all the ways she had let him down.

"He's a good man, Tansy," Aoife told the girl as she walked across the apartment to stand by the window. "I wish you were mine so you would know just how good he is. And Alex, too. Maybe you'll have superhuman memory and remember all the things that happened to you while you're little. Maybe you'll remember me and know how much I love you."

It was an empty wish, a wish Aoife knew she had no business making. She should be wishing that Shannon would get better, and Tansy could be reunited with her mom. She should be wishing she could have her life back.

There were so many other things she could be wishing, but none of them seemed important right then.

Aoife began to hum the song "Danny Boy" as she swayed in front of the window. Tansy wasn't changed or fed, but she was dropping off to sleep in Aoife's arms. She wanted to stay there with the baby, staring out at the sea, thinking of her mother, thinking of how waves give you a fresh start, but she turned away and began to ready Tansy for bed. The child squawked unhappily at being woken up, but she was soon cooing and babbling as Aoife spoke lovingly to her.

She didn't stare at the sea again that night. She ate her meal and crawled into bed next to the sleeping child.

Forever.

People would come and go from her life, but the sea would always be there.

-Chapter 7-

The Rock to His Roll

Sarah finished curling Aoife's hair and helping her with her makeup to complete Aoife's look for the evening. Her completely black ensemble of crop top, leather jacket and tight high-waisted jeans were paired with white, low-top converse simply because Aoife didn't have any other shoes that would work with the costume. The smoky eye shadow, dark lip stain and heavy eyeliner made her look like a different person, but Sarah had done an amazing job.

"Oh. My. Gosh! Aoife! You look so good!" said Sarah as she stepped back to take in her work. She was already in her mermaid costume and her face was covered in a rainbow of shimmering colors. "When do you find the time to work out?"

"Work out?"

"Yeah! You're like, solid muscle!" Sarah poked at Aoife's abs and felt them tense up beneath her finger. "How do you do it?"

"Oh, I... dancing. I guess." Aoife bit her tongue before she could blurt out that Sarah should have seen her five years earlier at the height of her physical strength. She could tell all the ways her body was losing muscle mass from the lack of use, but to Sarah it was all amazing.

"I have to go to a spin class three times a week just to look like this," Sarah pouted as she looked down at her slim waist and toned legs.

"Sarah, you look great!" Aoife pulled her into a hug. "And your costume is stunning."

"Max is dressed as Prince Eric." Sarah's smile appeared again. "Did you know that it was at a costume party where Max and I properly met?"

Aoife shook her head no, hoping she would get the story.

"We were both dressed as pirates, but we couldn't recognize each other because of how dark it was in the garden, and the makeup and the wigs. We spent the whole evening together having a blast because there was no pressure since we couldn't tell who the other was. When the party was over he asked for my mobile number and called me on the way home. He told me it was him and that he really fancied me."

"That is the sweetest story I have ever heard in my life." Aoife sighed and pressed her hands over her heart. "I love that you guys were matching before you were even together. You were made for each other."

"And in less than two months we'll be getting married." Sarah stared down at the ring on her finger. "I'm so excited to be his wife."

Tansy fussed on the floor beside Aoife's feet. She bent over carefully to pick up the little baby. Tansy stared at her with wide eyes and mouth searching for her fist to suck on.

"She doesn't recognize you!" Sarah laughed at the expression on the baby's face. Her phone clicked as she took pictures of Tansy's reaction to seeing Aoife's face. She posted the picture to Instagram with the caption, *"You'd react the same if you just saw Aoife's makeup."* Martin texted Sarah asking for a picture of Aoife after seeing the Instagram post, but Sarah just laughed at him and told him to wait. She did, however, take a picture of Aoife and Tansy on Aoife's phone so Aoife could send a picture to Alex and Peter. "So, Peter and Alex; did you ever date either of them?" she asked.

"Did I ev-..." Aoife glanced up from her phone. "Oh! No, there was never anything like that between us, but for a good portion of our lives we were basically inseparable."

"Best friends?"

"Made ourselves into a little family, like you and Martin."

Sarah's expression lit up, but she said nothing as she slipped her feet into her shoes and pulled on a jacket. It was cold outside and they wanted to be warm for the drive over to Max's. Aoife buckled Tansy's seat into the back of Sarah's car and kissed her forehead before jumping into the front seat. She was glad to be arriving at the party with Sarah and not by herself. At least she had Tansy to use as a shield and an icebreaker.

There were already vehicles lining the road when they arrived at Max's place. Sarah knew Max had saved a spot for her in the driveway, so she pulled in and parked behind his black Range Rover. Aoife could see the excitement and anticipation all over Sarah's face as she hopped out from behind the wheel. Aoife thanked her for taking the diaper bag as she unbuckled Tansy's car seat. She brought the front pack as well, but Sarah had said she wanted people to see the full effect of the outfit before she started wearing Tansy.

"Besides," said Sarah matter-of-factly, "It will be hot and crowded and Tansy will most likely not want to be all up against you."

"She's a baby," Aoife reasoned, gazing at the little one with soft eyes. "Of course she'll want to be all up against me."

"Well, just hold off until later on. I want people to see how fit you look all dressed up like this."

Aoife had complied and was now carrying Tansy in the car seat. Max had offered to let Aoife put the baby's things in his room in case she needed to feed her or calm her down. There weren't many people in the entryway when they walked in, and Aoife went straight up to the room to leave Tansy's things. She glanced at herself before leaving. There was a text on her phone from Alex telling her to call them the next day and give them the scoop on how everything went with Sam.

She laughed and shoved her phone into the pocket of the diaper bag without responding and went back down to join the party. Having Tansy in her arms gave her a bit more confidence, knowing that anyone who looked at her would be drawn to the cute little ballerina in her arms before looking at her face and costume. Her plan of safety was ruined, however, when Martin snatched Tansy away from her and gasped.

"Aoife! You look so good!" He was dressed as Sherlock Holmes, complete with the pipe stuck in the breast pocket of his jacket. "You could be a model! Like, honest to God, you look like a girl from a poster."

"Geez, Martin!" Aoife blushed and looked down, pulling at the hem of her crop top.

"Sarah!" Martin shouted over the din of more guests arriving. "You did ace on Aoife's makeup and hair!"

"Didn't it turn out so good?" Sarah appeared from around the corner, her hand dragging Max along behind her. "Look, Max! I did Aoife's hair and makeup."

"Well done!" Max gave the costume a once-over with his eyes, a huge smile on his face. "Bloody heck, I'm going to have to introduce you to my single friends!"

Aoife hoped the foundation Sarah had slathered all over her face hid the red of her cheeks as she walked slowly into the spacious dining area. The tables had been pushed back against the walls and were covered with food. Aoife wasn't hungry, but she thought about grabbing a plate for something to do.

"Look who's matching now!" a voice hissed in Aoife's ear at the same time Sam's hearty hello boomed throughout the house. "It was meant to be!"

Sarah slunk off to find Max again, leaving Aoife basically in the middle of the room on her own. Sam stopped when he spotted her. His own completely black ensemble was almost identical to hers with the main difference being that he had a black fishnet t-shirt in place of Aoife's crop top. There were rips in the knees of his jeans, and his hair was held back with a bright purple headscarf. A few temporary tattoos could be seen on his torso and neck through his outfit.

"Look at who we have here." Sam walked forward, a confident swagger in his step. "You look like you know how to have a good time the way I like it."

"Easy there, rock star." Aoife didn't allow her pounding heart to mess up her words as she smirked back at him. "Who says I'm here alone?"

"Who is he?" asked Sam in a mock whisper, playing along as he circled behind her. "One of these jokers?"

Aoife snorted with a laugh as she noticed a young man dressed as the Joker from the Batman movie. She pointed in the lad's direction and Sam grinned.

"You don't want to be here with him. I can rock your world."

"You'll have to work really hard to impress me," Aoife said seriously, her eyebrows raised. "I own a rocking chair."

Sam's laugh filled the kitchen and drew the attention of those around them. That was when people started pointing out their outfits, exclaiming over how perfectly they matched each other. People asked them to pose together and before Aoife knew what was happening, there were pictures of herself and Sam all over social media being posted by Max's friends.

"It's only right the two of you do karaoke!" Martin was still holding onto Tansy when he passed them by the snack table twenty minutes later. "Please! Oh, but tell me when you're going to do it! I need the whole thing on camera!"

"Do you want to?" asked Sam. "Sounds like fun."

"I'm not a great singer." Aoife pressed a hand against the butterflies in her stomach at the thought of singing in front of a room full of strangers. She had met a lot of them, mostly the young men, but it was still unnerving to think about.

"Can you hold a tune?"

"Yeah, I mean, I can stay on a note, but I'm not good at it."

"Staying on a note is good enough for me!" Sam reached over to take Aoife's hand in his own. "I'll beat you at pin the tail on the donkey first."

He didn't beat her, though. And nobody beat her at limbo. The fact that Aoife could still control her body like that encouraged her. She wouldn't have been surprised if she had fallen on her butt after the first go, but there she was, the champion with the fake, plastic gold medal hanging around her neck.

"Karaoke competition!" Max shouted from the doorway of the den. "Come and join us!"

"You're going to be singing with Sam, right?" asked Sarah as they pressed into the crowded room together.

"I don't know." Aoife didn't know where he had gone off to.

"Do it with him! He's a great singer!" Sarah slipped away through the group of aliens and astronauts that stood between them and the front of the room and left Aoife to stand alone.

The first three people went solo, picking to focus on performance rather than singing ability. Everyone in the room was eating it up, applauding and cheering on their friends with drinks in their hands. When one particularly drunk young man dressed as David Beckham took the mic and sang the Titanic theme song, everyone turned the flash on their phones and waved them over their heads. The next girl had a voice like Christina Aguilera and sang "Genie in a Bottle." Then a couple sang "I Think I Want To Marry You," ending the song with a kiss. Aoife was still standing in the corner, enjoying the show immensely, when she felt an arm slip around her shoulders.

"I picked out what song we should do."

"What song?" Aoife turned, pressing her shoulder against his chest in the tight space they were attempting to share.

"'Livin' On A Prayer.'"

A grin filled Aoife's face as she remembered singing it at the top of her voice, her hairbrush her microphone and her stuffed animals her audience. It was one of the songs Carl really liked, which was ironic after the divorce.

"Do you know it?" asked Sam. "Because we could do a different one..."

"It's perfect! Ready to show these people a little rock and roll?"

Max was beaming when he introduced Sam and Aoife as Madonna and Bon Jovi, eliciting a loud round of applause. Some of it was just because Sam was famous and he was there, some of it was because they looked like a rock and roll power couple as they took the microphones. Sam went all out with the air guitar and Aoife let herself dance like she had seen Madonna do in the "Like A Virgin" music video she watched back in high school. She saw Martin with his phone out, Tansy not with him. After looking over the whole room, she saw Sarah holding Tansy, her phone also pointed in the direction of her friend and her brother.

They sang the chorus to each other, stepping closer and screaming into the microphones. Sam wrapped an arm around Aoife's shoulders and she continued to dance. They finished big and left the fake stage with huge smiles, bowing to the shouts and whistles. A few people called out for an encore, but they were done. Minutes later, however, Sam was back up with Conor, who was dressed as Captain America. They sang "The Star-Spangled Banner", dedicating their performance to their honorary American, pointing to Aoife who was taking Tansy from Sarah for a cuddle.

Once everyone who wanted to participate had finished, Max said that he and his team of judges would announce the winner after the game of Mafia that was about to start in the living room. Aoife and Sarah went up to Max's bedroom to change Tansy's diaper and get away from some of the noise. Sarah was laughing as she tried to reenact Conor's version of the statue of liberty he had done while he sang.

"They really did a horrible job on that song," Aoife chuckled as she pulled out the nappies and wipes and set them on the floor beside her.

"I think you and Sam are going to win." Sarah flopped down on the bed belly-first. She reached over the edge and rubbed the soft, downy hair on the top of Tansy's head. "And, I'm pretty sure you guys are going to win the best couples costume as well."

"But we're not a couple! We didn't even come together!"

"I don't think it matters at this point. Everyone loves your costumes! I can't believe you guys didn't plan it, because you look ridiculously hot together."

"Stop! Oh my gosh!" Aoife rubbed her hands over her face.

"Do you not like it that you suit each other?"

"No, I just... we're not a couple."

"Do you want to be?"

The question was loaded and Aoife gave Sarah a look that told her she knew it was. Sarah shrugged and rolled onto her back.

"Besides, I wanted you and Max to win best couples costume."

"Oh, we're already winners." Sarah smiled at her ring for the second time that night. "We don't need to be at a costume party for that."

"You know what I mean, Ariel." Aoife threw one of Tansy's socks at Sarah's face.

"I think he really likes you," Sarah said quietly.

"I guess we'll just have to wait and find out," Aoife said in response.

Sarah took Tansy as soon as they were downstairs again. With a drink in her hand, Aoife made her way out into the back garden where lights were flashing and someone was playing music loudly. She was surprised when Conor pulled her into the yard to dance with him. He was as uncoordinated as they come, but he didn't seem to care as she pulled out a few of her more impressive moves. They were laughing over him flailing his arms and smacking Aoife's shoulder when Sam pressed into the circle beside them.

"Now kiss!" Conor was clearly drunk as he pressed Sam and Aoife closer together.

"Conor!" Sam pushed his friend, laughing when he tripped over his own feet and nearly fell onto his backside. "Go find someone your own size."

"He's like a giant puppy," Aoife said with a smile.

"He's gotten that before."

"Hey, thanks for doing karaoke with me." She wanted to bring it up before Sam said something else. "That was a blast."

"Do you think we'll win?" Sam's eyes were sparkling with the thought.

"We have a good chance, that's for sure."

"Pretty crazy how our costumes match like this without us even planning it."

Aoife nodded. She was sure Sam knew how his sister and Max ended up dating. It wasn't that she was opposed to dating Sam, it was just a big thought to have at the moment with people bobbing for apples and making out in the back garden beside them. Something crashed inside and Aoife immediately thought of Tansy, hoping nothing had happened to her.

"Just a punch bowl or something, I'm sure." Sam was amused by the look of concern on Aoife's face. "You want to dance? You already did awesome with the singing, so you need to bring your A game on the dance floor."

Someone would come get her if Tansy were hurt, Aoife reasoned as she took Sam's hand and began dancing. She didn't know the song, but Sam sang along loudly, pulling Aoife close every time the chorus rang out.

"I need to go find Tansy!" Aoife shouted over the noise of the music and people cheering at the apple-bobbing station.

"She's with Martin! She's fine!" Sam tried to tug her back onto the dance floor.

"I need to check on her. She's probably tired." Aoife felt Sam release her hand. He nodded with understanding and watched as Aoife walked into the house.

The clock told Aoife that Tansy was up past her normal bedtime and she would be more than a little hungry. Martin was jiggling the girl on his knee when she found him. He was talking to two girls who were dressed as fairies and sat on either side of him. They were cooing over the baby and making a fuss over Martin. Maybe he hadn't planned to use the baby as a girl magnet, but it worked and Aoife was happy for him.

"Kind of don't want to take her from him now," Aoife said to Sarah when her friend stopped beside her and put an arm around her shoulders.

"He definitely has been getting a lot of attention with her," Sarah agreed with a smile. "It's her bedtime, isn't it?"

"Yeah. She's probably going to cry all the way home because she's hungry."

"I'll get my keys."

When people realized that Aoife and Tansy were leaving, they asked for a few last-minute pictures with the baby. They called Sam into the house to get some of the rock and roll couple, too.

"Let me know if we win." Aoife hugged Sam.

"I can't. I don't have your number." Sam gave her a pointed look when she stepped back.

"That's a shame." Aoife teased him with a smile. "Isn't it horrible when you don't have someone's number? How do you ever fix that?"

"Let's go, Aoife! Tansy's crying in her seat!" Martin called from the doorway.

"Go on now. You've got a baby to take care of, apparently." Sam jerked his chin towards the door, his eyes still smiling. "I'll see you around."

"Bye, rock star." Aoife waved and ran out of the house, half wishing she could justify pulling out her phone and giving her number to Sam right then.

Sarah and Martin helped Aoife take her bags up to her flat and watched Tansy as she showered quickly, trying to wash away the makeup and hairspray. There were still black smudges around her eyes when she emerged, her hair pulled into a wet knot on the back of her head. She was glad to see Tansy settled in Sarah's arms with a bottle in her mouth. Sarah looked up at Aoife with an expression of pride, her mermaid makeup still glimmering on her face.

"Look! I've done it! She's almost asleep!"

As if on cue, the baby started to squirm and cry. Aoife took her with a smile and sat down in the rocking chair. Her two friends told her goodnight before they left to rejoin the party. Tansy was cozy in her arms when Aoife finally scrolled through her phone after ignoring it all evening. She was surprised to see so many texts from Alex and Peter, and even Genny and a few other old friends from New York had contacted her.

r u dating Sam Tadwell?!

Basically, that was all they wanted to know. She only understood what they meant when she saw the screenshot Peter sent her of a picture of her and Sam from Instagram. Oh, from Sam's Instagram. She held the phone close to her face and studied the way she and Sam were pressed together, scowling at the camera in an attempt to look like rock stars. There had been so many pictures, she didn't even realize that one of them had ended up on Sam's phone. He had posted it hours earlier, probably right after they had taken the photo. The caption made her heart still for a moment, *"she's the rock to my roll"*, and Aoife definitely hadn't been expecting that.

She texted Sarah, asking her if she had seen Sam's Instagram post, but of course she didn't respond. Alex and Peter were at their own Halloween party, dressed up with three of their other friends as members of a boy band according to the fifty-four pictures they had spammed Aoife's phone with. It was just her, Tansy and the sea that night. Aoife's toes grew cold as she pushed against the floor, rocking her and the baby back and forth to match the waves.

When she and Sam were together, they got on perfectly, but she was never sure where he was coming from. The weekend he found out about Peter was sad, but it made sense. Now he was in Brighton again and he was fine. Maybe it was because of something Sarah told him? She didn't know. It was still crazy for her to ponder the fact that Sam was a sort of a celebrity in certain circles, yet he seemed to like her.

"It doesn't quite make sense," she said to no one. "I do like him, but I don't know him very well. I feel like our lives are really different right now."

Aoife went to sleep and woke up to several texts from her Brighton friends telling her that she and Sam had won the karaoke contest, as well as the best couple costume contest. Peter sent her another screenshot of Sam's second Instagram post from the night before. It was a picture of them singing, laughing at each other while trying to stay in character at the same time. The caption was less shocking than the one from earlier as it simply stated, "*winners*" with the trophy emoji beside it.

Supper was at Sarah's that night and Sam and Conor were in attendance, having stayed one more day after the party. Tansy was fussy and wouldn't let anyone other than Aoife hold her. Martin tried, but gave her back with a frown when she wailed in his ear for two minutes. Even Sarah gave it a go, but Tansy would not be placated until she was back in Aoife's arms, wrapped in the folds of her oversized sweater.

"I'm sorry I made you cranky by having a party last night." Max was trying to get Tansy to smile at him, talking in a sing-song voice and reaching for her finger. She was having none of it, though, ignoring him and nuzzling against Aoife's arm. "But she was so cute! Did you see the pictures people posted of her on Instagram?"

"She doesn't have an Instagram." Sarah scowled at Aoife in mock anger. "Deleted it to hide her secrets."

"Hold on, now!" Aoife laughed. "There were other reasons for deleting."

"You should make a new one," Martin suggested, setting plates around the table. "You could post pictures from now on it. That would be nice."

The thought made Aoife furrow her brow. She considered things like that as part of her old life, something that could never be relevant again. There were no pictures from stage performances, shots from the airplane window or of backstage preparation. There would be no selfies of her with her best friends, Peter always holding the phone because he was the tallest with the longest arms. And there was no Roe...

"And you could see all the hundreds of pictures of you and Sam on there," said Conor. "You guys won, by the way."

"Rock and roll." Aoife looked to Sam and smiled. His expression shifted to confused, but she didn't want to explain right at that moment. Maybe if he worked up the courage to ask her for her number she would tell him that her friends had hounded her the night before to know what was going on between them. She hadn't texted any of them back. Alex and Peter already knew what was going on and they were the most important.

"All right, kids, here's your supper." Sarah carried a big plate holding a Sunday roast to the table.

Aoife ate slowly, shifting Tansy and making sure she was happy every time she fussed. It was not the most enjoyable for the atmosphere, but at least she knew that everyone there loved the baby and didn't mind. She wanted to take the baby home to let her nap on her bed; however, she didn't want to be rude and ask to leave before the meal was done.

"I'm going to go into the other room. See if I can't help her fall asleep in there." Aoife stood up with Tansy.

It didn't help, but at least she wasn't crying at the table. She wondered if maybe someone tried to feed her something at the party. The thought made her shake her head in disappointment at herself. She should have kept Tansy with her. Yeah, it was nice to have enjoyed the party with Sam, but Tansy depended on her to take care of her. She should have left earlier in the night and put her to bed on time, fed her when she first started getting hungry instead of letting her stay hungry until they went back home.

"You okay?" asked Sam from the entrance of the sitting room where Aoife was pacing.

"I'm just worried about Tansy. I should have taken better care of her last night." Aoife sighed and swallowed down the lump in her throat. She was about to cry.

"I didn't realize that Tansy proper lives with you." Sam stepped into the room. His voice was low and steady so it wouldn't bother the baby who was sucking on her fist for a moment. "I thought you just watched her from time to time."

Aoife stared down at Tansy.

"But she like... she's like your child."

"Except she's not." Aoife forced herself to look at Sam. "And one day she'll go back."

"Unless Shannon decides that she's better off with you."

"Don't say that." Aoife closed her eyes and shook her head. "This is hard enough without thinking about things like that."

"Sorry."

"It's okay."

Sam stayed, watching her pace back and forth, patting Tansy's back and bouncing her lightly in her arms. He didn't say anything and Aoife let her mind forget he was there. She just wanted to go home and take care of her baby.

"Did you see the pictures I posted last night?" asked Sam, his voice still quiet.

"Yeah." Aoife acknowledged him again. "Peter sent me screenshots."

"Ah." Sam didn't seem to know what else to say. "I really enjoy my time with you, whenever we get the chance."

"I do, too." Aoife stopped pacing and stood where she could see Sam. "I don't know what to think about you, though."

Sam chuckled and ducked his head.

"I mean, you act as if you're interested, and the word on the street is that you don't just flirt with anybody, but I... like, I don't know."

"Word on the street?" Sam's lips twitched with a smile.

"I will never reveal my sources."

"Fair enough." Sam was grinning now. "I do like you, Aoife. You are obviously busy raising a child and I'm busy kicking a ball around a giant field with sweaty men, so that means this might not be a good time to actually start anything, but I wanted you to know. Even before you asked me, I wanted to tell you."

"Now what?" Aoife struggled to keep herself from smiling, trying to remain calm, but there were feelings inside of her that she hadn't felt in a long time.

"Can I have your number?"

-Chapter 8-
Sarah Finds Out

Aoife found it calming to talk to Sam at the end of each day. He always made the time to talk to her when she asked, even leaving groups of friends to chat with her for a few minutes where it was quiet. They weren't dating, but as they got to know each other more, there was very little that stopped them from liking each other. Sarah was beside herself with excitement that things were going well between the two of them and even offered to babysit Tansy for a date night if she was needed.

"No." Aoife shook her head. "It's too hard leaving her. She's still so small."

And she was, even though it was now the middle of November and she was going to be three months the first week of December. The doctors praised her growth and development at her appointments, the only time Shannon actually had anything to do with her. Every time the baby would go away with Martin and Shannon in the car, Aoife would be practically sick with worry until Tansy was back in her arms. The child seemed to feel the stress of those times as well and would often refuse to eat or calm down for half an hour to an hour when she was returned.

There were a few times that month when Aoife turned on her music and slipped on her pointe shoes to remember bits and pieces of old dances. Tansy would watch from her seat or from the blanket. Aoife never told anyone, not even Alex and Peter when they asked her if she had thought about going back to it. Losing one baby had stolen her love of ballet; maybe, if she had to lose another one, it would bring the love of it back?

The weather grew colder and the winds whipped at the water, giving the waves white foam caps as they crashed on the beach. The lack of sunshine was something she discussed with Sam on many occasions. When she and Tansy spent a day in London, the gray weather and drizzling rain followed them. They split their day between Peter and Alex, and then Sam. She didn't tell Sam who she had been seeing, but he almost found out when a crowd of ballet enthusiasts saw her friends walking away from the cafe where they had just eaten and started taking pictures with them.

"Who's that?" Sam stopped and turned. "Should we go get our picture with them? They must be famous."

"No, let's just go someplace warm."

"Come on, I don't get to meet many people who aren't footballers. Don't you want an autograph?"

Aoife smiled and shook her head no, remembering the millions of times she and Peter had drawn each other pictures to hang on their bedroom walls, always signing their names in their childish scrawl. As for Alex, well, she had that scar on her shoulder to remember him by.

"I feel weird not taking you out somewhere to enjoy London," said Sam once they were at his apartment. He made her a cup of tea and she settled on the rug on the floor next to Tansy.

"No, I love this." Aoife smiled up at him. "Really."

Sam pulled out his board games and they ended up spending hours playing Guess Who?, Battleship, and Connect Four. Tansy was content to lay on Aoife's lap until she was ready to eat. It was getting dark outside when the pizza Sam ordered arrived. After they finished the entire pizza between the two of them, Sam glanced at his phone to check the time.

"Time to go?" asked Aoife, seeing the disappointment on his face.

"Unless you want to stay here tonight. You and Tansy can have my room."

"Thank you, but I don't want to keep her out all night."

"All right."

They drove to the train station and Sam parked to help Aoife buy her ticket and get her to the right place. He hugged her and said he had had a lovely time before they parted ways. Aoife texted back and forth with Alex on the train ride to Brighton, telling him how Sam had almost gone up to them to get their autographs.

haha! that wld have been so funny!

y dont u want him to kno us?

Aoife sighed and rolled her eyes. Because if Sam asked her how she knew Peter and Alex, he would know what she used to do, who she used to be. She wasn't ready for that yet. She would tell him one day, and Sarah and Martin and Max, but she wasn't going to tell them yet. Miss Wilcox was still talking about leaving, but Aoife pretended she didn't hear her when she did. It was the week before Christmas when things finally went into motion.

"Tomorrow?" Aoife was glad Tansy was on the floor or she was afraid she would have dropped her at the news.

"I want you to have a little bit of time before the new year starts, time to think about what you want to have in your life." Miss Wilcox patted Aoife's arm affectionately. A tear rolled down the woman's face. "I will miss you, but I love you enough to know that you're only going to hurt yourself more if you don't take it back."

The selfless love of Miss Wilcox hurt more than soothed as Aoife spent the rest of the morning crying and telling Miss Wilcox that she didn't have to leave. She tried to promise anything she could, but the elderly woman was unmoved. By the time Aoife had to say goodbye, she was torn between being angry and hurt. Why did Miss Wilcox think she could manipulate Aoife's life like that? But then again, Aoife could feel the truth behind her words.

"Tell me when you're going to be in a show. I'll come back for it."

"What am I going to do without you?"

"Don't worry, you'll still be paid. I've set it up so your rent is taken care of for a full year from when you started. The rest is for you and Tansy to live on."

That wasn't what she had meant.

Aoife wept and hugged Miss Wilcox again. She thought about Genny as she drove home, the windshield wipers squeaking against the glass as the rain pounded down. Genny had passed off this opportunity to Aoife because she hadn't wanted it. It was clear Genny didn't realize just how special her great-aunt was, or she would have never done that.

Aoife and Tansy spent the rest of the day up in their apartment, cups of tea for Aoife and plenty of snuggles for Tansy. She played music in the background to accompany the waves. It reminded her of living in Carl's house as he never turned off the radio in the kitchen, even when they went away on trips. She wondered how her dad was and if she should try to call him. Maybe she should ask for his address and send his family a Christmas present.

She ignored the call from Sam. Aoife didn't want to try to come up with some excuse for Miss Wilcox leaving or why she was all wrapped up in her thoughts all of a sudden. She didn't answer the call from Peter, either. She didn't know what he wanted, but she wanted to be alone.

If it wasn't going to be Christmas the next week, Aoife would have considered holing up for a while and not leaving the house until she was out of groceries and toilet paper. But Christmas was next week and Aoife was expected to be places and be cheerful. Tansy gurgled happily up at Aoife's face whenever she tried to figure out what to do by talking to the child. Then she would cover the baby's belly with kisses and sigh. At least she still had Tansy.

Sarah noticed that Aoife was not herself and asked her about it. Aoife tried to pin it all on Miss Wilcox leaving and brush the topic away, but she could tell Sarah wasn't convinced. It wasn't until two days before Christmas that Aoife found out what her present from Sarah was going to be, and the curl of terror in her stomach made it almost impossible to seem excited.

"VIP tickets to the ballet?" Aoife's mouth was dry. She hoped that if she cried, she could pretend they were happy tears.

"Well, you're a dancer so I thought you'd appreciate it. I love the ballet, but Max isn't keen on it so I wanted to take you. Are you happy with it?" The shy question made Aoife feel even worse.

"Ballet is perfect."

"I've even managed to arrange a time to meet some of the dancers after the performance." Sarah's eyes were shining. "Max met a couple of the managers of the show when he was in London the beginning of the month and then I met them when I was there last week. I talked to them and they said they would see what they could do."

"Oh. Lovely." Aoife's chest tightened. Perhaps that was what Peter had tried to call her about. If she was lucky, maybe they wouldn't run into Peter and Alex at all.

"Are you sure this is a good gift? I wanted you to like it." Sarah stared hard at her face.

"Yes! Sarah! I'm just... blown away. No one has ever given me a gift like this before."

The situation only grew more complicated when she called Peter to ask him about it and he told her that Sarah was definitely going to meet them.

"I don't know what to do, Peter. I'm going to have to pretend to meet you tomorrow night, or I'm going to have to tell her everything."

"Do you want to tell her?"

"I don't know! Miss Wilcox left so I can go back to ballet, but I'm still struggling." Aoife closed her eyes and pinched the bridge of her nose. "It doesn't matter how hard I try, I still hear her screaming at me every time I dance."

"You were very close to them, Eef. You don't have to explain yourself."

"To have them all snatched away, just like that! And because she was angry at me, just knowing that! Just knowing that this woman I had looked up to and saw as a mother in my life was angry at me," Aoife's voice broke. "enough to say she hated me! I just couldn't. I still can't."

"I know, Eef." Peter's voice was low and Aoife knew if he was with her in that room instead of on the other end of a phone call he would be hugging her. "I wish had she picked me to be angry at."

"But you were her favorite." Aoife sniffed and looked over her shoulder to make sure Tansy was still asleep.

"Nah, that was always you."

"I miss Chloe." Aoife spoke so quietly she wasn't sure Peter would be able to hear her. It had been a long time since she last said that name out loud.

"I know she misses you, too."

"It has been over five years." Aoife shook her head at the thought. "She's never once tried to contact me."

"You don't know that. She may have tried and it just never worked out."

"Maybe," Aoife said quietly. "I don't want to go back to it all if she's not going to be with me."

"Eef." Peter sighed.

"I know it's stupid and immature to be like that, but it's true. My heart aches because she's gone and I don't know if I will ever see her again."

"But ballet is more than just Chloe."

Aoife went back in her head to when she was little, only five or six years old. She loved the way her body could move and look beautiful and graceful, just like her mom's. But then her mom was gone, and she still danced because it made her heart open when it was too hard to talk about what she was feeling, and gave her a place of refuge when home wasn't a place she wanted to be. All through high school she had danced, pushing her body harder and harder, making it stronger and better, doing everything she could to be accepted into the company of her dreams. And she had done it all with Chloe.

Before Aoife was even born, her mother was a ballerina. Rebecca became best friends with two other girls who had also left their home countries to join New York City ballet around the same time she had. Their children were raised together, the mothers teaching them to dance as soon as they could stand, and instilling the love they carried for ballet into their lives. When Aoife found herself without a mother, Chloe's mom stepped in, covering for her friend and raising Aoife as if she were her own.

"I want it back," said Aoife in a thick voice. "They took it from me, and I want it back."

"You can have it back. I believe in you."

Whether Peter was right or not, Aoife knew she couldn't ignore that pain in her heart anymore. The next day she woke up early, dressed nicely, and packed Tansy's things. The baby would be spending the day with Martin and Shannon. Martin had whispered that maybe Shannon was ready for her baby again, and Aoife forced a smile. It felt like more than just a rug being ripped out from under her feet; the whole bloody house was about to be shaken down.

"Have a great time at the ballet! I can't wait to hear all about it!" Martin waved as the two girls drove off in Sarah's car.

The tension in the vehicle made Aoife feel ill. She wanted to explain it all to Sarah before they got there, but she didn't know where to start. Sarah kept frowning and glancing over at her friend. Aoife kept checking her phone, but there was nothing there to distract her. Finally, they parked.

"Aoife, if you don't want to go to the ballet, we can do something else." Sarah's voice was calm and understanding. "You don't have to say yes to this just because you don't want to hurt my feelings."

"Sarah," Aoife managed to say before tears filled her eyes. "I do want to do this. Not only because you're one of my best friends, but because ballet has been the thing that I love most in all the world since I was a baby."

Sarah's face showed confusion at Aoife's statement. "You've never spoken about ballet before."

"I know." Aoife nodded. Her makeup was going to be ruined and Alex would laugh at her when he saw her, she knew it. "Because I left it a few years back."

"Did something bad happen?" Sarah reached across the center console and touched Aoife's arm. She squeezed it when Aoife only nodded. "I'm sorry. I didn't know. We don't have to be here."

"I want to. I need to." Aoife took a deep breath. "And I want to be here with you."

"I'm only going to go in there with you if you cross your heart that you're ready for this."

"Cross my heart." Aoife laughed through her tears as she made the motion with her finger. "And I'm glad I'm finally telling you. It wasn't because I didn't trust you; it's just not a nice thing to remember."

Sarah helped her fix her makeup before they left the car. They admired the Christmas decorations and the way the lights sparkled against the dark blue sky as they walked from the car park to the entrance of the theater. Aoife pulled out her phone as they settled into their seats to text Peter and Alex good luck.

see u after the show! wish u were up here with us.

Aoife smiled sadly at Alex's quick response. He was probably all done up in his costume and makeup, trying to shove food into his mouth before it was time to get into their places. It was *The Nutcracker* and Aoife took long, steady breaths as she listened to the auditorium fill up.

"You good?" asked Sarah with a hand on her arm. "Hungry? Thirsty?"

"Thanks." Aoife smiled. "Just miss Tansy."

"She's probably having the best time with Martin."

"I hope so."

The lights dimmed and the show started. Sarah leaned over a few times to ask Aoife if she was okay, and if she had ever performed like this before.

"I love Alex Minsky! He's a brilliant dancer! I hear him and Peter Olev have been dancing together for years, and they started this company."

"I heard that, too," said Aoife, her face burning. Explaining everything in the middle of the ballet just wasn't going to work.

"I can't wait to meet him! Oh my gosh, I'm so nervous I'm not going to know what to say! He's just such a good dancer! I bet he's the perfect dance partner!"

She didn't tell Sarah that she used to be the one who danced with Alex in almost every show, didn't tell her that the last time she danced with Alex was in this very show in the role of Clara. Leanne was Clara that night and she was perfect for it. Aoife was glad she had met her, doubly glad that it was because of her that she had Peter and Alex back in her life. Tears shone in her eyes as she stood and clapped. Sarah's face glowed as she smiled and cheered for each cast member as they bowed at the end of the performance. Then...

"Okay, now the guy I spoke to on the phone said we could meet him by the doors to be let in the back to meet the dancers." Sarah gathered up her jacket and purse.

Aoife followed Sarah out of their row, her stomach in knots. She still wasn't sure if she should pretend to be surprised when she saw Peter and Alex or not. Knowing that someone did ballet was a lot different than knowing that someone had been a professional ballet dancer. She didn't have time to come up with anything because Sarah located their guide and they were ushered backstage.

Everything was familiar and different at the same time. It smelled the same as every other establishment where Aoife had performed; the distinct smell of sweat, damp clothes, hairspray and makeup permeating the air. She wanted to grab the girl that walked past them and tell her how perfect her échappé sur les pointes were. But she didn't, she kept her face neutral, only smiling when Sarah grabbed onto her arm with excitement.

"I know you've probably met a lot of dancers before, but have you ever met famous ones? Like, Alex Minsky famous? I want to meet the girl who played Clara as well! She was so good!"

There was no air left in Aoife's lungs to push words out, so she just smiled. Sarah's eyes dimmed and she frowned. Aoife shook her head, telling her she was fine. They followed their guide around a corner and barely had a chance to look around the room before Aoife was being crushed in a pair of familiar arms. Alex's laugh reached her ears as he picked her up off the ground and danced around with her.

"Aoife! You're here! This makes me so happy!"

"I can't breathe!" Aoife tried to make it sound urgent, but Alex only laughed and placed a big kiss on her cheek.

"Did you see how good I did? Did you see, Aoife?" Alex wouldn't stop pestering her as she tried to push him away.

"You are acting so unprofessional!" Aoife hissed at him through her teeth, giving a sideways glance towards Sarah who was standing in the doorway, a look of shock on her face. "Go say hello to my friend Sarah, she has been looking forward to meeting you all evening."

"Hello, Sarah." Alex shook her hand and smiled at her. "It's nice to meet you. Heard a lot about you from Aoife, here."

Honestly, Aoife didn't know why she thought Alex was going to make it worse by adding his last sentence; she had done most of the damage on her own without his help.

"You know Alex Minsky?" Sarah looked like she needed to sit down. "*The* Alex Minsky?"

"Yeah, we've been friends for about, uh, ten years."

"What?!" Sarah was gaping at her. "How? Why?"

"We went to dance school together," said Alex, amusement lighting up his face. "Then we joined the same company."

"Wait, you were in a ballet company? You were an actual ballerina?" Sarah's eyes narrowed at Aoife.

"Surprise." Aoife smiled weakly, not bothering to correct Sarah's use of the word ballerina. Technically, she had never been a principal ballerina.

"You didn't say a word! The whole time he was on stage, you never said a word!" Sarah looked from Alex to Aoife and back. Alex held up his hands and took a step back to show that he had no part of Aoife's silence. "I can't believe you were an actual ballerina and you never told us."

"Right?" said Alex, nodding in agreement with what Sarah had said. "She's great, too. Always has been."

"'Great,'" Sarah quoted Alex to Aoife. "Alex Bloody Minsky just called you great! Aoife! Why didn't you tell me?"

Aoife bit her lip and shrugged.

"How many more surprises like this am I going to get?" asked Sarah.

"Eef!"

At least one more, thought Aoife as she ran across the room to hug Peter. He caught her easily and spun her around, his smile lighting up the room.

"You were brilliant," whispered Aoife, taking his face with her hands. "You always are."

"Are you going to come back?" Peter's eyes were hopeful as they watched her, keeping his voice low to match hers.

"I haven't decided yet."

"It's not a no, that's good enough for me." Peter hugged her again.

"Please help me fix my friendship with Sarah. I can't tell if she wants to punch me or hug me."

Peter chuckled as he walked over to Sarah and shook her hand, telling her it was lovely to meet her. It wasn't Peter or Alex that Sarah couldn't stop staring at, it was Aoife. Every so often she would shake her head at Aoife with a huge grin on her face.

"Are you upset at me?" asked Aoife worriedly as they followed Alex to meet Leanne.

"Upset at you? Are you crazy? I'm absolutely buzzing with excitement over the fact that you used to do this! I have a friend who is an actual ballerina!"

Leanne appeared bashful when she saw Aoife.

"I'm glad I didn't know you were in the crowd, or I would have been too nervous to dance with Alex!"

"You were beautiful," said Aoife with a smile.

"Oh my goodness, I could cry! That is the highest compliment I have ever received in my life." There were tears in her eyes as she spoke.

"It was an honor to watch you dance with him."

"She's good, isn't she?" Alex winked at Aoife as he nodded his head at Leanne.

"Leanne, this is my friend, Sarah." Aoife remembered her manners and watched as Leanne shook Sarah's hand politely.

"Any friend of Aoife Stewart is a friend of mine," said Leanne.

Sarah was staring at Aoife again. "She knew who you were! She knew you used to be a ballerina."

"Of course I do!" Leanne started giggling. "Does she not know anything about you, Aoife?"

"Apparently not," said Sarah before Aoife could form an answer. "Since I was never told about her doing ballet with Alex Bloody Minsky and Freaking Peter Olev!"

Peter pulled Aoife aside, a gift in his hands. She knew what it would be, but she took it anyway.

"I left your presents in Brighton," she said.

"I think you being here was enough for us."

"It was good." Aoife let out a deep breath. "Thank you for still being my friend, even after I left you."

"You've always been my best friend, Eef." Peter put a hand on her arm. "Don't tell Alex that, though."

"Never." Aoife almost went back to Christmases past, remembering how empty it had felt the last few years to not have a present from Peter to open on Christmas day. Peter had always given her a gift.

"Let me know how things work out with Sarah." Peter stepped back, still smiling at her.

"Merry Christmas, Peter."

"Merry Christmas, Aoife."

Sarah was watching them from the doorway, ignoring everything Alex was saying.

"Bye, Alex." Aoife smiled against his cheek as he pulled her in for another hug. "Merry Christmas."

"You being here made this the best Christmas in years. Since Milan, probably."

Milan had been the best Christmas. The last good one.

"I got you that blue scarf to match your favorite coat," Alex remembered. "You said it was your favorite present that year."

"It was." Aoife smiled with nostalgia. "See you soon, Alex."

The two girls put on their jackets and hurried down the hallway towards the exit. They stepped out into the cold and watched as their breath froze in front of their faces. Cars drove past, filling the air with the sound of engines and the smell of exhaust, headlights flashing in the dark streets. Aoife felt her toes pinch inside of her shoes as they walked quickly down the sidewalk.

"Well, tonight definitely was not what I expected!" Sarah said brightly, pulling her gloves over her hands to protect them from the dry cold. "I don't even know what part is my favorite!"

"You had a good time?" asked Aoife cautiously.

"Of course I did! I got to meet Alex Bloody Minsky!"

"You aren't upset at me?"

"Aoife! You nutter! Of course not!" Sarah turned to wrap an arm around Aoife's shoulders, bringing her closer as they walked down the sidewalk. "Why would I be upset that you used to be a professional ballet dancer who will most likely give me opportunities to see many more ballets and see Alex Minsky many more times?"

"I guess when you put it that way it doesn't sound so bad."

"Not even a little bit," said Sarah with a happy laugh.

They climbed into the car and headed back to Brighton. Aoife was quiet again, her mind whirring with thoughts as Sarah sang along with the Christmas carols on the radio. They were twenty minutes from home when Aoife turned down the music.

"Can you not tell anyone about this?"

"What?" Sarah turned the music down even more.

"About who I used to be. About Alex and Peter. Please."

"Why not? Are you ashamed of it?"

"No." Aoife knew how stupid it must seem to Sarah for her to not want to own this part of herself in front of her friends. "I'm just trying to sort through my feelings, how it all ended, you know? I want to tell them, but I need to have a few days to just think it through."

"Do you promise?"

"Yeah." Aoife sighed. "Just give me a few days."

Aoife was glad Tansy was with Martin, only because she spent most of the night crying. She allowed herself to feel and remember things she had shut out of her mind because they hurt her. The memories stretched all the way back to losing her mom, and her dad not having a clue how to raise her. Intertwined with the bitter memories was a deep desire to return to dance. She missed it.

The present from Peter was on her table. She knew it was a leotard and probably a pair of tights. She opened it and found both items she had guessed, as well as a card. The message was simple, saying he believed in her dreams and that he loved her.

A touch of gray was on the horizon when Aoife finally sighed and decided she could go back to ballet. Not right then, but one day. Soon. She didn't know, all she knew was that it wasn't the same bold "never" that used to be there when she thought about going back to her first love. She held her pointe shoes in her hand, running her fingers over them and letting her heart realize that she would dance in them again one day.

She fell asleep just as it was becoming light in the sky on Christmas morning. A knock woke her at noon. She tried to straighten her wrinkled clothes and smooth her hair before answering, but she was sure she was still a rumpled mess when she opened the door and saw Sam standing there. He smiled at the sight of her and pulled her into a tight hug.

"Happy Christmas, Aoife."

"Mmm." Aoife wasn't sure how to talk, too pleased to see Sam and too groggy to pull her words together.

"You okay?" Sam leaned back to look in her face.

"Yeah, just... stayed up late thinking." Aoife gave him a smile. "I'm sure I look like a mess right now."

"You look beautiful to me." Sam was still grinning at her.

"Thank you." Aoife paused a moment to register what he said.

"I'm here to take you to Sarah's for Christmas. She told me you wouldn't mind if I picked you up instead of her."

Aoife gave a short laugh. She would have to change her clothes and brush her teeth. She had planned to wash her hair before lunch, but it was too late now. Oh, coffee sounded so good right at that moment. She spun around in a circle as her thoughts moved around her head, trying to figure out what to do first.

"Can I help you? You're literally spinning in circles!" Sam laughed as he stepped into the apartment and put a hand on her arm. "What are you trying to do?"

"I need... I was... Can you make me coffee?"

"Of course!" Sam looked over at the tiny kitchen in the corner and saw the instant coffee and her mug sitting there beside the electric kettle. "Do you drink instant coffee?"

"I haven't bought a coffee maker yet." Aoife waved off Sam's question. "I never remember when I'm out of the house."

"Could've mentioned it to someone. I never bought you a housewarming present."

Aoife just laughed before going into the bathroom to shower and change as quickly as she could. She realized she hadn't checked her phone since falling asleep that morning. She hoped Martin had sent her pictures of Tansy. It hadn't been decided if Martin and Tansy would end up at Sarah's Christmas dinner or not as Martin and Shannon usually went to visit their mother on Christmas day. Naturally they would take Tansy with them. It was her first Christmas and she should spend it with her family. It felt so quiet and empty, though, without her little baby noises and her tiny arms and legs kicking against the air.

Aoife's hair was still wet when she came out of the bathroom, dressed in black pants and a red sweater. It looked Christmassy at least. Sam was standing at the window, his eyes fixed on the sea. Aoife's heart squeezed a little at the sight, wishing she could take a picture to remember the moment.

"I love doing that," said Aoife quietly.

"Is that why you love this place?"

"Yeah." It was the only reason some days.

"What do you think about?" Sam turned then, as he asked. "When you stare at the sea."

Aoife shrugged and looked down at the floor for a second. How did she explain everything the sea meant to her in a simple answer? Sam watched her walk across the floor in her socks to join him by the window.

"I think about a lot of things," she said. "Anything I have on my mind."

"What's on your mind right now?"

"Christmas dinner with my friends." Aoife pushed her mouth up into the shape of a smile. "Did you make my coffee?"

"No." Sam shook his head. "Because I do not want you to have instant coffee on Christmas day. I wouldn't wish that on people I didn't like, let alone a girl that I really, really like."

"But instant coffee is better than no coffee."

"And coffee from Pret is even better," said Sam with a wink.

"That will be the best Christmas present I get this year." Aoife pulled on her jacket and tried to find a pair of shoes to wear.

"Don't say that! Didn't Sarah take you to the ballet in London last night and help you meet Alex Bloody Minsky?" asked Sam with a grin.

"Yes. She did. And it was wonderful, but it was not coffee from Pret after a night of no sleep."

"Tell me about the ballet, by the way." Sam waited patiently by the door. "Did you enjoy it? You're a dancer so I'm sure there's a part of you that finds things like that much more exciting than the rest of us non-dancers."

"It was fun. I really enjoyed it." Aoife remembered to grab her phone at the last minute. She saw that there were several missed texts and calls, but she didn't have time to check them right then.

Sam offered to go into Pret to buy the coffee and let her stay in the car. She smiled at him and pulled out her phone. There was a text from Genny saying that her Aunt Bonnie wouldn't stop talking about her, and who was Tansy? There was a missed call from a number Aoife didn't have saved in her phone, and she wondered if it was Carl. The last two texts were from Alex and Peter respectively.

Merry Christmas!

did u open ur present?

Aoife saw Sam still in line for her coffee so she decided to call Peter instead of trying to type it all out. The video call connected and Peter's face appeared, a huge smile nearly blinding Aoife. In the background she could hear several cheerful voices, including Alex's. She smiled back and gave him a little wave. Peter's expression turned confused.

"Why are you in a car? Are you driving?"

"No, Sam's stopped to pick me up some coffee. I figured this would be easier than trying to text you."

"You're spending Christmas with Sam?" Peter's eyes lit up, pleased with the news.

"Well, Sarah, but he picked me up to take me there." Aoife allowed herself a pink-cheeked grin. "He's buying me coffee for Christmas."

"True love."

"It is when you thought you were going to have to drink instant coffee."

"Eef! You are a sinner!"

"You live with a baby and try to make it without coffee of some sort when you don't have a coffee maker before you point fingers at me!"

"Alex! We need to buy a coffee maker for Eef!" Peter interrupted their call to shout over at his friend.

"Are you talking to her?" Alex suddenly appeared on screen. "Aoife! Merry Christmas!"

"Merry Christmas!"

Just then the car door opened and Sam was there. Aoife dropped her phone and put her hands over her racing heart.

"Geez! You scared me!"

"Aw, sorry!" Sam handed her her cup of coffee. "I didn't realize you were that distracted with your phone."

He leaned over to retrieve the mobile device from the floor. He was surprised when he realized Peter and Alex were still on the screen, blurry and out of focus. The confusion was masked with a smile and a cheery "hullo!" before he handed the phone back to Aoife.

"I have to go. I'll talk to you soon, though." Aoife's hands were shaking. "Merry Christmas."

"Okay, Aoife." Alex's voice was garbled. "See you next time you come to London, yeah?"

"Yeah." Aoife hung up.

"Didn't mean to cut your call with your friends short." Sam kept his eyes on the road as he drove.

"Oh, it's okay. They just wanted to say merry Christmas." Aoife took a drink of the hot beverage. "Thank you so much for the coffee. I feel like a new person."

"I'm glad you're happy with it."

"I have a present for you as well. I don't know if you want it now or later." Aoife grew nervous. It was a cheesy, sentimental present, but she had gone for it anyway. Even if they never worked out, they still had a friendship she could look back on.

"You have it with you now?" Sam glanced at her hands. All she had was a cup of coffee. "Where is it? Did you swallow it?"

"No, silly." Aoife licked her lips. "I'm wearing it."

"What?" Sam's face went a shade pale.

"I didn't want to lose it before I was able to give it to you." Aoife unzipped her jacket and fiddled with the clasp of a necklace she was wearing. It was a simple gold chain with a hoop pendant on it. She had seen it right after Sam had gone off about how complicated jewelry shopping for his mom was with so many choices. He had called her for advice, but never having met his mother, she wasn't much help.

"*I wish I could just buy a necklace with like, a circle, or something, and it would be fine,*" he had said.

"*A circle? I have never seen a necklace with a circle on it.*" Aoife was laughing.

"*See! This is my whole problem!*"

Sam was clearly remembering the phone conversation when he held it up in front of his face while stopped at a stoplight. His grin was crooked and happy and shy all at the same time and Aoife was sure there wasn't any other place she wanted to be than with him right at that moment.

"This is perfect." Sam slipped it around his neck. "I thought you said necklaces like this don't exist!"

"I pulled some strings."

"Well, I wish my present for you wasn't just a cup of coffee now." Sam sighed.

"Believe me, I'm very pleased with this."

"The fact that you're acting like this is the only present I have for you offends me!" Sam reached over and tried to poke Aoife in the side, but she blocked him, laughing that he was going to make her spill her coffee. "I will have you know that I am very good at giving gifts."

Knowing that Sam was the blood relative of Sarah Tadwell was all Aoife needed to believe Sam's claim. Sarah was the queen of gift-giving, and if Sam was even a fraction of what his sister was, then he would be good.

Sarah was calling them, asking them where they were by the time they made it to Sarah's apartment. She had decorated it in November, but there were new decorations on the walls Aoife hadn't seen. It didn't surprise her; Christmas decorations were one of Sarah's weaknesses.

Sarah mentioned how it was her last Christmas in that apartment since she and Max were to be married in four days and she would be moving into his house. Aoife found herself in the kitchen with Sarah and her mom, finishing the puddings and vegetables and talking about wedding details. Max came in at half past one and hurried them, telling them they could talk about first dances and flower girls after they ate.

"So happy Aoife is with us this year!" Sarah was beaming around the table at her parents, Max and Sam. She didn't know that under the table Sam was holding Aoife's hand. "Happy Christmas!"

"Happy Christmas!" Max cut the turkey, and the many bowls of vegetables, sauces and puddings circulated until every plate was full.

"Don't eat that one, it's rubbish," Sam whispered as Aoife was about to put something she didn't know on her plate.

"Thanks." Aoife smothered her laugh and passed the bowl on to Mrs. Tadwell.

Presents came after the meal. Aoife had taken her gifts over to Sarah's a few days earlier so she wouldn't have to worry about moving them on the day of. She sat at one end of the couch and was surprised when Sam sat close beside her, his arm across the back of the couch behind her. His warmth soaked through her clothes and she pulled her sock feet up to have him warm them as well.

In between the presents, Aoife found herself worrying about Tansy. She hadn't heard from Martin since she dropped her off the day before. Every possible scenario was going through her mind when Sarah turned on *It's A Wonderful Life* and snuggled up by Max. It was halfway through the movie when Aoife realized that everyone except for her and Sam was snoozing on the couches. The movie and full tummies had lulled them to sleep. She leaned back against Sam and sighed. He put his arm around her properly and leaned his chin against her head.

"You okay?"

"I haven't heard from Martin yet."

Sam tightened his arm on her and said nothing. It was comforting that that was all she had to say. She thought about telling Sam why she had stayed up all night and how she wanted to go back to ballet, but then she thought about Tansy and how this affected her as well. With another sigh, she closed her mouth and let her eyes slip shut.

She was woken up when Sam began whispering loudly and moving excitedly. His arm jostled her head and she slowly sat up, blinking and looking to the window. It was still light out, but the sun was low. Sarah and her mom were both gone, leaving Aoife with Sam, Max and Mr. Tadwell.

"Steady on, mate," Max was saying. "You've gone and woken Aoife now."

"Aoife! Look!" Sam didn't seem apologetic in the least as he shoved his phone in her face. "Alex Minsky follows me on Instagram!"

Aoife groaned and rolled her face into the back of the couch. Alex was a menace. She pulled her phone out of her pocket to tell him so, shifting up from her position of leaning against Sam so he wouldn't be able to see over her shoulder. There was a screenshot and a text from Peter waiting for her.

looks like u r having a good xmas

The winky face emoji made sense when she saw the picture Sam had posted to Instagram two hours earlier. It was her with her face half-hidden by the blanket, snuggled against him and the back of the couch. She looked for the caption and saw that Peter had fit it into the screenshot as well.

"christmas is nice, but not as nice as her"

"He liked my last post!" Sam shouted, nearly jumping up from the couch as he did.

"What is your last post?" asked Aoife, hiding her phone.

"Nope. If you don't have your own Instagram, you don't get to see it." Sam stuck his tongue out at her, but there was pink in his cheeks.

"Are you sure it is *the* Alex Minsky and not a fan account?" Max said, getting up to look over Sam's shoulder.

"No, it's bloody him!" Sam pointed to the little blue circle and white check mark that meant he was a verified user. "What! He's liked another one!"

Max's gaze flicked over in Aoife's direction, but she had no idea what picture they were looking at. She unlocked her phone again and pulled up her message thread with Alex.

what r u doing?

he's going crazy over here

srsly

Sam cheered again, this time jumping up off of the couch. He waved his phone in Max's face; Max tried to grab his wrist so he could see what had happened. When he finally was able to hold the device still, his laughter filled the living room.

"Cor blimey! What a Christmas!" Sam turned his phone back to face him.

Aoife's phone lit up with a text from Alex.

just spreading Christmas cheer xx

Great.

"Where did Sarah and her mom go?" asked Aoife through a mouthful of yawning.

"What did you say?" Sam chuckled at her as he returned to his spot beside her on the couch.

"I asked where Sarah went."

"Oh, Martin called her," said Max carefully.

"What? What did he say? Is Tansy all right?" It was Aoife's turn to nearly fly off the couch, and she would have if Sam hadn't placed a hand on her shoulder. "Is everything okay?"

"We don't know, but he was talking about Shan. I don't think it had anything to do with Tansy." Max spoke with measured statements.

"So, you think she's okay?"

"Yes," Sam answered with a comforting smile barely showing on his face. "Martin would have told you, I'm sure."

"Right." Aoife focused on remembering how to breathe. "Right, you're right. He would tell me."

Three months, two weeks and five days. Three months, two weeks and five days. Three months, two weeks and five days.

It had been almost that exact amount of time since Aoife took Tansy into her arms and agreed to keep her for as long as was needed. Tears pressed at her eyes and Aoife could feel her face turning red with emotion. She pulled up the blanket that was pushed around her legs to cover her face. An arm wrapped around her and pulled her against them, their heartbeat solid and steady against her ear. She knew it was Sam, the way he smelled and the way he shushed her quietly filling her senses.

An hour passed and no one heard from Martin, Sarah, or even Mrs. Tadwell. Max tried not to appear worried when he called Sarah for the fifth time and no one answered. Finally, Sam offered to take Aoife back to hers in case Martin went to drop Tansy there. She didn't talk during the ride, just held tightly onto Sam's hand and worried her lip with her teeth. Where was her baby? Was she still hers?

"Do you want me to come up with you?" asked Sam quietly when he stopped in front of her apartment.

"No. I'll be okay." Aoife started to unbuckle.

Sam walked around the car to open the door for her and give her a solid hug; one that said she could call on him at any time if she needed him. Then he kissed her cheek and waited until she was inside her building before driving away. She stood by the window, wrapped in a blanket, staring at the sea.

"This feels too big, mam," whispered Aoife. "This feels too big for me."

What Aoife wouldn't do to hear her mother's lilting voice singsong over her, telling her it would be okay. She never let herself dwell on how different her life could have been if her mother had stayed a part of it, but at that moment she couldn't stop herself. She felt a rush of emotions she couldn't handle on her own and her hands reached for her phone. She wasn't even sure if it was the right number, but she called it anyway. There was the voice of a confused man on the other end when the call connected.

"Hello?"

"Carl?" Aoife knew he could hear the tears in her voice. "Carl Stewart?"

"Aoife?" The man sounded aghast.

"Dad," sobbed Aoife, putting her hand over her eyes. "I need to talk to mom."

"Oh, Aoife." Carl sighed.

"Please, dad!"

"Don't do this."

"I know she'll talk to me! Just give me the number!"

"She's been moved, Eef. I don't have a number for her anymore."

"What?" Aoife felt like the air had been sucked out of her lungs. Her last connection was severed, the one thing she carried in the back of her mind that kept her from losing it completely. "What? Dad, no! What?"

"She's not in New Jersey anymore."

"H-how long have you known this?"

"Aoife."

"How long, Carl?!" Aoife shouted angrily.

"Seven years, okay? They contacted me saying she had been accepted into a new facility and she hadn't wanted contact information passed on to us. I didn't think it would help you to know, Eef."

"But they can't do that! Right? She was your wife! You have to be informed!"

"Was, Eef. She *was* my wife. After the divorce, there was nothing that said she had to keep in contact with me beyond the fact that I was raising you, but I had full custody."

"But what if there is an emergency? Surely we would need to know!"

"Just because we don't know where she is anymore doesn't mean nobody does. She had other emergency contacts. Just... not us... anymore."

Aoife couldn't answer, her heart crushed. She didn't know what she expected to gain from a talk with a barely lucid mother who may or may not remember her anyway. If the parts of Rebecca that had lived and breathed ballet, and loving Carl, and being a mom were stripped from her without warning, what was to guarantee she even remembered Carl and Aoife at all? The girl leaned against her window and wept.

"Oh, Aoife." Carl's voice sounded rough. "You shouldn't be like this. Not on Christmas day."

"It doesn't feel like Christmas anymore."

"Listen, Aoife, if you want, you can come over. I know Deb and I live a ways out of the city, but..."

"I'm living in England, dad."

"Oh."

"Yeah. Genny, you remember Genny? Genny hooked me up with a job over here."

"Good. Teaching dance?"

"No. Caregiving." Aoife bit her lip. "But I'm going to give ballet another try."

"Really?" She couldn't miss the way Carl's voice picked up, even over the phone. "That's great. That's really great."

"Peter and Alex are in London right now, doing stuff with a company they started. I think I'm going to join it."

"Good. They'll take care of you. They're good boys."

"Yeah."

"I'm sorry you had to find out about your mom this way."

"Me, too." Aoife closed her eyes but swallowed down her tears. "Merry Christmas. Dad."

"Merry Christmas, Aoife."

As the call ended and the silence of the cold, dark apartment wrapped around her, she suddenly didn't want to be alone. The sea wasn't enough— it was too much. She paused with her finger over the call button next to Peter's name, and then she changed her mind. The call rang through and a familiar voice came on the line.

"C-can... can you come back? Please?"

"Of course," said Sam gently. "I'm on my way."

Aoife didn't move from the window until she heard a light knock at her door fifteen minutes later. She opened it and fell into Sam's arms. He walked her backwards into the apartment and closed the door behind them. There was no sound apart from Aoife's soft weeping.

"I can't call my mom," she choked out. "I just want to talk to my mom, but I can't call her."

"How come?"

Aoife slipped from Sam's arms and walked over to her bed. There was no other place for the both of them to sit unless they wanted to risk the wobbly chair next to the rocker. Sam sat beside her, waiting for her to explain.

"When I was six, my mom had to go into a mental institution." She glanced over at Sam, but there was no judgement in his eyes. "One day, out of nowhere, she was a completely different person. She didn't love my dad, or her job... or me."

"How come?"

Aoife shrugged. She had been too little when they talked about all the technical terms and when she was old enough to know, she didn't want to talk about it, especially not with Carl.

"She still remembered us, knew who we were, but her mood swings... It was too much. Too unpredictable."

"I'm so sorry."

"I missed her a lot." Aoife wiped a tear from her face, her fingers pressing against her cheek and trying to remember what it felt like to have a mother touch her face out of love. "We had been so close."

"Does she still remember you?"

"She did last time I saw her, when I was nine. She used to be at a place in New Jersey, but I just called my dad and he told me she was moved seven years ago. I have no idea how to find her now."

Aoife knew there wasn't much for Sam to do or say in response to what she told him, but knowing that he knew was good enough for the moment. He hugged her before taking a deep breath. Aoife forced a grim smile as she sat up from his arms and tried to put herself back together.

"Is there anything I can get you? Anything to help?" Sam put a hand to the back of her head, stroking her hair thoughtfully.

"I didn't get to have gingerbread men this year." She didn't know why that popped into her head. Gingerbread men and gingerbread houses were things she used to do with Chloe.

"Gingerbread men?" Sam hid an amused smile, just barely, as he repeated what Aoife said to him.

"They're cookies shaped like men, made out of gingerbread. Don't you have those here?"

"Yeah, we have them." Sam chuckled. "We can buy a tub of twenty of them at Sainsburys. Is that all?"

"You can't have cookies without hot chocolate," Aoife murmured.

"All right, let's go to Sainsburys and buy anything you want. Sound good?"

Aoife nodded.

"I know you love your view of the sea, but... it's a bit cold in here, Aoife. We can go back to Sarah's and watch another Christmas film, make hot chocolate. She has couches, too?"

"Yeah, that's fine." Her toes were numb already.

"Okay." Sam smiled.

He intertwined their fingers and waited for Aoife to lock the door behind them. They walked down the empty aisles of the grocery store, Sam doing his best to cheer her. A few teenage girls spotted Sam and asked if they could take a picture with him. He obliged politely, telling them merry Christmas and wishing them a happy new year. They giggled and Aoife thought they might have taken a picture of her and Sam as they walked away, but they left too quickly for her to ask. She didn't mind, though; she liked Sam, and he liked her.

By the time they reached the checkout lane, they had a basket full of chocolates, cookies, two tubs of ice cream and a gingerbread house that was marked 75% off. Sam was polite and chatted with the lady at the checkout, signing a piece of paper for her son who was a big fan of Sam and his team.

"He won't believe I actually got to meet you!" The woman thanked Sam again. "This will make it up to him for working on Christmas."

"She was sweet," said Aoife as they climbed back into the car.

"She was. Things like that make me happy."

Aoife noticed the same group of girls standing on the corner as they pulled out of the parking lot. She wondered what they were up to on Christmas evening. When they arrived at Sarah's, Max had the news that Sarah had called. She hadn't been able to explain anything, but she said they wouldn't be back until the next morning, and she was so sorry to leave them without a hostess for the evening.

"Did she say anything about Tansy?" asked Aoife hopefully.

"No, but I know that Martin is really good with her and if there were any problems that he would let us know."

"I know." And she did know. It was just so hard because it had been two days since she last held her and kissed her face and made sure she was safe and fed and warm.

The gingerbread house and old *Doctor Who* Christmas specials kept them distracted until after midnight when Max took off for his place and Sam and his father made up the pullout couch. Aoife slept in Sarah's room, tossing and turning on the big, comfy mattress covered with the cozy cushions *Pop's Shop* no longer carried.

Aoife woke up at half past six and tried to go back to sleep, but she was still mostly awake when Sarah unlocked the front door at eight am. She ran to the hallway and saw Sarah, Mrs. Tadwell and Martin, but no Tansy. Mr. Tadwell and Sam woke up from their bed in the living room and rubbed sleep from their eyes as they joined them. All three of the newcomers had red-rimmed and bloodshot eyes. Aoife felt sick.

"What happened? Is everyone all right?" asked Sam, his morning voice rough and scratchy.

"Shan's in the hospital." Sarah pulled off her jacket. "Tried to kill herself."

There was a tiny sob as Martin covered his face with his hands and hunched his shoulders.

"Come now, darling. Have some tea." Mrs. Tadwell took the young man by the arm and led him into the kitchen.

Aoife hovered on the edge of the group, silently screaming that she needed to know where Tansy was, to know if she was okay. Mrs. Tadwell put the kettle on and pulled a mug out of the cupboard. The sound of the glass on the counter was loud as everyone held their questions.

"Did Max go home?" asked Sarah, looking around and noticing he was missing.

"Yeah. Aoife stayed here with dad and I," said Sam.

"Oh. Good."

"Can I do anything? To help? Martin?" Aoife couldn't hold back any longer.

"No. Shan will stay at the hospital until she can get into a rehab center. Nothing will really change." Martin shook his head.

"Wh-ere's..." Aoife saw Sarah shaking her head out of the corner of her eye, but she went ahead anyway. "Where's Tansy?"

"She's with my neighbor, Miss Nancy."

"Your neighbor?" Aoife's heart thumped twice, painful and strong against her ribcage. "You could have brought her to me! I wouldn't have minded! You could have just brought her back to me!"

"I found my sister trying to hang herself in the bathroom on Christmas day!" Martin snapped, and for the first time ever, Aoife saw him angry. "Please! I did what was best for my family!"

Aoife took a step back, trying to breathe. Her phone rang in her pocket and everyone looked at her.

"Sorry, excuse me." She pulled her phone out and slipped into the living room. The tree was still there, lit up and beautiful, as if Christmas hadn't ended up being the worst day in a long time. She looked down at the screen and saw it was Peter. "Peter, this is not a good time."

"Aoife, you've been found out." His voice was serious as he said her full name.

"What?"

"You're in some gossip magazine, Leanne just saw it. They got pictures of you and Sam at the grocery store yesterday and they've figured out who you are."

"What do you mean they figured out who I am? Like, my name or... Or like..."

"They know you used to dance with us, that you were in a company. It's going around the internet. I wanted to let you know in case you still have friends you hadn't told yet."

"You mean everyone?" Aoife couldn't believe this was happening. "Sarah is the only one who knows. Wow, this is really bad timing. Sam's going to see it."

"Do you think this will matter to him?"

"Not like that, but I just... I didn't want him to find out this way. I wanted to tell him when I knew for sure what I was going to do with ballet."

"I'm sorry, Eef."

"Martin's sister just tried to kill herself yesterday and everyone is tired and emotional and now this. This is the worst time in the world."

"Do you want to come spend a few days with me? I can get a baby seat for Tansy."

"No, I... I can't go. Max and Sarah's wedding is in a couple days." Aoife couldn't bring herself to say that Tansy was with some stranger named Miss Nancy.

"I have a few days off before we start rehearsing for *Giselle* so if you need me, just call."

"Bye, Peter."

Aoife walked out into the kitchen to hear everyone talking quietly. Martin had his back towards her, sipping his tea and wiping his eyes. When Sarah disappeared into her bedroom, Aoife followed her. She knocked on the door and waited for Sarah to call out a weary "come in" before she entered.

"You okay?" asked Aoife, shutting the door and standing awkwardly beside it. "I'm sure you had a rough night."

"Rough doesn't even begin to describe it." Sarah rubbed her eyes and moaned. "I haven't cried like that in ages."

"I'm glad you were there for him." Aoife took a step closer. "I know how hard it can be to stay with a friend when they go through something like that."

"He's going to be a mess for days." Sarah sat on the edge of her bed and laid back, staring up at the ceiling. "I should cancel the wedding."

"Let's have everyone get some rest before we talk like that."

"You're right." She closed her eyes and yawned.

"Sarah, I know this is really bad timing, but I need you to help me with something." Aoife hated the words coming out of her mouth. "Not a thing, just... Okay, some gossip magazine got pictures of Sam and I and they've figured out who I am as like, a ballet dancer. They know I used to dance with Alex and Peter."

"Hmmm?" Sarah's eyes were still closed.

"I just... I need to know how to tell people. I don't want them to find out through some gossip column at the grocery store, but today is really bad timing. What do you think I should do?"

Sarah dragged her eyelids open and struggled to sit up. She blinked at Aoife a couple times before dropping back onto her bed. Aoife twisted her hands and waited.

"Sarah?"

"I don't have any idea, Aoife. It's your own fault for not telling people sooner."

"I realize this, but I don't want to make it worse by not telling them, but I don't think now..."

"I said I don't know." Sarah sighed.

Just then Martin walked into the room. He stopped short when he saw Aoife there. He ignored her, and walked over to the bed where Sarah was.

"I need to go," he said quietly. "If you're not busy."

"Oh, yeah, course." Sarah sat up, a yawn pulling at her mouth and chin again. "Aoife was just saying how she didn't know how to tell people about her past now that it's in a gossip magazine."

It took all of Aoife's self-control to keep from crumbling with frustration. She didn't blame the poor girl; Sarah hadn't slept all night and was about to get married.

"What?" Martin turned to stare at Aoife. "What past?"

"Nothing, Martin, I just..."

"Did you do bad things? Are you a bad person?" His questions came off quickly, harshly. "Are you a criminal? A manipulator or con-artist?"

"No! Nothing like..." Aoife was cut off again.

"You know, I don't know hardly anything about you and I don't think Tansy should stay with you anymore." Martin was clearly too tired to know what he was saying, but his words cut Aoife's heart to pieces. "I don't know what you used to do! Or where you're from! I can't believe I let her stay with you!"

"Come on, Martin." Sarah shuffled to her feet and pushed Martin out of the room. She gave one last look at Aoife before she closed the door behind her. "You should not have brought this up today."

Aoife was still standing in a state of shock when the door opened and Sam peered in. He quickly crossed the room to pull her into his arms. She stood stiff, unyielding to his embrace.

"Aoife, I'm sorry."

"What are you sorry for?"

"Sarah said something about you being in some magazine and they said things about you that you don't want people to know. I know what that's like, and I'm sorry you're having to deal with a situation like this."

"Did Martin leave?" Aoife pushed away from Sam.

"Yeah, Sarah's taking him home now. My dad's driving with her."

Aoife nodded.

"I'm sorry for how Martin acted towards you as well. He's really worried about his sister. He doesn't mean it."

"There's some sort of truth, though."

"Don't hold onto this. He hasn't slept it off yet."

"It will feel worse when he wakes up and he still feels the same way." Aoife pressed a hand to her throat and burning hot tears welled up in her eyes. "That he doesn't trust me with Tansy."

"Aoife, please, let it all go."

"He didn't even let me explain! He didn't let me explain what the magazine said! I'm not a criminal! I-I'm not a bad person."

"We know that, Aoife. I don't care about the article. I won't read it. Anything I find out about you I want to come from you."

"Other people will read it, though. They'll tell you." Aoife's chin quivered. "I wanted to tell you when it would be happy, when I knew what it meant for my future."

"Then wait."

"I can't. It's out there. I want you to know from me." Aoife took a deep breath and wiped her eyes. "It shouldn't even be this big of a deal, but I... My mom was a principal ballerina."

"Okay." Sam nodded, listening attentively.

"And when I was born, all she wanted was for me to love ballet as much as she did. A-and I did. Even after she went away, I kept dancing. I got better and better at it, until I was really good at it." She watched Sam's expression.

"You were a ballerina?"

"Technically you only call the highest rank of ballet dancers ballerinas, but for the sake of simplicity, yes. My friends and I performed on stages across the world. Paris. Milan. St. Petersburg... I lived and breathed ballet, and dancing. I thought it was going to be my life forever."

"Why did you give it up?"

"It's a long story," Aoife whispered. "But anyway, Peter Olev and Alex Minsky are my best friends and that's why Alex follows you on Instagram now. That's basically all you need to know from the article."

"Okay." Sam nodded thoughtfully.

"Like I told Sarah," added Aoife in a quiet voice. "I didn't keep this a secret because of trust, I was just looking to put a very painful memory behind me."

"You don't have to explain it to me. It's fine. Are you fine?"

"I mean... more now that I know you're not freaking out at me."

"Oh, Aoife." Sam held his arms open for the girl to step into a hug. He lightly kissed the top of her head. "Let's take you home."

Aoife woke up from a nap that evening to insistent pounding on her door. It was Martin and the apologies were falling from his mouth before the door was even fully opened. Over and over he apologized for what he had said, asking her to please forgive him.

"Of course, Martin." Aoife hugged him. "I know you didn't mean it. You were trying to take care of your family."

He returned Tansy to her and Aoife spent the entire night holding her baby close. The little one smiled and cooed after she finished crying, as if she was telling Aoife how much she had missed her while they were apart.

"I love you so much, Tansy girl," Aoife said in a whisper. "And I always will."

-Chapter 9-

New Year, New Direction

Max and Sarah's wedding was almost as beautiful as Sarah in her floor-length chiffon dress that included a cathedral-length train. The horrible trauma of Christmas day turned into a memory that everyone put away from them as they focused on the flowers and fairy lights and stringed quartet playing while the bridal party made their way down the aisle. Aoife wore a red dress as she carried Tansy, the flower girl. She smiled at Max, but looked beyond him to find Sam's face in the lineup of groomsmen. He looked handsome in his black tux and hair styled back from his face and up into a quiff. A wink just for her made her stomach tilt for a moment. Then she was at the end of the aisle, finding her spot in the front row to sit until the end of the ceremony.

The reception was filled with laughter and happy tears. Aoife couldn't have been more pleased for her two friends and joined in on the toasts. Everyone ooed at her American accent and smiled as she wished them years of happiness and cozy cushions. When Sam talked about how much he loved his little sister, even Max teared up.

Sam and Aoife found each other later on the dance floor. He pulled her in for a slow dance, singing quietly along with the band on the stage. Aoife hooked her chin over his shoulder and tightened her hold on his waist. He was perfect for her.

Then the wedding was over and everyone went back to their homes. Aoife had Tansy again, but their days were empty without Miss Wilcox. She spent her mornings stretching and dancing while the people who lived below her were at work. Tansy seemed to enjoy watching Aoife leap and pirouette across the tiny apartment. It was painful getting back into a core-strengthening routine, but she loved it. She wanted her body to be ready for whenever it was time to go back.

Two days after New Year's, Aoife received a text from Martin asking her to come over for tea. Aoife had a sinking feeling that she knew what it was about, but forced the idea from her mind. Instead, she wrapped herself and Tansy up in their warmest jackets and walked down to the beach. She stood with her feet on the rocks and her face towards the giant, blue expanse. She thought about her mom and how she could be anywhere in the entire world.

A gust of cold, wet wind blew against them and Tansy protested in the front pack.

"It's okay." Aoife patted Tansy's back, staying for just one more moment. "Remember, Tansy, that no matter how big life's problems or hurts seem to be, the sea can always remind us that we're just little and we'll make it through. The waves of life can wash us clean like the waves wash the sand."

Tansy gurgled and kicked her legs.

"I love you." Aoife pressed her lips against Tansy's forehead and felt her eyes blur from unshed tears before she turned and walked to Martin's.

Martin had the tea things all set out already and was waiting for them when they arrived. He took Tansy from Aoife and bounced her lightly up into the air to make the baby giggle. Aoife watched with a smile, removing her jacket and the front pack. She left them both by the front door and walked slowly into the living room. Martin saw the look on her face and smiled sadly at her.

"Come sit. I have your favorite biscuits here."

"Thanks." Aoife watched Martin place Tansy in the playpen.

The baby was soon back in Aoife's arms, however, when she made sad noises, telling them she was ready for her afternoon bottle and nap. Aoife rocked her softly as she and Martin spoke about the wedding, about Sam, and even about what the new year might bring.

"Aoife, I need to talk to you about something," said Martin. "I think you've already guessed what this is about."

Aoife said nothing. Her throat felt thick and filled with cotton.

"Shan's in the hospital and I don't know when she'll be out. I don't know when she'll be out of rehab, or even if she'll ever be." Martin sighed. "But I do know she's not coming back to Tansy, and because of that, I need to start thinking of a permanent home for the babe."

Tears filled Aoife's eyes. She nodded. She tried to swallow and speak, but she couldn't. All she could do was nod and let her eyes speak for her.

"I'm so sorry, Aoife. I've looked into things before calling you over to talk to you, but because you're American you can't... Oh, Aoife." Martin's eyes watered.

"No, I know," Aoife finally managed to say. "I know. This is good. I'm... I know this is what needs to happen."

"You have been the best thing to ever happen to Tansy, and I don't want you to think for a second that I'm looking for someone else because you wouldn't do an amazing job raising her."

Aoife nodded and tried to speak, but the lump was back. She looked down at the baby in her arms and watched a tear splash onto her blanket.

"This has been an incredibly difficult decision for me. I wanted to keep her, I really did. I-I..." Martin opened and closed his mouth twice before pressing his lips together and taking a deep breath. "She's my niece. I want to keep her more than I even know how to put into words and I haven't had a full night's sleep from thinking about it."

There were tears in Martin's eyes and Aoife couldn't keep herself from crying. Martin pressed his fingers against flushed cheeks and sniffed loudly. Their tea was lukewarm and the sun was completely gone for the day, leaving the room feeling dark and cold.

"I feel like I'm failing her..." Martin said from behind his hands.

"Stop." Aoife reached out and put a hand on Martin's arm.

"But I'm only twenty-four. I have to run the shop and make sure my sister and my mum are cared for. Tansy deserves to be in a home where she's not being juggled around everything else in my crazy life." Martin wiped one finger under each eye to dry his tears. "Obviously it makes sense to find someone who will adopt her sooner than later, give her the best chance at really feeling a part of their family."

"No, you're right." Aoife nodded again. "I know. You're right."

"I want you to stay in her life, though, Aoife." Martin waited until Aoife was looking him in the eye before he continued. "Please, Aoife. Promise."

"Of course." Aoife took a shaky breath. "I promise."

"And I don't just want you in her life to give her free ballet lessons when she's older."

Aoife's jaw dropped the slightest bit and Martin laughed even as he wiped his eyes again.

"I read the article in the magazine."

"Ah. Yes." Aoife's mouth pushed up into a small smile on one side. She stared down at Tansy and remembered another child that had slept in her arms just like that. She licked her lips and looked back up at Martin. "You know how you asked me if I had experience with babies, and I told you not really?"

Martin nodded, confused by the change of subject.

"That was a bit of a lie."

Martin urged her to continue with a nod.

"I didn't quit ballet and dance because I was too old, or because I had an injury, or whatever other rumor is going around. I quit ballet because it stopped being a source of joy and pleasure to me. I wasn't excited to perform anymore, it was like torture, because all it did was remind me of people who I loved, who felt like family to me... people who had been there since..." Aoife paused to take a deep breath and steady her voice. "Sorry, I've never really told this to anyone before."

"It's okay, love." Martin's eyes were compassionate.

"I guess I should start at the beginning of the story. My mom moved to New York City to join a ballet company there. While she was in that company, she met her two best friends who ended up having their babies within months of when my mom had me. Peter and Chloe and I grew up together, going to dance classes, rehearsals, traveling, competitions, having sleepovers and movie nights. We always said we were going to join the same ballet company when we were older and dance together forever."

Forever. Aoife swallowed hard.

"When we were in high school, Alex moved to New York from England to go to the ballet school we were a part of. We don't know why, but he just fit our group perfectly. For the rest of high school we were inseparable. If one of us wanted to be in a competition, we all did it. We all auditioned for the same shows. That's why when we graduated from high school, our graduation present from our parents was a trip for the four of us."

"Aw! How special!" Martin smiled at his friend.

"It was special," Aoife agreed, letting a smile cross her face. She could still remember the way her stomach filled with butterflies as she stood in line for security, her hand gripping Chloe's tightly. They had flown hundreds of times, but this was the first time they were flying internationally by themselves. Chloe had insisted on taking a Polaroid picture at every stop along their journey, documenting their summer in Europe together. Aoife wondered where the stack of pictures had ended up.

"Where did you go?" asked Martin, his voice soft, as if he knew Aoife was someplace far away in her head.

"Everywhere." Aoife's eyes were shining, gazing at the brilliance of an old memory. "We went to all the best ballet schools and visited some of the most prestigious companies. It was a huge, once-in-a-lifetime opportunity that our parents somehow pulled enough strings for us to experience. They let us rehearse with them and perform little roles on stage. It was magical. We went to Russia, the Netherlands, France..." Aoife's eyes dimmed. "It was in France that Chloe told us she was pregnant."

Martin's eyes widened, but he said nothing.

"It was like everything suddenly stopped and life was just... ruined." Aoife shook her head, a bitter taste in her mouth. "I remember being so angry at first. She was supposed to dance with me forever, but there she was, eighteen years old and pregnant with the baby of a man that was... Well, he was a lot older than us."

"By how much?" gasped Martin.

"Thirty years, probably."

"No! How did he know her?"

"He was a private dance instructor her mom hired to work with her when she was twelve. He was an amazing ballet dancer and Chloe loved him. Not like that at first, of course, but when she got older he... I don't know what happened. I tried to talk her out of it, but once her mind was set, there was no changing it."

"What happened?"

"She was terrified. The boys were terrified. I was heartbroken, and then terrified. Her mom was one of the strictest instructors at our ballet school and all she wanted was for Chloe to be a ballerina like she had been. If she found out that Chloe was pregnant, and with Dave's baby no less, it would have been madness." Aoife paused. "Sometimes I think back and wonder what we could have done differently to make the situation better. We were just kids on the other side of the world supposedly chasing our dreams. Chloe had never been afraid of anything before, but finding out she was going to have a baby paralyzed her.

"She contacted Dave and he flew out. He had his opinion on what should happen, but Chloe was almost sick at the idea of an abortion. We had had a couple friends who had one and their stories really shook Chloe up. One night, I was trying to sleep but I could hear Chloe crying in the bathroom of our hotel room." Aoife could hear the soft weeping in her mind, as if she were back in that room in the middle of Paris. "I went in to try to comfort her, and all she kept saying, over and over, was that she couldn't do it alone."

Aoife slipped back into her memories and relived the conversation. Her heart ached as she pictured her best friend, tears on her face, fear in her eyes. There was already a bump showing in Chloe's middle and soon anyone who saw her on the street would know her secret.

"Eef, I can't do this! I'm too scared I'm going to mess up!"

"You're not going to mess up."

"How do you know that? You don't know that!"

"It's okay, Chloe, no matter what happens, I'll help you."

"You'll help me?"

"Yeah."

"Do you promise?"

"Of course I promise."

"No matter what?"

"No matter what, Chloe. I promise I'll help you."

"I had never seen Chloe like that." Aoife's voice trembled. "She had been there for me through so many hard things, and I knew if our places were switched, she would do anything to help me. So I promised her that I would help with the baby after he was born."

Martin's eyes were shining with tears, probably from thinking back to the day when he had broken down and said that he couldn't do it alone.

"After that, life found a new normal for the most part. We were supposed to have traveled to London after the *Opéra National de Paris*, but we went to Italy instead. Dave had some connections in Milan and was able to get us into the *Milano City Ballet*. We took the train across Europe to get there. I think that was my favorite part of the trip."

"What did you tell your parents?"

"That we had been taken on as apprentices there. They were thrilled." Aoife laughed. "Told us they were proud of us for working so hard and chasing our dreams. And it was an incredible experience. Being able to dance under Professor DiLanardio is hands down one of the greatest things to have happened to me as a ballet dancer. Peter and Alex will say the same if you ask them."

"What about Chloe?"

"She didn't... she wasn't a part of that." Aoife frowned. "She worked with Dave in a private studio he rented for her. It was really hard, because that was the first time we were ever separated when it came to dance. At least I still had the boys, though. We would all come back to our apartment at the end of the day and talk about when we would be together onstage again. It was a very special time in our friendship where we had to really take care of each other. We had always been family, but that was when we were all the family we had. The good things were really good, and the hard things were really hard, but we had each other."

"And the baby?" asked Martin.

"He was born January 28th. We named him Roe." Aoife couldn't help but smile sadly as she said his name. "He was the most perfect little baby I had ever seen. Chloe had me in the room during the birth and the nurse put him in my arms when he was just minutes old and I... I don't know. I just loved him from the second I saw his face.

"Chloe loved him, too. I could see it in her eyes when she looked at him when she thought she was alone, but she was... it was a big change for her. Dave went back to the states and she was left with this tiny human to take care of and the reality that she was going to have to tell her parents what had happened. The boys and I helped her with him, and because I had promised her, I took the biggest share in the responsibility. I even left the company to take care of him so Chloe could get back into shape."

"Was that hard?"

"It was, because ballet had been my life, but then Roe became my life and I didn't regret it at all. I mean, Chloe was still Roe's mom, and she took care of him, but..."

"You had promised," said Martin.

"And I wanted to do it. There was something about holding him in my arms and knowing he was trusting me to take care of his every need that melted me. Chloe and I would take him to the private studio and he would sleep while we danced. When he woke up, I would feed him and Chloe would keep dancing. At night I would keep him next to my bed so Chloe could get enough sleep. For a couple months it worked, and I foolishly thought it was going to be okay." Aoife let out a deep sigh and closed her eyes for a moment. "Dave flew over in May to help us move back to The States. He came in on another flight with the baby so when our parents picked us up at the airport he wouldn't be there. Chloe just wanted a few days to figure out how to tell her parents, but those few days turned into a week and I couldn't stay in the apartment anymore.

"Chloe told me not to take him with me when I went to the studio, but I was afraid she would still be sleeping when it was time for his bottle. I went in early, thinking I would just stay for a couple hours. I didn't realize Chloe's mom was there until she saw me, and..."

"Oh, Aoife." Martin put a hand over his heart.

"She was like a mother to me after my mom left. Taught me ballet, took me to dance recitals and competitions. Did my hair, gave me pep talks, fed me, hugged me, gave me presents on every birthday, told me she was proud of me. And then suddenly, in a moment, she hated me." Aoife took a minute to steady her voice. "When she found out who Roe was and what had happened, she was livid. She made Chloe come to the studio and tell her everything. I tried to calm them down, but then she turned on me and told me I was the worst friend for helping Chloe hide something like that from her. She said I was ungrateful for everything she had done for me, and then she told me that she hated me and I was to never talk to them ever again."

"No, Aoife!"

"Chloe was so upset she wouldn't even look at me when she went back to the apartment to pack her things. I couldn't have felt more miserable if I had tried." A tear slipped down Aoife's cheek. "Right before Chloe left she told me she still loved me, and that she forgave me. Then they were gone. Chloe's whole family moved away and I never heard from them or saw them again."

Aoife swallowed and wiped the tears from her face. "I had him for three months, two weeks and five days."

"I feel terrible that I'm taking Tansy from you." Martin's voice wavered as he spoke. "Just like that lady."

"No, Martin." Aoife shook her head. "This is nothing like losing Roe. You're doing what is best. I'll miss her. Of course I wish I didn't have to give her up, but she needs this."

"How long have you had her for?" he whispered.

Aoife closed her eyes before she answered. "Three months, two weeks and six days."

As Aoife and Tansy walked home from Martin's that night, Aoife kept her thoughts positive. She would have Tansy until a new family was found and she would be able to stay in her life forever. Forever. Maybe, just maybe, Tansy could be a forever. Not in the way Aoife had wanted, but a forever nonetheless.

"She's going to be leaving me," Aoife told Peter that night over the phone.

"Eef, you okay?"

"I think I am, actually." Aoife stood at her window and stared out at the sea. "It will be hard, but I'm not losing her the same way I lost Roe."

"I'm so proud of you for doing all that you've done for her these past few months."

"Thanks, Peter. I couldn't have made it through without you. And Alex."

"And?"

Aoife was confused by Peter's question.

"And who else helped you through?" asked Peter, trying again.

"I don't understand..."

"Well, there's a certain gentleman who posts an awful lot of pictures of you who seems to have helped you a lot recently."

"Ah. Sam." Aoife smiled and blushed.

"Can we meet him now?"

"No." Aoife's answer was firm. "You know too much about me and I really like this guy."

"Eef, if you don't introduce us on your terms, Alex will come up with his own way to meet him and you know that won't be pretty."

"Okay, fine." Aoife let out a loud sigh. "Next week?"

"Sure, just not Thursday or Friday; that's when auditions for *Giselle* are."

"All right. I'll talk to Sam and see what we can work out. Just promise you won't chase him off."

"Unless we find he's not worthy, of course," said Peter matter-of-factly. "We will definitely chase him away if he's unworthy."

"How about if you find him unworthy we talk about it first?" said Aoife. She knew they would be protective of her, but she had never really had a boyfriend before, at least, not one that they hadn't known as well as she had. Her dad was right; they were good guys. "And please don't embarrass me."

"I've been waiting for this day for years now. I'm fully prepared."

"That's actually what I was afraid of."

The preparation Peter had done turned out to be a hundred pictures of Aoife growing up. Sam was excited to meet Peter and Alex, and was quickly at ease with them. Knowing that protesting or putting up a fuss would only make things worse, Aoife sat quietly, watching three of her favorite people in the world get to know one another. Sam held her hand under the table and squeezed it whenever Peter showed him another cute picture of Baby Aoife. It wasn't until Peter put his phone away that Aoife realized he hadn't added any pictures of Chloe and Roe. She waited until he glanced at her before she mouthed her thanks to him.

"So?" Aoife asked, leaning against Sam for warmth as they stood outside the restaurant waiting for their car.

"You were the most adorable baby in the world." Sam leaned forward to kiss Aoife's forehead. "And I would love to see you dance one day."

"One day."

"Thank you for letting me meet them. I enjoyed seeing this side of you."

"What side of me?" Aoife added a defensive tone to her words. "I'm me, same as always."

"The way they tease you and get under your skin just to wind you up. You play into it every single time, don't try to lie."

Aoife didn't contest his allegations, but smiled to herself.

"Has Martin found a family yet?" Sam asked softly.

"Not yet." Aoife leaned harder and felt Sam put his arms around her. "But soon, probably."

"What are you going to do once she's left?"

"Not sure yet," said Aoife quietly as they saw their car pull up. "I'll decide once I know how much more time I have with her."

"You'll find something and you'll be amazing at it." Sam opened her door for her and helped her in. She looked at him when he squeezed her hand meaningfully. "Hey, I mean it."

"Thanks, Sam." She kissed his cheek, feeling the stubble on his face against her lips. "I'm glad I have you."

"I'm glad I have you."

The screenshot of Sam's Instagram that night was a picture of Aoife laughing at the table during supper. Peter's hand was in the edge of the photo, reaching over with whipped cream on his fingers, ready to smear it against Aoife's cheek. He had, too, but Sam hadn't posted that picture. Underneath it read, *"I'm glad I have you"* with a red heart after it. There were apparently already hundreds of comments and likes that Aoife couldn't see.

did u like him? She sent as a text to Peter.

let's just say... he typed back.

Aoife rolled her eyes when he made her wait two minutes for the next text. She thought about calling him and insisting he stop acting like a child, but her phone finally received his second message. A smile crossed her face as she read it.

im glad he has u 2

February second was Aoife's last full day with Tansy. The family adopting her was beautiful and sweet and lived in Brighton, which meant both Martin and Aoife would see her often. They threw a little party in her honor, a going away party of sorts, to mark how much time they had had with Tansy as only theirs before she started her new life. Sarah baked a cake, and Max rented a bounce house for no apparent reason. There were tears, but it was a happy celebration, and when Aoife handed the little girl over to her new mother, there was a sense of closure.

"Well, this is it, Tansy girl," Aoife whispered against her soft blond curls. "If you ever miss me, just look at the sea. I will never stop loving you, just like the sea never stops coming to the shore. Okay?"

Tansy cooed and shrieked happily. Aoife's eyes were so filled with tears that she couldn't see how big the baby's smile was as she giggled. It was a magical sound that made Aoife's heartache all worth it. She felt Martin's arm around her shoulders as Tansy's new family drove away with her.

"They'll be good to her."

"I know. I'm happy." Aoife wiped her eyes and sniffed. "You did a good thing for her."

"I did that when I gave her to you, Aoife," Martin whispered.

Aoife gave herself one week to catch up on sleep, cleaning the apartment, and sleepovers with Sarah before she decided what she was going to do. She and Sarah spent an entire night on Pinterest looking at different things and talking about options. Aoife didn't have many as she didn't have a work visa. Miss Wilcox had paid her rent until the next August, but she didn't know if she would be able to stay that long. In fact, unless she found a way to stay, she would have to leave by the end of the month when her six-month visa expired.

147

She spent a long time sitting in the rocking chair and staring out at the sea. She hadn't ridden the rusty bicycle for months, relying on Martin or Sarah to loan her their cars. Her time was divided between dancing in her apartment and hanging out in *Pop's Shop*. She ached for Tansy when she woke up alone in the middle of the night, and she threw out her instant coffee.

The last week of February rolled around and Aoife had her plane ticket. She told her friends with a heavy heart that she would be moving back to New York City. Maybe it was for the best to go back and start over where she had first began. Sarah wanted her to have a going-away party, but she refused. Instead she had a special time with each person, one-on-one, before she left. She knew that one day she would be back, there was no way Brighton could be forgotten after all it had brought her that winter. Sam let her help choose the photo of them from their time together to post on Instagram. He already had his caption in mind, though, and had her read it over his shoulder as he typed it out.

"'She loves staring at the sea, I love staring at her,'" said Aoife, a blush creeping down her cheeks as she read it out loud. "Sam."

"It's true."

Aoife shifted closer to him on the sofa and hugged his arm to her. It was going to be hard not living close enough to visit him every so often, but they had agreed to keep in touch and take things slowly, even over long-distance. Conor had joked that Aoife could marry Sam for residency, but Sam told him to shut it and mind his own business.

"I'll see you soon," said Peter as he dropped Aoife off at Heathrow the morning of her flight. "Whether it's here or in New York, I'll see you."

"Yeah. Keep me updated on *Giselle*. You know that was one of my favorites."

"You'd make a brilliant Giselle."

"Maybe one day." Aoife smiled at him. "Thanks for everything. Keep an eye on Sam for me. Not because he needs it, but because I like his face and I'll be too far away to look at him myself."

"I love seeing you like this, Eef." Peter pulled her into a hug. "I will make sure Sam feels loved and beautiful every day while you are gone."

"Peter!" Aoife laughed even as her eyes blurred slightly.

She waved over her shoulder and walked into the airport, ready to go back to the place she had run away from six months earlier. Genny was waiting for her on the other side. Her smile was a mile wide as she went on and on about how Aoife would fit into the ballet company she was a part of. Aoife smiled and tried to stay awake, putting it all to the back of her mind.

Over the next few weeks, Aoife felt the strain of hard work and long distance like never before. All of the people she loved the most were far away and her body felt like it would break at the intensity of the workload she found herself thrust into. She did private practice times after the day with Genny, relearning things she had let slip through her fingers.

Sam would let her cry to him during their video calls, telling her that he knew she was doing great and it was all worth it. She would swallow her tears and nod because she knew he was right. Her calls with Peter and Alex were few and far between as their crazy schedule left them with no extra time to connect. She wasn't worried, though. They had gone longer without talking and had been fine. It was when Aoife didn't have time to return Sarah's calls to tell her about her new apartment or her favorite bakery that made her sad the most.

A package arrived at Aoife's new address the end of March. It was filled with little goodies and presents from Sarah and Martin. There were new pictures of Tansy in the box and Aoife wept as she held them against her heart. That afternoon she climbed into a taxi and went to the Hudson River. It wasn't the sea, and it didn't have waves, but it was the closest thing she had.

"I just want to go home," she told Genny.

"You are home, silly! What do you mean?"

Aoife didn't answer.

"I know what would cheer you up. I'm going to see Aunt Bonnie tonight."

"Can I come? Please?"

"Oh, good! I was hoping you would want to come! I was afraid I would have to sit there and watch her knit all on my own again."

Aoife worked hard that day, knowing she would see Miss Wilcox and tell her what she had done since she left. She put the new pictures of Tansy into her bag, even though she knew Miss Wilcox wouldn't be able to see them. It just seemed right.

The house Genny pulled up to was much less grand than the house Aoife had known in Brighton. It was a single story with nothing to attract attention to it. Even the neighborhood wasn't much. Aoife realized how much Miss Wilcox gave up to make sure she followed her dreams. The ache in her throat started right then.

"Aoife! My dear!" Miss Wilcox called out her name before Aoife had hardly stepped through the door. "I'm so happy you're here to visit!"

"Miss Wilcox!" Aoife knelt down by her knees, like she used to when she would play with Tansy on the floor. "It's so good to see you!"

"I was hoping you would come."

149

"I'm sorry I didn't come earlier."

"Oh, hush, dear! You were working hard, Genny told me. Now, how is our little one doing in her new family?"

Genny sat in stunned silence as Aoife and her aunt spent nearly two hours catching each other up on everyone's news. Aoife blushed as she told her that she was dating Sam Tadwell and teared up when she talked about handing Tansy over to her new parents.

"And now you're here dancing as you should be."

"Thank you for pushing me back into it." Aoife felt the ache again. "You made this happen."

"Well, I'm very proud of you, dearie."

The next few days were hard for Aoife as she tried to reconcile the fact that she loved dancing, but she wasn't happy. Not the way she wanted to be. She was a dancer and she loved embracing it again, but what was she dancing for? There was a picture of her and Tansy in her bag she would pull out when she needed inspiration. When everyone else was gone she would turn on Tansy's favorite songs and dance until she cried from exhaustion and homesickness.

"You all right?" asked Sam as they talked over the phone.

"Just really missing you and everyone."

"I miss you, too. If you had an Instagram you would know that."

Aoife hadn't thought about the fact that Sam might post things about her after she left. Peter had most likely been so busy with *Giselle* that he missed the posts as well. After their call, Aoife downloaded the Instagram app onto her phone and reactivated her account. Snapshots of memories suddenly filled her screen and Aoife had to take a deep breath.

She forced herself to not look at what she had last posted five years earlier, but searched for Sam. She followed him and spent the next hour looking through his pictures. At first she thought about going through and liking all the pictures of her that he had posted, but decided against it. Before closing the app, she found a picture of Sam from Max and Sarah's wedding. It was one of her favorites of him, and she had a copy of it printed off and hanging on the wall by her bed. She tagged him in it and settled on a caption.

"Pretty Blue Eyes"

There was a string of messages from Sam the next morning including the heart eye emojis and several texts in all caps declaring his love for several old pictures. She looked at the ones he said he liked the best; a few of her with Peter, Alex and Chloe, one of her in Paris and two from the biggest show she ever did: *La Bayadere* in St. Petersburg.

By that afternoon, she had four hundred new followers, most of them fans of Peter and Alex, or Sam, and a steady stream of likes on her old pictures. A few people even direct messaged her, asking if she would ever do ballet again. Aoife took a picture of her reflection in the full-length mirror opposite her in the studio. She posted it without a caption and put her phone away.

"I don't know what to do with an Aoife like this!" Genny said two days later. "You're all angsty and wild and, and, and you just push yourself so hard!"

"I've always pushed myself, Genny. You knew me when I was part of competitions and trying to get into companies."

"Yeah, but then you had Chloe and Peter to kind of balance you out. Now you're just like a missile and I'm terrified to get in your way."

"Well, if I can't be with the people I love the most then I might as well be dancing."

"No, Eef. Not like this. I can't work with you like this."

"Then what am I supposed to do? What do I do?" Aoife's voice broke. "Because I want this! I want this so much! But maybe it's too late."

"I think you just need another focus."

"Like what?"

"Like... I don't know. I don't know." Genny shook her head. "But think about it."

Aoife tried to see Miss Wilcox, but the elderly woman was in bed resting after having a bad cough. She wanted to call Sam and tell him she gave up, but she knew she was just being emotional. She remembered how everyone had acted the day after Christmas when they hadn't slept well and emotions were high. Maybe she just needed sleep.

There was surprise in Carl's voice when he answered the phone the next evening and heard her on the other end. She had been thinking all day and she needed to talk to someone who could answer her question. He was the only one.

"Did I love ballet when I was little?" she asked.

"Yeah."

"Why?"

"Well, I suppose at first it was because you got to be with your mom, and you loved anything that had to do with her. You were like two peas in a pod back in those days."

Aoife closed her eyes and held in her sigh. She didn't remember those days, and it wasn't fair that life had taken her mother away from her so suddenly like that. When she was little, she used to wish her mom was dead just so she could stop hoping that Rebecca would get better and being disappointed when it didn't happen.

"And when mom left?"

"I gave you a choice," said Carl thoughtfully. "I asked if it was what you loved to do, and you said you would love it forever."

"I said that?"

"Yes."

"But why? Why did I love it?"

"It was you." Aoife could hear the way Carl was shrugging as he answered. "You were good at it; it made you a better person, made you love yourself in a way you never would have. You had your little group of friends and that was all you wanted in life: ballet and Chloe."

"Life was so simple back then."

"What made you ask these questions, Aoife?"

"I'm back in New York. I'm doing some stuff with Genny's dance company, but she says I'm too off balance with it and I just don't understand what I'm supposed to do. People were telling me to not give it up, and now I'm too invested or something, and I just don't... I don't know, dad."

"Well, you're asking the right questions to find the right answers."

"You think so?" It had been a long time since she asked for his opinion.

"What's your goal in life, and does what you're doing with Genny put you closer to that?"

"I guess it does, but maybe not anymore." Aoife stood to look out of the window of her apartment. There was no view of the sea, just a row of shops on the other side of the road. "I feel like I'm floundering now."

"Okay, then find something else."

Aoife nodded.

"It's good to hear your voice, Aoife."

"Yours, too, dad." Aoife hung up and pressed the phone against the palm of her hand. Her thoughts went back to what her dad said, how she had told him that she would love ballet forever. She supposed it was true, that the love she had for the sport had never completely died even when buried with pain and bitterness. It was one of those rare moments where she wished she could know what her mother thought.

-Chapter 10-
Auditions & Boyfriends

Sarah's birthday was the end of April and Max bought Aoife's plane ticket for her to spend two weeks back in the UK with them as a present. The look on Sarah's face when she showed up at Sam's house and saw Aoife sitting in the kitchen was worth all the hours of travel and lack of sleep. They spent every moment they could together for two days, but eventually Sarah had to go back to Brighton and Aoife stayed in London to watch Peter and Alex as they worked on *Giselle*.

She found herself in the practice rooms doing the dances on her own, watching herself in the mirror. Alex caught her in there a couple times and he made her do the steps with him. She felt like she was nineteen again and about to perform for the first time in Paris, just days before Chloe told them she was pregnant. No one saw them dance, but she knew it was only a matter of time.

"I think I want to do shows again," she told Sam as they held hands on his sofa. "I want to go back to that."

"That would be amazing, Aoife." Sam's eyes were sparkling and Aoife felt like she was home when she looked into them. "Are you going to do it in New York or travel to someplace else?"

"I don't know yet. I'm finally feeling like my body is ready for it again. I just know I need a goal or I'll keep running around in circles."

"Yeah, do it." Sam kissed her cheek. "I'll be there to support you all the way."

The next day found Aoife in Brighton visiting Tansy. The little girl was nearly eight months old and Aoife could hardly get over how she was sitting up by herself and babbling over everything as if she was really talking. She thought that maybe the little girl remembered her, but it was hard to tell since Tansy had always been friendly and happy.

"I'm sure she does," said Tansy's new mother, Patricia.

"I'd like to think so," said Aoife.

Later, she stood in her apartment and stared out at the sea. She wondered what it would be like to have Tansy not remember her, or even grow to dislike her one day. It could happen, Aoife realized. There was no guarantee that just because she had raised her for five months of her life that the girl would love her forever. Her forever had barely even started.

The waves helped calm the hurricane of swirling thoughts before Aoife went to Max and Sarah's for supper. Martin was there and it was so easy to slip back into the circle of friends. They laughed until they cried and ate until they could hardly move. She mentioned to them what she had told Sam about wanting to perform again.

"Yes! Aoife, yes!" Sarah clasped her hands in front of her. "You're such a great dancer!"

"You've never even seen me dance." Aoife looked at her, amused confusion in her expression.

"Yes, we have!" said Sarah. "Martin and I found clips on the internet. We watched them all in one night."

"It's true. We were mesmerized." Martin nodded.

"How did you find them?"

"I asked Sam to ask Peter and Alex."

"Those two!" Aoife rolled her eyes.

"Speaking of them, though," said Sarah pointedly. "You should join them so you can stay close to us. Besides, they're your best friends."

"I would love to, and I know they would welcome me with open arms, but they're about to finish rehearsal for *Giselle* and they are performing that the entire month of June. It would be the end of summer before I had a chance to join in anything new and I don't want to wait that long."

"Fair enough," said Martin. "I don't want to wait that long to see you up on stage, either."

When Martin dropped Aoife back at her apartment, Aoife asked him how he felt about Tansy in her new family. The smile filling his face up to his eyes was all the answer she needed.

Aoife had been in England for a week when she was awakened by a phone call at five in the morning. She rubbed sleep from her eyes as she answered. Alex's whisper filled her ear and she sat up. He quickly explained what had happened and told her to come to London as fast as she could. Aoife could hardly think straight as she shoved things into her backpack and called a taxi. She had her fingers crossed that she hadn't forgotten anything as she rushed down the stairs when the taxi man arrived.

It was almost seven in the morning when Aoife arrived at the studio. She had spent the entire drive thinking about the fact that this could be it; this could be her chance back on the stage. Of course she was saddened that the girl originally cast to play *Giselle* in Alex and Peter's production had injured herself and needed to be on bed rest for three months, but that meant there was an opening and only a select few were going to be given a chance to fill the role. Auditions were by invite only and she had been Alex's invitation.

"Are you ready?" asked Alex. Aoife only nodded and pulled her leotard and shoes out of her backpack. He waited as she changed, greeting her with another smile when she reappeared.

"Shall we practice?"

Alex already knew which part he wanted to practice with her; the one from the second scene by the lake where Giselle and Albrecht dance until dawn. Aoife took a deep breath. There were lifts in that part of the dance that she didn't feel she had remastered yet. She cleared her mind and went with the music. They ran through the scene until they reached the lift and Aoife stumbled a bit.

"I'm sorry. I'm sorry." Aoife shook her head and walked over to reset the music.

"It's okay, I know you're nervous." Alex kept his voice steady.

They went through the steps three more times before Aoife felt comfortable with them and Alex said he had to go join Peter in the auditorium. They agreed to one more run-through of the lift without the music before stopping. The door opened as Alex lifted her above his head, her body hitting every mark and making every line. She was grinning until she looked in the mirror and saw a face that made her stomach twist violently inside of her. Alex looked too, and his entire face paled. An old, familiar voice crowded into her mind.

Vamonos! Más rápido! Aoife, shoulders back!

Then the scene changed and the same voice shouted at her again.

You are a horrible, ungrateful girl! How dare you do this to me?! You are the worst friend my daughter has ever had! I hate you!

Aoife had to remind herself to breathe as Alex set her back on her feet.

"I see you're finally back in the game, Aoife," said Therese Knight coolly. A young girl who appeared to be in her early twenties stood behind the dance instructor who was still as tall and willowy as she had been in her twenties at the peak of her ballet career. "Just in time to land the comeback role of a lifetime. How convenient."

"Mrs. Knight." Alex nodded out of forced manners. "What brings you here?"

"Same reason as Aoife; the auditions." Therese gestured towards the girl next to her.

Aoife felt her throat tighten and a wave of nausea hit her as she stood frozen. She wanted to disappear.

"Perhaps you remember seeing the name Sasha DeClan on the invite list? She's been under my instruction these last three years."

"Welcome, Sasha." It was clear by the strain on Alex's face that he had seen the name.

"Aoife shouldn't be practicing with you, one of the judges. Doesn't look professional." Therese telling them what to do wasn't new, the harsh tone and cold frown were. "Makes it hard to be unbiased."

"Thank you for your concern, but we have a team of people making these decisions. There is no room for bias."

"I hope she's ready."

Aoife looked into Therese's eyes and saw a worn-out expression there, as if she were already tired even though the day had just started. Her hair was all gray now, and the wrinkles by her eyes and mouth were more pronounced. She looked old and unhappy.

"Will you show us to the changing rooms?"

Alex didn't look back at Aoife as he left. As soon as she was alone, Aoife let all of the strength leave her body, and she slumped onto the floor. Of all the days to smash her way back into Aoife's life, it had to be that day. She crawled over to her bag and found her phone. Sam answered with a groggy voice.

"I have an audition today," said Aoife, trying to feel the original excitement she had felt when she first heard the news. "With Peter and Alex. I'm in London."

"Aoife, that's great!"

"I'm really nervous, Sam," she whispered.

"You're going to do great. Can I come be with you?"

"Yeah. Yes. Please." Aoife felt her heart slow its breakneck pace. "Do you remember when I told you about Chloe and her mom?"

"Yeah?"

"Chloe's mom is here. We didn't know she would be here."

"Oh wow, you okay?"

"Trying to be." Aoife let out a shaky laugh. "I'll feel better when you're here."

"Okay, give me time to get dressed and drive over." There was a rustling noise and Aoife could hear him climbing out of bed. "And Aoife."

"Hmmm?"

"I'm so proud of you."

Aoife had to hangup before she told Sam she loved him. She wasn't afraid of being in love, not with Sam, but she didn't want to say it over the phone when she couldn't see his face light up at the words.

Sam arrived minutes before Aoife was supposed to be on stage. He hugged her tightly and let her cry for a moment before helping her wipe away her tears. He whispered that he knew she was going to smash it.

"It's going to be weird auditioning for Peter and Alex instead of with them," said Aoife, leaning against Sam.

"They know what you're capable of more than anyone, I think. That's going to make it better."

"I suppose you're right." Aoife pressed a quick kiss to his cheek, not telling him how Therese had hinted at the auditions being judged unfairly. She knew the part wouldn't just be handed to her, and she could only trust that the others who were involved knew that as well.

There were six girls altogether. Aoife could tell she was the oldest one and hoped that would be to her advantage. All of them were asked to step out on stage. They would dance together first, coming forward one by one to do a solo from the first scene where Giselle dances in the village. The other girls were good, but there were two in particular whose nerves were showing and they shook as they performed. They were two who had auditioned for the role initially.

A murmur of approval came from the judges as Sasha began her solo. She was impeccable in technique and expression. Aoife focused on her breathing as the girl danced. She could see Peter and Alex along with five others in a row, taking notes and nodding their heads. When it was her turn to dance she looked everywhere except where she knew Therese was sitting. She kept her adrenaline channeled, letting it push her body as she danced. Then, it was over and they all stepped off the stage.

Peter and a man Aoife recognized as a manager of the company came to talk to them. They told them that three of the youngest girls were finished and Aoife, Sasha and the girl named Caroline had half an hour before they would be called on again. It felt weird to have Peter talk so formally about her when she knew how much he wanted her to be with him on stage again. He had to remain professional, though, or Aoife's audition would mean nothing.

Thankfully Sasha and Aoife were given separate rooms to wait in. Sam found Aoife and helped her try to relax by massaging her shoulders. He asked if she wanted to text Sarah or Martin and let them know she was auditioning, but she said no.

"Better to wait and let them know when it's all finished. I think I'll burst if I have someone asking me whether or not I've made it in."

"Okay." Sam continued to knead his fingers into her shoulders, feeling the tension leave little by little. "How do you feel?"

"Today should be exciting. Whether I get in or not, this should be something I feel good about, but I can't. I can't because Therese is here and she hates me."

"Did she know you were going to audition?"

"I don't know what she knew." Aoife rubbed her hands over her face and sighed. "Sasha has a connection here somehow because she was invited to audition, but I don't know why Therese came with her. I don't know what's going to happen."

"Just relax." Sam stopped massaging and wrapped his arms around her from behind. "I'm so proud of you."

"Thanks for being here for me," whispered Aoife, closing her eyes and focusing on the sound of Sam breathing.

"Thanks for letting me be here."

Aoife didn't see Therese again until she was called back to the stage. The woman was standing next to Sasha, a protective hand on her shoulder. Aoife kept her eyes straight ahead, wishing that Peter and Alex weren't busy whispering with the other judges so she could calm herself with the familiarity of their faces.

"Nice to see you're not as horrible as I thought you would be after leaving ballet for so long." The icy tone in Therese's words was still there.

"You taught me how to dance, this should be a proud moment for you." Aoife didn't turn to look at the woman.

"I'll be proud when someone who has worked hard and didn't quit because she 'lost herself' is placed in this role."

There were so many things Aoife wanted to say. No, not say, scream. She wanted to scream. Scream at Therese for being the reason Aoife even had to stop dancing. She swallowed hard and turned to face straight ahead.

"Where's the other girl?" She heard Sasha ask. Aoife looked and noticed for the first time that there were only two of them up there.

"Who knows." Therese didn't seem concerned.

"Oh." Sasha nodded and went back to flexing her feet in her shoes.

It was quiet backstage and Aoife was thankful that Therese seemed content to keep her words to herself. Aoife closed her eyes and pretended that she was alone. There was a loud noise from somewhere in the building and Aoife looked around. Sasha smiled at her when their eyes met.

"You're a really great dancer," she said.

"Focus, Sasha," snapped Therese. "Shoulders back. Remember, soft hands."

For a second, Aoife could see herself standing at the edge of a stage before a big competition, Therese by her side whispering last-minute reminders. She looked at Sasha's hands and half expected Therese to be holding them steady, not letting go until the very last second. It was those hands that had given Aoife the courage she needed to dance across stage after stage. When Aoife looked up again, Therese was staring at her. In a moment, there was a flash of something between them, as if they were both remembering the love that used to be there. Then it was gone and all that was to be seen on the woman's face was disappointment and disapproval.

Aoife turned and stared straight ahead, hoping that no one else could hear the way her heart was beating heavily. A moment later, the girls were called onto the stage.

"Alex will be accompanying the girls in one final dance before a decision can be reached," said Peter into a microphone.

"You allow one of the judges to dance with the girls who are auditioning?" asked Therese with a show of surprise.

"Alex Minsky plays the role of Albrecht. It's important to see how the girls dance with him."

With a nod of acquiescence, Therese left the stage. Aoife was up first and she was thankful when she saw Alex walking across the stage to join her. He kept his face neutral and eyes serious, leaving no room for anyone to say he was treating her differently than a stranger. Aoife matched his expression, only squeezing his fingers for a moment when the lights dimmed. He nodded, and then the music swelled and...

Aoife remembered the last time she had seen her mother on the stage. It was *Sleeping Beauty* and she wore the prettiest costume Aoife had ever seen in her life. Aoife had sat in the big seat, Peter on one side and Peter's mom on the other. Rebecca's stage presence had been second to none that evening, leaving the audience gasping at the way she spun and leapt, all the while wrapping the character she was playing around herself. For two hours Aoife forgot that the princess on the stage was her mother and watched in open-mouthed wonder as Aurora fell for the trick of the mean, old fairy and stumbled into a deep sleep.

"Your mom is so pretty," whispered Peter, his own eyes wide as he watched the prince fight against the enchantment.

"My mom?" Aoife was startled.

"The princess!"

"Oh. Yeah. She's always pretty."

By the time the memory was finished, so was Aoife's dance. She knew she had done the steps correctly, she had done the lift and played the part of Giselle the way she once had years before, but she remembered nothing except the face of her mother smiling at her as she bowed at the end of the performance. Aoife's whole body was shaking as she walked offstage with Alex.

As soon as they were out of sight, Alex hugged Aoife as tightly as he could.

"You were amazing. Amazing, Aoife. You did so good."

Aoife said nothing, fighting back tears as she hugged her friend. She wanted this. She had worked hard to get back to where she used to be and now she was here, right on the edge of it all over again. This was what she wanted.

"Go back out there." Aoife wiped her eyes after releasing Alex from their hug. "Show Sasha what it feels like to dance with the best dancer in the world."

"Good luck, Aoife." Alex pecked a quick kiss against Aoife's cheek before trotting back out on stage.

Instead of leaving to hide in the back until Sasha was done dancing, Aoife stayed to watch. She had done her best and it was all she could do. The music started once more and Aoife was impressed with her skill and movement. If it had been under different circumstances, Aoife thought that maybe she wouldn't be upset to lose a role to someone as talented as Sasha.

"Alex has always been a strong dancer," said Therese, coming up beside Aoife and crossing her arms over her chest. "One of my best students."

Aoife simply nodded. She didn't want her there ruining this moment for her.

"You know what I realized has always been your problem when it comes to ballet?" asked Therese. She continued without looking to Aoife for a signal that the girl did or did not want to know. "You make it too personal. You always have. Do you see how Sasha leaves room for space between her and the character she's playing? She doesn't make it personal. You, on the other hand, you have always made everything so..."

"Personal?" Aoife cut the woman off with a bitter tone. She turned to look Therese in the eye, angry tears burning there. "Well, maybe that has something to do with the fact that ballet was handed down to me from my mother? Or maybe that my ballet instructor became like a second mom to me when my mom became sick? Or maybe it's because my longest lasting friendships come from this? Yes, it's personal. Auditioning for Alex and Peter is personal. Not because I expect them to hand me the role, but because they have stood by me and believed that there would be a day when I would come back. Do you know how I treated them after you took Chloe from us? Do you know how hard it was for me to tell them I was walking away from ballet forever? But I couldn't stay. Not after being hurt by someone who I thought was going to love me forever and having two of the most important people in my life taken away from me."

Therese flinched, but didn't look away.

"They waited for me to be ready again and here I am, *absolutely* ready to be on stage. I'm ready! Yet all I can remember is the way my mom performed *Sleeping Beauty*." Aoife's voice broke. "It's all personal, Therese."

"Well," Therese cleared her throat and sniffed before turning to face the stage again. "If your mother were still alive, you could tell her you were making your comeback in her honor."

"What?" Aoife's mouth was instantly dry. "Wh-what? What do you mean?"

"She's gone, Aoife." Therese looked annoyed. "She died. Two years ago."

"How do you know?" Aoife was going to be sick.

"They notified me. Honestly, how else would I know?" Therese tried to sound angry, but she was watching Aoife's face and her expression changed, growing almost soft. "Aoife, I didn't kn-..."

"I hate you!" Aoife hissed through her teeth before turning on her heels and running down the hallway. She found her backpack in the room where she had been practicing with Alex earlier that morning. She didn't change out of her leotard, but simply yanked off her pointe shoes and shoved her feet into her flats. Her jacket was barely on her shoulders as she ran out of the building and onto the busy London street. All she wanted was the sea.

The building was a block from the Thames, and even though it was not the sea, it was the closest thing she had. Aoife ran down the street, dodging people and wiping tears from her eyes. Finally, she found herself standing by the railing of the bridge, looking over the side at the water.

The thing about rivers was that they kept moving, continually going in one direction, never stopping, never turning around. With the sea or the ocean, the waves come back again and again and again. The river was more like real life, though, with the way it kept moving, not really giving you a second chance. Once something had been done, it was done, and you may or may not ever have a chance to fix it. She watched the water move, her throat aching tightly.

"Don't worry, wee one. I've got you. I always got you."

"Mam." Aoife rubbed her fists into her eyes and struggled to stop the tears.

Her phone buzzed in her pocket and Aoife answered without looking to see who it was.

"Aoife, where are you? Did Therese say something to you?" Peter sounded frantic. "What happened?"

"They told her when my mom died, but not me. Not Carl." Aoife's words hurt pushing past the lump in her throat. "She died two years ago, and I didn't even know."

"Eef." Peter sounded close to tears. "I'm so sorry."

"I just want my mom." Aoife closed her eyes and let the tears fall.

"Tell me where you are. I'll come get you."

"What about the auditions?"

"There is a twenty-minute break while everyone deliberates."

"Don't you need to discuss who you want to be put in the role?"

"Aoife," Peter laughed. "I already know who I want in the role."

"Therese said..."

"I don't care what she said, okay, Aoife? I watched you dance today. You're the perfect Giselle. Just tell me where you are. I won't leave your side for the rest of the day."

"I'm at the bridge." Aoife looked back at the water.

"I'll be right there."

Aoife tried to picture her mother dancing on the stage, but all of her memories were suddenly blurry and filled with empty spots. A hand on her arm distracted her from her broken attempts to piece her mother back together in her mind. Peter pulled her into a hug and kissed the side of her head. He didn't care that people were watching them, noticing him, wondering who she was.

"I'm sorry, Eef. I'm so, so sorry."

"Part of me always thought she'd come back," Aoife whispered into his shoulder.

"I know. Part of me always hoped that, too."

True to his word, Peter didn't move his arm from Aoife's shoulders the whole walk back to the studio, onto the stage and for the last five minutes of deliberation. He shot an angry glance at Mrs. Knight and called to the judges from the stage. None of them seemed to care that Peter was with Aoife, that he was clearly comforting her and he was putting personal feelings above professional ones. Therese looked like she wanted to say something, but she kept her mouth shut, deep lines forming by her mouth. Her eyes no longer seemed quite so hard and angry.

Aoife focused her gaze outward, away from the pair to her right. From his seat in the auditorium, Sam caught her eye and gave her an inquiring look. With the tiniest shake of her head, Aoife looked away. She would tell him once everything was finished. It was too hard to put into words at that moment.

Minutes ticked by until suddenly the announcement was made that Aoife Stewart was to fill the role of Giselle. Aoife could hear the cheers of Alex and Sam, could hear the way Therese said her name, could hear the way her heart was pounding in her chest.

"Let's go, Eef." Peter left the stage with Aoife, his arm still around her.

"Aoife?" Sam ran over to her.

"Thanks for being here, Sam," whispered Aoife, hugging him tightly. "I just... I found out my mom... my mom is..."

"What?" Sam looked from Peter to Aoife and back.

"I need to go. I-I'll be back." Aoife squeezed his hand before leaving with Peter. Behind them, she heard Sam ask Alex what had happened and Alex saying he didn't know.

The drive to Brighton was quiet as Peter took them straight to the beach. He didn't say a word as she cried quietly, letting the news wash over her again and again like the waves. She stared out at the sea, wishing she could dive into the depths and somehow find her mother, or another life where her mother never left her, or where her mother came back. But she couldn't. Peter sat beside her, leaning back on his elbows, just being with her. She had stared at the rocks and the waves for close to an hour when she called Sam to explain.

"Hi," said Aoife.

"Hi, Aoife. All right?" Sam's voice crackled through the phone.

"I, um..." Tears filled her eyes and Aoife shook her head no, wishing she still didn't have to say it out loud. "Therese told me my mom died. Two years ago."

"Oh, Aoife."

"Peter knew my mom and I just wanted a little time thinking about her with someone who knew her."

"Yeah, okay." It was hard to read the tone in Sam's voice.

"Are you busy tonight?"

"Conor was going to have some friends around, I think."

"Well, I want to be with you."

"With me?"

"Mmhmm." Aoife squinted against the sun and tasted the salt on the air. "Because I just auditioned for a role in this ballet, and I, uh, I got the part."

"Did you really now?" There was the tiniest hint of a playful edge to his words. "Well, I'm not going to be in London tonight."

"Oh." Disappointment shot through Aoife's heart.

"Yeah, I'm going to be down in Brighton because, funny story, my girlfriend just auditioned for a role in a ballet and she got the part, so I want to celebrate her."

Aoife felt tears sting her eyes as a rush of emotions filled her. He called her his girlfriend.

"H-how did you know she was in Brighton?" she asked.

"She has this thing about staring at the sea. I know it's her favorite place to go."

"I think she's there right now."

"I think so, too. I might be looking at her."

Aoife set her phone down and swiveled her head to see if anyone was there. She spotted a lone figure up by the road who was walking towards her. Peter turned to see what Aoife was looking at and smiled when he saw Sam.

"I told him where we were going," Peter said quietly. "Wanted him to know I wasn't trying to steal you from him."

"You're really the best friend I could ask for." Aoife gave Peter's neck a hug. "I can never repay you for all of the ways you've loved me as a friend."

"Yes, you can. You can be in my ballet and dance with me on stage." Peter winked.

"Deal." Aoife grinned at him before jumping to her feet and running across the rocks to reach Sam.

The celebration that night at Max and Sarah's house was full of rejoicing over Aoife's new role. Peter stayed and allowed them to pester him with questions about dance and what Aoife had been like when she was younger. Beside him, Aoife sat and smiled warmly at everyone, her hand tucked safely into Sam's. Sam's other hand traced shapes on her back. Max laughed the loudest, while Martin had tears running down his face when Peter told the story of Aoife falling on Alex's head during a rehearsal when they were sixteen. Sarah begged Aoife to get copies of her old dances and let her watch them.

"I have to take the spot of your number one fan before Peter and Alex make you a famous superstar," she said.

Aoife smiled and shook her head, unsure of how to respond to a comment like that. It wasn't that she didn't want to be famous, it was just such an abstract thought. Technically Sam was famous, yet he was sweet and funny and kind. Peter and Alex were the same goofy guys that had tortured her for hours with spitwads as they rode the train across Austria while Chloe threw up in the toilets. Even her mom had been famous, but she was home almost every night, cooking a meal for her husband and daughter, humming Irish folk tunes and saying how much she hated washing dishes.

"I'll have to go back to New York at the end of the week to pack up and tell Genny I'm leaving," Aoife said to Peter before he left for London after supper.

"Okay. I'll talk to Leanne about a good place you can stay in London."

"Thanks."

"I'm sorry you had to hear about your mom today from Therese. That news should have come from someone who loved you."

"I know she loved my mom." Aoife's mouth twitched as she tried to keep herself from crying again. "I know they were best friends."

"Your mom was an amazing dancer, and she loved you with her whole heart." Peter tapped one finger against her forehead, smiling as she blinked in reflex.

"I know." Aoife gave him a small smile.

"I'll email you all you need to know once I've arrived back home."

"Bye, Peter."

Sam was waiting for Aoife as soon as Peter pulled away. He slipped an arm around her waist and surprised her with a quick kiss. Her cheeks grew warm and she tried to hide her smile.

"You know, if it was anyone else, I'd be worried, but with Peter I'm not worried at all."

"Hmm." Aoife thought about the fact that dating Peter would be like dating her brother. "What about Alex? Worried about him?"

"Absolutely! Do you not know how much chemistry you two share when you're dancing? Whew!" Sam pretended to be fanning his face.

"Stop!" Aoife laughed. "Well, get used to it, because I expect you to be there opening night."

"Wouldn't miss it for the world!" Sam tightened his hold on her and went in for a sloppy kiss to the cheek that made Aoife shriek and try to pull away. "Sh! The neighbors will hear!"

"Then stop being gross."

"Speaking of being gross, are you still using your return ticket back to The States?"

Aoife eyed him curiously.

"What does that have to do with being gross?" she asked.

"Nothing, unless you get sick on the plane."

"Right. To answer your question, I am using my ticket. I have to go home and pack some things to move back over here.

"Do you want company?" asked Sam casually.

"Why, you offering?"

"Yes. I am. I've been told I am an excellent traveling companion."

"Really?"

"Yes, I really have been told..."

"No! You really are offering to come with me?"

"Yeah, course I am. Why wouldn't I want to go to New York to help my girlfriend pack up and move to where I live? Besides, I want to see where Baby Aoife grew up."

Aoife threw her arms around his neck and hugged him tightly.

That night as Aoife stared at the sea through her window, she felt the bittersweet mixed together so closely there was no way to separate them. She would always remember that day as the day she landed her first role for the stage since leaving ballet, and she would always remember it as the day she found out her mother had died. She would remember staring out at the Thames wishing that life wouldn't move forward, but would give her another chance, like the waves. She would remember Therese's cutting words and hurtful eyes, but she would also remember sitting on the beach with Peter and being around the supper table with her friends in Brighton.

Exhaustion caught up to her and she finally crawled into bed and closed her eyes. As she did she made a mental note to tell Carl about her mom.

The weather in New York was beautiful and Sam and Aoife took their first day there to enjoy the city. They met up with Genny at the studio the next day to say goodbye. Aoife smiled as Genny bordered on flirting with the amount of attention she was giving Sam. He winked at Aoife when Genny turned away and Aoife grinned. She loved the way her friends adored him.

"Oh, Eef," she called as Aoife turned, ready to leave. "I need to tell you something."

Aoife stopped and stared at her friend. Genny shifted uncomfortably.

"What did you do?"

"Please don't get mad," said Genny. "Please..."

"Genny! What did you do?" Aoife couldn't imagine what the girl had done that made her so nervous. She had never seen Genny nervous apart from when she was about to perform on stage.

"Mrs. Knight was here..."

"Genny, no..." Aoife wanted to walk out of the room but Sam was holding her hand and he was standing still.

"Please, Aoife! I didn't want to do it!"

"What did you do?"

"She asked for your dad's phone number."

"You don't have Carl's number."

"Well..." Genny looked down. "It's in your file. Next of kin."

"You gave it to her?!" Aoife yanked her hand out of Sam's as she stomped across the floor towards the girl who was practically cowering against the mirror. "How could you? You know what she did to me! What she did to all of us!"

"She's a terrifying woman!" Genny defended herself. "If you had seen her recently, you would know!"

"I have seen her recently." All of the fight left Aoife's words and she covered her face with her hands as she exhaled deeply. "I'm sorry, Genny. Therese always had a way of getting what she wanted."

"She also left something for you. I put it in your locker."

Aoife walked over to her locker and opened it. There was a VHS inside. It was titled "*R, M & T 1993.*" Aoife picked it up and frowned. She didn't know what it meant.

"What does 'R, M & T' mean?" asked Sam quietly.

"I don't know. I'm assuming it means Rebecca, Mariya and Therese. Mariya is Peter's mom."

"Did they dance together?"

Aoife nodded.

"Thanks, Genny," she said. "Thanks for being a good friend to me, setting me up here when I came back. I'll see you when I visit."

"Of course." Genny gave her a genuine smile. "That's what friends are for."

"And thank you for sending me to Brighton in the first place." Aoife grabbed Sam's hand. "I'll never be able to tell you just how good it was for me."

"I'm happy for you, Eef."

They hadn't planned on visiting Carl, but Aoife knew if Therese asked for his number, she had probably called him and he knew about her mom. Sam said he was excited to finally meet her father, but he fidgeted the whole drive there. For a while, Aoife told Sam stories from when she was young, but she grew quiet as they approached the little farmhouse Carl had moved into when he married his second wife.

Carl wasn't expecting to see Aoife and Sam at the door when he answered it, but a pleased grin stretched slowly across his face as he realized who it was. He greeted Sam first, sticking out his hand and clasping it tightly.

"Well, she really does have a boyfriend." He gave Sam a once-over, but the smile never left his face. "Aoife's never brought a boy home before."

Aoife didn't want to ruin the moment by pointing out that this wasn't her home. She waited until her father looked over at her before holding up the VHS tape and handing it to him.

167

"I was told Therese tried to find a way to contact you."

Carl's smile dimmed.

"I didn't know she would try, or I would have warned you."

"She never did anything to me, Aoife, and I didn't even know she had done anything to you until she was at my kitchen table drinking a cup of coffee." Carl's eyes were sad. "Why didn't you tell me?"

"I was stubborn, I guess. Didn't know how to handle it myself, so I thought burying it would make it better." Aoife shifted her weight from one foot to the other.

"Why don't you come inside and tell me what happened." The door was pushed open until the couple could walk past him and into the house.

"Where are the boys?" asked Aoife, glancing at the pictures on the wall. Some were of her and her dad from before he married Deb.

"With their mom." Carl scratched at the back of his neck. "We're, uh, separated."

"Oh." Aoife looked to her father with concern in her eyes.

"Don't worry about it. We'll work it out. We always do," said Carl, waving off her unspoken apologies. "Now, tell me why Therese Knight sat at my kitchen table and apologized for how she treated you."

"Did she tell you about mom?" asked Aoife, pulling a chair away from the table to sit down. Sam sat next to her.

"Yeah." Carl let out a long sigh. "I wasn't expecting that either."

"I can't believe she kept Therese in her life after cutting us out."

"Don't go drawing conclusions, Eef." Carl shook his head at her. "You know your mother was sick, not that she didn't love you."

"I know, but... why not Mariya? They were best friends, too."

"Your mother always had her reasons for things; whether they were logical or no, she had her reasons."

"Did Therese say anything else about mom? I... I didn't give her a chance to talk to me again after, you know, she told me."

"She told me you said you hated her." Carl had a smile playing on his lips.

"I did. I meant it, too. Might still mean it." Aoife shrugged. "She told me she hated me first."

"And if I had known that I might have slammed the door in her face instead of giving her a cup of coffee," said Carl as he put two cups of the brew in front of Sam and Aoife. He supplied the milk and sugar as he continued to talk. "But, if I had done that, I would have missed out on the information she had regarding some of your mother's belongings. They are with her sister in Dublin. I don't know what it all is, Eef, but because you're her daughter, you're allowed to go look through it and see if you want anything."

"I'd like the address, please," said Aoife quietly.

"What's this VHS about?" Carl squinted at the label, reading it under his breath.

"Therese left it for me at the studio. Thought you might want to watch it with me." Aoife felt awkward and shy saying the words out loud.

Carl's face looked happier than it had when he opened the door and saw her standing there. He nodded and gestured towards the small living room where the television was. Aoife grabbed Sam's hand and he gave her a small smile as they followed their host. Carl muttered and poked some buttons for a few minutes before he was able to play the VHS. The giant screen TV didn't fit with the small farmhouse, but it suited Carl, or, at least the Carl that loved baseball games and football games and the occasional talk show.

"Sam is a professional soccer player, dad," said Aoife as her father settled into the chair next to the white, overstuffed couch.

"Is he really?" Carl grinned again. "I'll have to watch a game or two."

"You're always welcome, sir." Sam nodded politely.

"Sir? Please, call me Carl. Aoife does it." Carl winked at his daughter.

Aoife teared up when she realized the recording was of her mother in *Giselle*. Mariya had played the lead role, but she found her mother's sweet smile in the second act. There was a nostalgic happiness in Carl's eyes as he watched, glancing over at his daughter from time to time. They shared knowing glances more than once after Rebecca danced.

"I auditioned for Peter and Alex," Aoife said in a low voice to her father.

"You did? Great, great, Aoife. Did you get the part?"

"Yeah. I'm Giselle."

"Your favorite role." Carl turned to smile at his daughter. "Let me know when you'll be doing shows. I'll try to take time off. Come see you."

There had never been a time that Carl didn't support his daughter in her dancing. Even when he forgot birthdays, or to buy groceries, or school functions, he would do everything he could to make sure she succeeded in ballet. Aoife used to complain that he didn't care about her education or well-being, saying he worked too much and made life too complicated. She couldn't see it then, but she could see now just how hard he had worked to make sure that she had that one thing available to her for the rest of her life.

"Is that your mum?" asked Sam, pointing at the right side of the screen.

"Yeah." Aoife squeezed his hand.

"You look just like her. She's beautiful."

"Thank you," she said, leaning against him. "I'm glad you get to see this."

They ended up eating a frozen dinner with Carl before driving back to the city. Aoife hugged her dad before she left. He whispered that he was proud of her and that he was sorry she had to hear about her mom from Therese.

"Here's the address for her family in Dublin. Let me know if you need anything else."

"Thanks, dad."

"It was great to meet you, Carl." Sam shook Carl's hand again. "Any time you want to come see a game, let me know. I'll make sure you get good seats."

"Yeah, thanks, Sam." Carl grinned again. "Can't believe Aoife actually brought you to meet me."

Aoife waved as they climbed into the car and drove away. She exhaled deeply, letting her shoulders relax as she drove down the road.

"Have you really never brought a boyfriend home before?" asked Sam, a bit of a smile on his face in the passenger side of the car.

"I never really had a boyfriend." Aoife pursed her lips. "I mean, I did, but never anything serious. There was one guy, in Italy, but then Chloe had Roe and I didn't have time for him anymore so he dumped me."

"What an idiot."

"Whatever!" Aoife's face went red. "It was for the best. He only liked me because I was a dancer, so he would have dumped me eventually."

"Is that when the bikini picture is from?"

"What?" Aoife looked over at Sam for a second. "Bikini picture?"

"Yeah, on your Instagram. It has over one thousand likes now," said Sam.

"I have a bikini picture?"

"You haven't seen it in your notifications?"

"I haven't paid attention to what pictures are being liked. Are you sure I was wearing a bikini?"

"Yes, Aoife. I would not forget a picture like that."

"Pull it up! Show me right now! I don't remember this picture!"

Sam chuckled as he pulled his phone from his pocket, tapping out his password.

"It has over one thousand likes?" asked Aoife as she waited.

"Yeah. People think you're super fit, which you are, but like, this picture is... wow."

"I do not remember ever posting a picture of me in a bikini."

"Ah, here it is." Sam tilted the screen so Aoife could see. He grimaced when Aoife swerved, reaching out to steady the wheel. "Do you remember it now?"

"I'm going to kill Alex," Aoife muttered. "He said he deleted it. I should never have believed him."

"This picture is from years ago! You never realized he didn't delete it?"

"I didn't do much on Instagram back then. The boys would post pictures on my account all the time so I never paid attention. I saw the bikini one and told him to delete it, but I never checked and he and Peter probably posted a ton of pictures after that to bury it way down in my feed."

"I mean... you look great."

"And it has over one thousand likes?"

"And three hundred comments."

"I'm going to kill him."

"So... is that what you looked like when you were dating the jerk?"

"Yes, that is what I looked like while I was dating the jerk." Aoife gave a little laugh. "Are there any other pictures of me in bikinis that I should know about?"

"No, but your other popular picture from before is of you, Peter, Chloe and Alex with Pringles in your mouth to make duck faces."

"I remember that one." Aoife smiled. "I love that picture."

"I enjoyed looking through all these after you reactivated your account. I know you came to the UK with the idea of having a fresh start, but your past is still part of you and I liked seeing the things that were important to you back then."

"Or important to Alex and Peter."

"Well, they have good taste."

"Enjoy it while you can, I'm deleting it as soon as I get home."

"But it's a fan favorite!"

Aoife shot him a glance, and Sam smiled sheepishly.

"You're right, it should go."

"I'd rather be remembered for other things than what I looked like in a bikini when I was eighteen." Aoife turned thoughtful. "I've been thinking about my mom, you know, and how she's gone now. She's really been gone for so long, due to the sickness, but people remembered her for her dancing. Always told me how passionate of a dancer she had been. Said she could cheer up the grumpiest person in the world with her Irish tunes and her laugh... Peter's mom had this one story she loved to tell me. She would tell me whenever I spent the night at their house and I missed my mom. It was from before they had kids, and she was so tired one night after performing for five days straight. My mom saw her being all grumpy and moody, so she started whistling 'Irish Eyes Are Smiling' right behind her. That was my mom's favorite happy song. Next thing Mariya knew, my mom had grabbed her by the hand and was dancing around the dressing room with her and she wasn't tired anymore."

"She sounds great."

"She was great," said Aoife with a sad smile. "That's why her sickness was so unexpected, so drastic. One day she was cheering everyone up, the next day she couldn't hardly stand being near her family and her friends."

"You were little when it happened, yeah?"

"Yeah. I was about six when we realized what it was. Before that we just thought it was a mood thing." Aoife's brow furrowed as she remembered. "My dad was so worried my mom would go into one of her fits while he was at work that he stopped going. Mariya wasn't working then, so she would come over to help as much as she could. Peter and I would play outside for hours to keep me out of the way. Eventually my dad lost his job and my mom's fits were pretty much daily. No one could figure out what triggered them."

"That's a lot to process at six years old."

"It's a lot to process at any age," Aoife countered, her hands tightening on the steering wheel. "One time my dad left for the grocery store before Mariya and Peter arrived and my mom went into a fit. I thought I could help her stop if she just saw me and remembered that she loved me. I tried to hold her hand and she started screaming at me. She grabbed me and shook me, telling me I wasn't a good girl, that I wasn't beautiful or special."

"Aoife, you don't have to talk about this." Sam watched Aoife wipe a tear from her cheek.

"She stopped screaming, though. I-I don't know how the switch flipped, but I saw it in her eyes when she came back to herself. She hugged me so tight and told me over and over she was sorry and she never wanted to hurt me, but there was something inside of her making her sick." Aoife's voice broke. "She said she loved me and she was proud of me. I thought my idea to help her had worked, but then, just like that, the switch went back and her eyes went dead. She couldn't even look at me. That was the last time I spoke to her when she was fully herself."

"Wow." Sam put his hand on Aoife's shoulder and squeezed it lightly. "I'm sorry."

"I wish I would have said something, you know?" Aoife's lips still trembled with emotion. "Wish I would have told her I loved her, or that I knew she loved me or, or, or something. But I didn't say anything because I was too scared, and then I never had another chance."

Sam said nothing, just kept his hand on Aoife's shoulder. The road was quiet and empty, the night darkening around them as they drove. Aoife took a shaky breath and put her left hand over Sam's, pressing it against her shoulder to comfort herself.

"I wish I could have one more chance to let her know I understood that she didn't choose to leave me," whispered the girl.

"I think she knew."

"People always told me that, but I just, I never saw her, the real her, ever again. I don't know if anything I said really meant anything to her."

"When was the last time you saw her?"

"I was nine. Therese took me. I had made her a birthday card and was going to be in *Cinderella* in a big show and I wanted to tell her. My dad said he wouldn't take me because he knew I would just be hurt and upset, but Therese agreed to take me."

"What happened?"

"Nothing really." Aoife's smile was so sad. "I gave her the card and told her all about the show, and when I was done she stood up and walked away without saying a single thing. They said she was just tired and did that to everyone, but it didn't change how horrible it felt. Peter and Chloe used to tell me that the more she loved something, the more she acted like she hated it, so the fact that she acted like she hated Carl and I the most meant that she loved us the most."

"They were good friends to you."

"Are. They are good friends."

With a nod and a smile, Sam leaned over and kissed the hand that was holding onto his.

"I hope you're be able to meet Chloe and Roe someday."

"Me, too. The people in your life are truly wonderful, Aoife."

Aoife was emotionally spent by the time they reached the city, but there were parts of her heart that felt like they could breathe for the first time in twenty years. She set up the picture of her mom she used to keep by her bed when she was growing up and stared at it until she couldn't keep her eyes open. The next day she put it in her suitcase to take back to London with her. She would hang it up in her apartment in Brighton across from her window so that it was facing the sea. She knew that was where her mom would be happiest: staring at the sea.

-Chapter 11-

Best Friends Forever

Opening night of *Giselle* was filled with excitement. Peter and Alex's management team did a wonderful job talking up Aoife's return to the stage, creating buzz around her name. They were dedicating the performance to the late Rebecca Stewart and Aoife cried when they told her.

Aoife's dressing room was filled with flowers and cards from her friends both near and far. She couldn't stop grinning and she was already warmed up and in her costume, hair done and makeup painted on her face. Leanne had been in just a few minutes earlier, squealing over the fact that she was going to be on stage with her in less than an hour.

There was a knock on the door before Peter's head appeared. Aoife smiled at him. They were finally getting their wish to dance together again. Peter walked in after glancing over his shoulder.

"So proud of you, Eef," Peter said in a low voice. "I'm glad it's not a lie when I say I finally have my best friend back."

"I couldn't have made it through without you." Aoife stood to hug him. "Not when my mom left, not when Chloe left, not now..."

"There's someone here to see you." Peter cleared his throat and stepped back from the hug, his eyes wet.

"Hey, Aoife," Carl's familiar voice accompanied him as he walked in. "Just wanted to say good luck."

"Thanks, Carl," Aoife was pleased when he smiled at her. "I'm glad you could make it."

"I have something for you." Carl stuck his hand down into his pocket. "I was going through boxes after, you know, we found out that Rebecca was... well, anyway, I found something you might want. Waited to give it to you in person. If you don't want it, I'll take it back and put it in the box of things I'm keeping in the attic."

"What is it?" asked Aoife breathlessly.

"I bought this for her when we first started dating." There was a small, shiny object in his hand when he opened his fist. "She stopped wearing it when we got engaged, but she kept it and wore it from time to time."

"I remember this ring." Aoife's eyes were shining with tears. She took the ring and slipped it over her middle finger on her left hand. It was a simple

174

silver band with a Celtic knot inside a teardrop shape. "She wore it when we went on vacation to the sea."

"I want you to have it."

"Thanks." Aoife hugged her father for the second time in the same year, something that hadn't happened since she was young. "This means a lot to me."

"Well, I, uh, I know you'll do great tonight."

"I'm glad you're here."

Carl left the room and Aoife smiled at the ring on her hand before sliding it off. She looked up at Peter and saw him frowning thoughtfully.

"What's wrong?"

"I'm just sad your mom isn't here to see you."

"Your mom is here, and that's enough for me."

"I'm glad." Peter forced the troubled look from his face. "Excited?"

"Yeah. Are you? I bet this feels a bit old hat for you since you haven't had a five-year hiatus."

"Are you kidding me? I haven't been this excited since we met Professor DiLanardio!"

"Yeah," said Aoife quietly, smiling even though in her mind she was remembering how Chloe had been with them then. She would think about Chloe later; right then she had a show to do.

And she had a show to do the next night, and the next night, and the next night for a whole month. Her days off were filled with trips to Brighton to see Tansy and stare at the sea. She would sit in *Pop's Shop* and listen to Sarah read from her mystery novels and teach Martin dance moves until his long limbs were tangled together and they couldn't stop laughing.

The ring stayed on her hand unless she was on stage, but it was back on her finger the second she was in her dressing room again. Sam posted pictures of her, finding charming and sweet captions for each, gushing about how proud he was of her. Aoife was able to return the favor once his games started up again and she found herself next to Sarah and Max in the VIP box, cheering loudly.

"It still blows my mind that my pictures can get hundreds and hundreds of likes," said Aoife to Alex one day as they relaxed in Alex's dressing room before a show.

"What did you post this time?" asked Alex lazily as he stretched his legs.

"Do you remember that one time we went on a weekend trip to Rome? There were fireworks for some reason, and we found that beautiful fountain."

"Oh, yeah!"

"We had a random girl take a picture of us, but I could never post it before because it showed Chloe's belly."

"I remember that!" Alex reached for his phone without moving from his position on the floor. He pulled up Instagram to like the picture. He was quiet for a moment, thumbing through photos. "Aoife, do you ever read your comments?"

"Sometimes, why?" Aoife looked over at her friend and saw a pinched look on his face. "Alex, what?"

"I know you want me to tell you, but this might be something that should wait until after the show," he said, slowly and carefully.

"Is it bad, Alex?" Aoife sat up, holding her phone in her hands.

"No. Not bad. It can wait, unless you really want to know now."

"Wait." Aoife put her phone down. "I'll wait."

"Okay." Alex gave her a smile. "You ready for tonight?"

Aoife nodded and played with the ring on her finger. It was almost time to take it off. As she performed, she was able to forget what Alex said in his dressing room. They had been going four nights a week for three weeks now. The way time was flying by made Aoife's head spin, but she was happier than she had been in a long time. Even though he hadn't been able to see the show that night, Sam picked Aoife up from the theatre to drive her home. She was telling him how the show had gone when her phone buzzed in her hand.

"Oh, Alex is calling. I wonder what he needs." Aoife put the phone to her ear.

"It was Chloe," said Alex without saying hello.

"What?" Aoife felt her nerves tingle all the way down to her toes.

"Chloe. On Instagram. She commented on that picture of us."

Aoife hung up without saying goodbye and fumbled her way through her apps to find what she was looking for. There was a direct message in her inbox waiting for her before she even found the comment on the picture. Her hands were shaking as she opened it.

"Sam, Chloe just messaged me."

"Really? What, what... what did she say? Is it a good message?"

"It says, 'Hey Eef, love the pic. In town for a few days. Can we meet up tomorrow? I will be at your show on Saturday.'"

"She wants to meet with you!" Sam said excitedly. "Aoife!"

"I can't believe it. I've waited for this for so long and now I don't even know how to respond."

"Tell her yes! Send her your phone number and tell her you'd love to meet up with her."

Aoife did as she was told. Her mind was numb even though she felt adrenaline flood every corner of her nervous system. She didn't hear from Chloe again until after Sam dropped her home. A text came through, giving her an address to come to around noon the next day.

It felt strange calling Sarah for advice on what to wear to see Chloe, but she couldn't seem to make her brain function on a normal level. Sarah told her she was happy Chloe had contacted her and to let her know how it went. She made it sound so casual and normal, which eased Aoife's nerves, but also made her blink in surprise. There was nothing casual and normal about seeing Chloe Knight after six years of dead silence.

The address led Aoife to a hotel, a nice one, on the other side of London. She took a taxi and paid the man, wondering why Chloe had asked her to meet there. She would have thought Chloe would want to see the sites, visit the best places to eat, and be a tourist, but apparently not that day.

Aoife was led to a room at the end of a hall where there were no other guests. The woman who lead her to the room nodded and smiled at her sadly. Aoife drew her eyebrows together in confusion, but the lady didn't notice as she opened the door. She gave Aoife a tap on the shoulder to remind her to go in. The carpet was so thick Aoife couldn't hear her own footsteps as she walked past the closet and bathroom to the main part of the large, well-lit room. She turned the corner, and...

"Eef! Oh, Aoife! You're here!" A thin voice and loosely grabbing arms met Aoife, taking her by surprise.

"Chloe?" Aoife pushed back before she could even hug her friend; there was something too wrong about the way she felt, holding onto Aoife's neck and talking in a voice barely strong enough to be called a whisper. "Chloe, you're sick! Y-you're, you're sick! Chloe! Wh-what happened?"

"It's lovely to see you, Eef." Chloe tried to ignore the questions with a bright smile, but her face looked so tired and her expression soon faded. "Thank you for coming."

"Chloe, what's wrong with you?"

"That's a greeting," joked the girl. She felt around for the back of the nearby chair and leaned against it until she was settled down on the seat. "Where are your manners, Aoife Grace?"

"Chloe, stop." Tears pricked Aoife's eyes. "This isn't funny."

"Promise you won't leave when I tell you?"

"Chloe." Aoife's brow furrowed again. "Of course I promise."

Of course I promise.

"Leukemia. I have two months if God is generous."

And that was when Aoife hugged her friend, because she knew if she didn't hold onto Chloe, she would run from the room and never look back. She hugged her as tightly as she dared, feeling bones and sinew through the pale, clammy skin; the skin that was holding Chloe's sick body together. She cried and felt her friend put a comforting hand on her head, but Chloe's shoulders were shaking as well. They didn't rush their feelings, allowing the tears of what they missed in the past and what they would miss in the future to mix and bleed into a feeling Aoife had never known before.

"Love you, Chloe. So much," Aoife finally choked the words out. "Thank you for letting me see you."

"I didn't want to, you know." Chloe wiped her cheeks slowly, measuring the strength she had to spend on the simple task. "But you never got to say goodbye to your mom. I couldn't do that to you."

"Did your mom tell you she passed away?" Aoife settled on the floor by Chloe's feet, keeping herself as close to her friend as she could.

"Therese and I don't talk." Chloe shook her head. "I'm sorry, Eef. When did it happen?"

"I didn't find out until two months ago, but apparently it has been about two years. Your mom told me when she saw me at Peter and Alex's studio. I think she thought I already knew."

"Why didn't you know?"

Aoife shrugged. "Who knows."

"Sorry, Eef." Chloe frowned sympathetically. "And how is Therese?"

"I told her I hated her." Aoife grimaced.

"Good." Chloe gave a tired smile. "I haven't seen her for three years."

"Are you going to see her before..."

"Only if she comes to India."

"India? Chloe, what are you talking about?"

"I'm going there. This is just a stopover to rest my body." Chloe chuckled weakly at the surprise on Aoife's face. "I always wanted to go. If I don't go now, I'll miss my chance."

Aoife took a moment to let the words sink in. She tried to smile, but everything hurt. Not everything, but almost everything. When she left Chloe's side, then everything would hurt. Her confusion at the situation she was thrust into was evident in her eyes and Chloe reached out to touch the worry on her friend's face with shaking fingertips.

"You okay, Eef?"

"Chloe, where's Roe?" Aoife saw the flash of pain in Chloe's sweet hazel eyes and she wished the question wasn't a painful one.

178

"He always was like your baby after he was born, wasn't he?" Chloe's lips wobbled even as she tried to put on a brave face to go with her well-rehearsed answer. "He's with Dave, has been since his first birthday."

"Is that when you found out you were sick?"

"Oh, no." Chloe shook her head. Her eyes turned red with unshed tears. "I just couldn't do it. I didn't know how to be a mom. I'm still in his life, though. He knows me. We have long talks about life."

"He must be so big."

"Get my phone, I have pictures." Chloe gestured to her bedside table. "I wanted to show you."

"He looks like you when you were this age! Is he in school already?"

"Kindergarten. He has Dave's smile." Chloe's expression went wistful. "I always loved his smile."

"I'm guessing you're not with Dave anymore?" Aoife remembered just how in love Chloe had been with the father of her child.

"He told me we should break it off after my mom found out. Said it was too hard." A touch of sadness and bitterness told Aoife that her friend still wasn't over it. "You tried to warn me, Eef. Should have listened."

"I was fighting against Dave, I'm not surprised I lost." said Aoife with a small smile.

"I was a fool for him. Fell so hard I lost my mind in the process."

"You still love him?" asked Aoife gently.

Chloe nodded and closed her eyes just in time to shut the tears in. She reached for Aoife's hand and held it tightly. After a minute, she composed herself and opened her eyes again.

"Your boyfriend looks nice."

"He is nice." Aoife felt a little glow light up her eyes as she talked about Sam. "I really want you to meet him."

"Maybe at your performance tomorrow?"

"He's leaving in the morning for a trip. Can you meet him today?"

Chloe leaned back against the chair and nodded, her lips forming a smile. With her hand still in Chloe's, she pulled her phone out of her pocket to call Sam. He said he would be in a meeting for another half-hour and then drive straight there. Aoife thanked him and hung up. Chloe's eyes were still closed and Aoife studied how pronounced her cheekbones were because of the weight loss. Her eyes were sunken in her face and there was no more youthful glow on her countenance.

"Are you going to see Peter and Alex?" Aoife spoke quietly. "Chloe?"

"I'll see them tomorrow when I'm at your show."

Aoife wanted to fight Chloe's decision, but the look in her eye told Aoife that she was too tired, too worn out to spend more time telling people goodbye. Aoife squeezed Chloe's hand and forced her mouth shut. She knew Alex and Peter would want to say goodbye and have a moment with her before she was gone. It wasn't for her to decide, though.

"I can't think of a better last memory of my best friends than watching them all together on stage," said Chloe with labored breaths. "It will be perfect."

"Maybe they can see you after the show?" Aoife's throat was tight.

"Maybe." Chloe closed her eyes again. "I told Dave I would be giving you his number. I want you to look out for Roe for me, you and the boys."

"Of course." The request sent a sting of pain straight through Aoife's heart and it was all she could do to not burst into tears. "We would love to do that."

"I need people I trust to be there for him when Dave gets too old. I want to have people there for when he might have questions, you know, about me. You guys knew me better than anybody else. I figured you would be willing to do that for him... for me."

Aoife was glad Chloe's eyes were shut as tears trickled down her face. They sat quietly for a few more minutes. This was the easy silence Aoife had known with her best friend as kids. When they were both locked up in their own thoughts, they would just be together, sharing space and air, but alone in their own worlds.

"Eef, can you hand me my Polaroid camera?" asked Chloe, breaking the silence. "I want a picture of you to hang on the wall by my bed when I get to India."

She put the camera into Chloe's hands, remembering a different camera that had gone everywhere with them during their summer in Europe. Chloe had to use both hands to hold it up to her face. Aoife rested her chin on Chloe's knee and smiled big. She wanted her best friend to have that smile with her in her last days.

"Can I take a picture, too?" Aoife asked.

"No, Eef, I look so gross..."

"Please, Chloe. What if I just took one of our hands? I just... I want something to help me remember this wasn't a dream. Something to hold onto once you're..." Aoife couldn't make herself finish the sentence as she grabbed Chloe's hand in her own. She snapped the picture and showed Chloe how it turned out.

"I like this one." Chloe smiled. "Text it to me. I'll look at it when I'm lonely and wish you were there to hold my hand."

"Oh, Chloe." Aoife's voice broke. "You don't have to leave me. You can stay. I have three shows left and then I have a break and, and, and I can take care of you! I have an apartment in Brighton, that's a town by the sea. It's beautiful, and you'd love it. You can see the beach from the window and I have the coziest cushions in all of Brighton."

Chloe's lips twitched up into a sad smile.

"Maybe even in all of Great Britain." Aoife's eyes filled with tears.

"You almost have me convinced with the cushions." Aoife could tell that Chloe wasn't serious. "But I have to get to India. It's the only thing I'm holding on for."

Her hand tightened on Chloe's as she listened to her talk. She licked her lips and nodded.

"You're right. You've always wanted to go."

"You know how much I love you, Eef?" asked Chloe in a slow, sleepy voice.

"Not as much as I love you," Aoife whispered hoarsely.

"I know." Chloe's mouth turned down. "You gave up everything for me and Roe to help me stay in ballet in spite of the way I messed up my entire life."

"You were there for me when I needed someone."

"I never told you." Chloe opened her eyes and looked straight into Aoife's. "I used to be so angry at your mom, couldn't understand how she could suddenly just not love you when you loved her so much. Peter was always saying how much he loved your mom and how she had been a beautiful dancer, but I... I couldn't bring myself to forgive her for leaving you."

"It's okay."

"And then my mom..." Chloe's voice shook angrily. "She walked out on you and she didn't even have a disease to give her an excuse."

"It's okay, Chloe," Aoife tried to soothe her friend. "It's all worked out now."

"It's not okay," said Chloe, her eyes still holding Aoife's gaze. "She hurt you after taking you in and letting you think she was going to be the mom you didn't have. She screamed at you and said horrible things about you, and... I don't think I can ever forgive that."

"Don't take something like this to the grave, Chloe." Aoife sighed. "Yes, she hurt me very badly, but look what has come from it all? I'm here now. I live in London and I dance with Alex and Peter and I have wonderful friends and a great boyfriend. You can let it go."

"You still hate her." Chloe pulled up one side of her mouth into a twisted smile. "Don't try to be my priest. I'm not on my deathbed yet."

"Chloe, I'm making my peace with her. Eventually. Does she even know you're sick?"

"Insurance company told her." Chloe grimaced. "If she comes to India to find me, I'll make my peace with her."

"And if she doesn't... maybe write her a letter. Even if she's not going to read it until after..."

"You're not going to let this go, are you?"

"Death is forever, Chloe. Some things need to be said," was all Aoife said.

"Remember that song..." Chloe changed the subject with a little quirk of her lips. Her eyes slipped shut. "The song your mom taught you. It was about death."

"'Danny Boy.'" Aoife was surprised. Chloe had hated that song. "Of course I remember it."

"Sing it for me?"

"You hate that song." Aoife's throat filled with a lump and she tightened her grip on Chloe's hand.

"I've changed my mind about some things. Dying does that to a girl. Please sing it, Eef."

"I don't think I can." Aoife couldn't even swallow. There was a curl of anger in her stomach at Chloe saying she was dying. It was obviously true, but she shouldn't be saying it, at least not so calmly.

"I like the part where it says that Danny Boy will come back and find the grave." Chloe paused to take a breath. "And the person who died hears him say that he loves them."

"And I shall hear, though soft you tread above me," sang Aoife quietly. "And all my grave will warmer, sweeter be."

"Yes." Chloe nodded. "That part."

"For you will bend and tell me that you love me, and I shall sleep in peace until you come to me." Aoife watched her friend's face as she sang, tears in her eyes.

"Thanks, Eef." Chloe's eyes fluttered open long enough to show Aoife that she meant what she said. "I like to think that I'll hear you, hear Roe... hear my loved ones if they came to my grave."

"Is there no chance the Leukemia will go away?" Aoife knew it didn't work like that.

"Eef," sighed Chloe as she reached out to put a hand on Aoife's cheek.

As they waited for Sam to come, Aoife told Chloe about Tansy, Sarah, Max, and Martin. She told her about Miss Wilcox and how she had actually flown all the way from New York City to London for the opening night of her show. The ring on Aoife's left hand caught the light and Chloe brought it closer to study the design.

"It was my mom's. Do you remember it?"

"No," said Chloe shaking her head. "But it looks good on you. I like it."

"My dad found it when he was looking through my mom's things once we heard she was gone."

"I'm glad you have some pieces of her to carry with you." Chloe tried to smile, but she was too tired. "I wish I had a ring to give you."

"It's okay." Aoife kissed the back of Chloe's hand. "You'll always be a part of me."

"I have left a few things for you. Nothing big, obviously, but I wanted to make sure you got them when I was gone. Same with the boys. Just a little thank you for everything."

Sam arrived and Aoife greeted him with a hug and sad eyes. He shook Chloe's hand, said he had wanted to meet her and was happy for the chance. Chloe tried to be upbeat and energetic, but she could barely keep her eyes open. The visit only lasted a few minutes before Aoife knew it was time to go. She didn't want to leave, but she comforted herself with the fact that she would see Chloe one last time at her performance the next night.

"You'll tell the boys for me, won't you, Eef?" asked Chloe as she hugged her best friend goodbye. "That I love them with all my heart."

"You can tell them tomorrow, Chloe." Aoife tried to keep her tears at bay as she said goodbye. "And I'll tell you that I love you with all my heart tomorrow, so you better come."

"Nothing will stop me from being there. I promise, Aoife."

Aoife had to go straight to the theatre as soon as she was done. She kissed Sam goodbye and told him she would see him after the show. Tears tried to press through her walls, but she stayed strong, determined not to cry when Chloe was still alive. She could cry when her friend was gone.

It was difficult telling Peter and Alex about Chloe. They sat in Peter's dressing room in silence for several long moments. Even after losing her to distance all those years ago, Chloe's spot still felt empty and knowing she would never be joining them again made the spot gape wide open like a wound that would never close.

"This just isn't right," said Alex, looking at his friends. "She's our age. She's got a kid."

Peter nodded solemnly.

"I can't... I can't believe this." His hands went up to his head and he took several deep breaths to calm himself.

"I wonder if this is how Therese and Mariya felt after my mom left," murmured Aoife. "Like she should still be there."

"I'm sure." Peter slipped his arm around Aoife's shoulders. "She was important to them, just like Chloe is important to us."

"This isn't right," Alex muttered again.

"You saying that isn't going to change anything, Alex." There was a hard tone to Peter's voice.

"Thanks for the information, Peter! I wasn't aware of that!" Alex snapped back.

"Guys!" Aoife was shaking. "Don't."

Alex clamped his mouth shut and crossed his arms.

"I'm going to, uh, make sure we're alerted when she arrives." Peter cleared his throat. "Make sure we don't miss her."

"Good." Aoife nodded. "Come on, Alex. The show is going to start soon."

The grim expression of anger was still on Alex's face as Aoife led them backstage. The hustle and bustle around them did nothing to shift Alex's mood. Aoife stopped him and pulled on his arm until he was looking at her.

"Alex, it's going to be o-..."

"No, Aoife," said Alex. His voice was quiet, but firm. "It's not. Chloe is one of us! She's as important to me as you or Peter! She's gone through so much, and now this? No. I'm not like you, Aoife. I can't just accept things like this."

His words stung, because she felt like they were an implication that she didn't care. She did care, though. She cared so much she had to shut out part of the pain just to put one foot in front of the other. Alex wrapped his arms around Aoife in a hug, his whisper muffled against her shoulder. She didn't hear what he said, but she nodded anyway.

The show that night went smoothly despite the heavy hearts three of the dancers carried inside of them. It was the last weekend of shows and the house was packed. It was packed the next night as well for the second-to-last performance of *Giselle*. Alex bit his nails backstage as he waited for the girl in the ticket booth to tell them that Chloe had arrived. The show started and still no one came to tell them.

"She promised she would be here," cried Aoife, her emotions taut, like a string being stretched. "She promised. She said she wanted the last memory of us to be us dancing together on stage."

"Maybe she's sick." said Peter, his own eyes rimmed red with tears. "Intermission is almost over. Let's finish tonight and we'll go see her."

They agreed, doing their best to stay focused for the people who had paid money to watch the ballet. Aoife scanned the crowd as she bowed, thinking that maybe Chloe had come, had somehow slipped in unnoticed. It was impossible to see every face, and Aoife clung to the hope that maybe her friend had come after all.

"Her seat was empty. She never came," Peter said, coming into Aoife's dressing room as she changed. "I'm going to find Alex. We'll go see her as soon as you're ready."

Peter drove, taking directions from Aoife as she alternated between praying that Chloe had missed the show because she was sick and praying that she was okay. They arrived at the hotel and climbed out of the car. It was eerily quiet and Aoife slipped her arm around Peter's for comfort. He squeezed it against him, letting her know he was there.

"Excuse me, we're here to see Chloe Knight." Alex reached the lady at the reception desk first.

"One moment, please." The woman left the desk and walked over to another woman who was wearing a white jacket. She gestured at the three young adults by the desk as she spoke. They watched, waiting to see what the woman would say.

"Aoife Stewart?" the woman in the jacket asked.

"Yes?" Aoife's heart began to pound.

"Come with me. I'll take you to Nurse Jackie."

The woman who led Aoife to Chloe's room the day before looked up when her name was called.

"Jackie, Miss Stewart is here."

"Oh." Jackie walked over to them quickly. "I didn't even contact you yet."

"We came to see Chloe. She didn't come to the show tonight like she said she would." Aoife knew her voice was shaking.

"I'm sorry." Jackie's eyes filled with tears. "She passed away earlier today, around two pm."

Alex swore and covered his face with his hands.

"What?" Aoife felt her knees buckle. "But she said she had two more months! She said! She said she was going to India! She promised she would come tonight! She, she, she promised! She said!"

"Aoife." Peter tried to calm his friend.

"She was planning on going to the performance tonight. She had the ticket by her bed and even had me wash her hair." Tears slipped down Jackie's face as she spoke. "But she didn't have two more months. She wasn't going to India. She was lucky she made it here. She was holding on to say goodbye to you, Aoife."

"Why would she lie to me?" asked Aoife thickly.

"She told everyone she had two more months, ever since the doctor told her it could be any day. It was her way of coping."

There was the sound of something smacking against the wall as Alex groaned angrily. Aoife ignored it, her mind spinning with what she had just been told.

"But India." Aoife couldn't believe Chloe was gone.

"She didn't care about India, just seeing you. She had been planning this trip for months. Tried to come sooner, but she got pneumonia and almost died. Hung on, though. Had to see her Eef."

"I can't believe it." Aoife buried her face in Peter's chest. "No! No, it's not true! I-it's not."

"Would you like to see the body?" asked Jackie sympathetically.

"No," said Alex, his voice gruff and eyes wet. "I, at least, would like to remember her how she was. She would want that. I don't want to see what the Leukemia did to her."

"C-can I see her room?" Aoife sniffed and wiped her eyes.

"Of course. Her body is covered, so you don't have to see it if you don't want to."

Jackie led them into the room where Aoife had been the day before. Sure enough, there on the bedside table was the ticket. Aoife choked up at the sight. Pinned to the wall by her pillow were three Polaroids. One was of Aoife from the day before, the other of Dave and Roe when the boy was probably three years old, and the last one a picture of a post Alex had put on Instagram a few weeks earlier. It was of Alex and Peter cheesing for the camera after a show, their faces red and sweaty and makeup smeared in a half-washed-off state. The picture was terrible quality, but it showed their faces, and Aoife knew that was all that mattered. She pointed it out to her friends and they smiled through their tears.

"I'm glad she's not hurting anymore," said Peter as he pulled the picture off the wall. "Not from sickness, or Dave, or her mom... She's free from all that."

"She didn't deserve any of it. She went through more than was her fair share of pain." Alex pressed his fingers against his eyes to keep his tears from falling. "And it's not fair that it ended like this."

"She loves you with all her heart," whispered Aoife, remembering what Chloe had asked her to tell the boys. "She told me to tell you."

"Love you, too, Chloe," Alex said as he put a gentle hand on the sheet that was covering Chloe's body. "Love you."

Peter said nothing, his eyes filling with tears and lips trembling. He stared down at the bed, as if he was imagining what Chloe looked like under the sheet. His Adam's Apple bobbed as he swallowed. After a moment, he hid his eyes with one hand and dropped to his knees beside the bed. He cried, unable to hold back his grief any longer. Alex was by his side in an instant, a firm hand on his shoulder. He reached for Aoife with his free hand. She let him squeeze her fingers, but she didn't feel very comforted. They would never be all together ever again.

They didn't stay long, just long enough to take a small bag of personal things Chloe instructed Jackie to give to Aoife after she was gone. Dave and Roe had been notified earlier and were trying to find a flight from New York that would get them to London in the next few days.

"Chloe made me promise I wouldn't tell you until after your show if she didn't make it tonight," said Jackie with one last sorrowful smile. "She talked about you three and her baby all day long. You made her world go around."

"Thank you for taking care of her." Aoife hugged the woman. She could see that Jackie would miss her friend as much as she would. "I can't tell you how much that means to me."

"She was a very special girl," the nurse replied. "I'll be in touch if anything comes up."

Aoife posted the picture of her and Chloe holding hands when they were back in the car. She captioned it, "*best friends forever. I love you with all my heart*" because she had promised that she would tell her. There was a stack of Polaroids in the bag of Chloe's things, and Aoife recognized the top one as the four friends outside the airport in New York City, the day they left on their trip.

"We were babies," she said as she showed Peter and Alex. There were smudges on the reflective surface that spoke of the many times their friend had looked at their faces and remembered them. "We had no idea what was about to happen."

"I think she was actually happy then," said Alex from the backseat.

Aoife looked at their wide grins and nodded. They had all been happy back then. She smiled softly as she thought about the fact that she had been part of Chloe's happiness.

Her call to Sam went through to voicemail. She left a message and then called Sarah. Despite the late hour, Sarah told Aoife she would drive down right away and spend the night with her.

Having Sarah's warm presence beside her was what gave Aoife the strength to make it through. Sam offered to come home early when he called her back, but Aoife told him that Sarah was with her and she would see him when he flew in on Wednesday.

"You have important things to do, Sam. I want you to be able to do them," said Aoife.

"I know, but I... I love you, Aoife, and I want to be there for you." Sam sounded slightly frustrated by the decision. "I didn't want to tell you that I loved you for the first time over the phone, but I want you to know. I'll come back early if you need me to."

"I love you, too, Sam." Aoife felt a tiny bit of pain melt away. She wished she could see his face. "Sarah will take good care of me until you come back."

The final performance of *Giselle* was an emotional one for the three friends. They danced harder than they ever had for themselves and for their missing loved ones. Aoife thought of her mom, who had given her the gift of dance and nurtured that gift when she was little. When she closed her eyes, she could imagine Chloe there on the stage with her, just like she had been her whole life. She couldn't hold back her tears at the final bow. She would never dance with Chloe again.

-Chapter 12-
The Sea

Aoife drove with Sarah back to Brighton that night. The drive was quiet and tense, and Aoife was thankful to finally see the sea again.

"You need me to stay?" asked Sarah, dark circles under her normally bright eyes.

"No," Aoife said with a smile. She hugged her friend and climbed out of the car. She watched until Sarah drove around the corner.

Everything was dark and quiet as Aoife looked around. She took a deep breath and let it out slowly. It was humid, but cool. The street light on the corner made it impossible to see the stars. She left her bags at the bottom of the stairs in her building and walked across the street to the beach. She walked until the water washed over her feet and sandals, chilling her skin. It felt like she was so far away from everyone and everything down on the rocks with the water moving around her.

"I hate this," Aoife said only loud enough for herself to hear. She clenched her fists and stared out into the darkness. "I hate this."

Another wave touched her feet and Aoife felt tears fill her eyes. Over and over the waves came back. Each one reminded her that she was alone and Chloe was gone. The anger that Aoife had shoved down when Chloe told her she was sick bubbled up and Aoife shouted out at the sea.

"Why? Why did this have to happen?!"

She didn't care that the sea was bigger than her pain, and she didn't care that the waves of life could wash her clean. She wanted her best friend to come back. Tears rushed in hot, angry streams down her cheeks and she gritted her teeth together to try to keep herself from screaming. Her stomach churned and she thought she was going to be sick she was crying so hard.

"This isn't fair!" Aoife cried. She looked up at the sky and shouted again. "It's not fair! She was my best friend!"

She would have kept shouting, but someone put a hand on her shoulder.

"Shouting helps a little," said Martin in a quiet voice. "Relieves the pressure."

"How did you know I was here?" Aoife didn't turn to face her friend.

"Sarah." Martin stepped closer so he was beside Aoife. "Said she thought you might come here."

"I'm fine."

"I had a certain spot I would go after my mum's accident," said Martin as if he hadn't heard Aoife. "I would drive there after bad days and just scream as hard as I could for five minutes. Then I would cry."

Aoife finally turned to look at Martin. He wasn't much more than a shadowy figure on the dark beach, but she could imagine the kindness in his eyes as he spoke.

"After I felt like there was nothing left inside of me, I would drive back home and take care of Shan."

"How old were you when your mom had her accident?"

"Nineteen. It was one of the hardest days of my life. My dad was already gone, so it was just the three of us. My mum was the glue in our family, and knowing that I might lose her..." Martin's voice broke. "I was angry for a very long time."

"I'm sorry," whispered Aoife. "That wasn't fair."

"No." Martin shook his head. "But that's how it goes sometimes. Life isn't fair, and it's okay to be angry about it. Just don't let the anger turn you into an angry person."

"I hate missing her."

"Scream it."

Aoife paused. She didn't feel the need to scream anymore. She looked at Martin.

"It's okay. It comes in waves," he said.

Like the sea, thought Aoife as she nodded and wiped the tears from her face. She looked out at the water one more time before turning. Martin fell into step beside her, quiet and comforting at the same time.

"Thank you," said Aoife once they reached the road. His car was parked on the curb. She hugged him when he reached out his arms towards her. "I needed someone to tell me those things."

"Scream as often as you need." Martin ended the hug with a single pat to her head.

Aoife lay in bed that night thinking about how many things came in waves. Pain, anger, sadness, life... They would ebb and flow forever. Sarah came over the following afternoon when Aoife was trying to unpack her things. She had a couple weeks before she moved back to London to start discussing new projects with Alex and Peter.

"What are you going to do when it's time to move out of this place?" asked Sarah.

"I don't know." Aoife looked around. "I love it here. I can't imagine not having it to escape to on odd days and weeks off."

"I know." Sarah's eyes were on the picture of Rebecca that hung on the wall opposite the window. "It needs more furniture, but this place is you. If you left it, there would be a part of you missing."

"My view from the window." Aoife gave a sad smile.

"I've started going to the beach when I'm having bad days, staring at the sea and letting it calm me down," said Sarah with a slightly sheepish smile.

"Bad days?" Aoife's eyes filled with concern.

"I've had some heavy thoughts going around my head these past couple weeks."

"What's wrong?" Aoife left her suitcase and walked over to where Sarah was standing by the window. "Is everything okay?"

Sarah hesitated before answering.

"Max is ready to try for kids, but I don't feel ready yet."

"Sarah." Aoife's surprise showed in her voice. "But you... last year, with Tansy... What happened?"

"Tansy happened!" Sarah gave a sardonic laugh. "I watched you with her and I realized babies aren't just about when they're cute, they're about every moment of every day. I saw what happened with Shan, and I heard about your mum, and then Therese, and I just... I'm not ready. What if I do the same thing?"

"Sarah," Aoife spoke her friend's name fondly. "My mom was a great mom. The only thing that happened was she became sick. Same with Shan, you know that. Therese made her choices, but I know you, Sarah, and I know you wouldn't make choices like that."

"I know it's dumb, but I can't think about being a mum without thinking I might get sick, too." Sarah's eyes watered and she forced the tears away. She let Aoife hug her tightly.

"If you do get sick, you have a whole team of people around you who will make sure your baby is loved and taken care of, but I know you're going to be great when you are ready to have children."

"Thanks, Aoife." Sarah wiped her eyes as she stepped back from the hug. "I'm really glad we're friends."

"Me, too." Aoife smiled. "You have no idea how glad."

"I never told you this, but I almost didn't introduce you to Sam that night at the pub."

"How come?"

"Because I really liked you and I wanted Sam to like you, but he never fancied the girls I tried to set him up with in the past. I was afraid that if I tried to set you two up, he wouldn't like you and I was so sure you would be great together."

"I guess I was wrong about you not being a good matchmaker." Aoife blushed as she smiled.

There was a pause before Sarah spoke again.

"What would you say if he asked you to marry him?"

Aoife was quiet for a moment. Sarah had asked the question in all seriousness, not to squeal over or whisper about later, but as a friend who cared very much about Aoife's future happiness.

"I would say yes," she said with a little nod.

"You would?" Sarah smiled. "Even though you've only been together for a few months?"

"I know Sam isn't perfect and he has his faults, but I also know he's the kind of guy you don't just let go of." Aoife looked down as she answered. "He's sweet, honest and thoughtful. He loves what he does and cares about people. I would be pretty foolish to give up a guy like that."

"He is a pretty good guy, isn't he?" Sarah watched Aoife with a smile.

"Do you think he'll ask me to marry him?" Aoife couldn't deny the way her heart fluttered as she said the words.

"He'd better," Sarah said with wide, serious eyes. "Because if he lets you get away..."

Aoife laughed lightly and turned to look at her phone where it buzzed on the table. It was Peter. Sarah saw the picture on the screen.

"Do you need me to leave?"

"No, he's just calling to tell me he's picked up Dave and Roe at the airport." Aoife answered the call. "Right?"

"Are you with Sarah?" Peter chuckled, having heard what Aoife said.

"Yeah, she's helping me unpack."

"Tell her I say hello," said Peter. "And yes, I'm heading to my place with Dave and Roe as soon as they are done in the bathroom."

"Okay, I'll finish up here and catch the train."

"Eef, Roe is huge. He is adorable and really bright."

"I can't wait to see him," said Aoife with a smile. "See you all in a bit."

"They here to get Chloe's body?" asked Sarah in a soft voice once Aoife had hung up.

"No, we're having a memorial service tomorrow." Aoife's eyes went sad as she spoke. "Chloe said we should keep her body wherever she ended up dying. Said trying to move it someplace else after she was already gone was a waste of money."

"Is she going to be buried here?"

Aoife shook her head no.

"No, uh, she wanted to be cremated and a few people will get a portion of the ashes to scatter in a place that is meaningful and special to them."

"Are you one of the people?"

Aoife nodded.

"I guess since she wasn't close to her family it makes sense. Is her family coming?"

"I don't know." Aoife pressed her mouth into a frown. "I called her brother and told him everyone was invited if they wanted to come. I don't know if they will or not. Things between them were really bad last I knew."

"That means you might have to see Therese."

"I know." Aoife had thought about letting the mother go for years without finding out that her daughter was gone, just like she had let Aoife go for years without knowing her mother had died. It didn't set right in her heart, though, and she knew she couldn't do that.

"Are you nervous to see Roe?"

"Not really." Aoife answered honestly. She had had a couple days to prepare herself to see the little boy she once loved as her own. "I know he won't remember me, but I'm thankful I'll get to be in his life again. A second chance."

"I'm really happy you get that, Aoife. He's a lucky kid."

"Thanks." Aoife pulled Sarah into a hug. "I'll see you when I come back from London."

"Call me if you need anything," said Sarah as she walked down the stairs with Aoife. She carried Aoife's overnight bag for her. "Martin will let me take time off from the shop."

"I will." And Aoife would, too, because Sarah was dear to her heart and she trusted her to be the kind of friend she could keep in her life forever.

Forever.

It was a nice thought.

Aoife kept her mind busy with other things during the train ride to London. She made lists of what she needed to buy for the apartment, wrote a letter to Miss Wilcox, and ordered a welcome home present for Sam. It was a silly, romantic gesture, but she found herself not being too bothered by that as she pushed the button on her phone to order the new pair of shoes Sam had been looking at a couple weeks ago. There was a safe, happy feeling in her heart when she thought about him, especially after Sarah's question about marriage.

The others were at Peter and Alex's apartment when Aoife arrived into town. She took a taxi to their place and stood on the sidewalk for a minute before going inside. After a few deep breaths, she rang the bell and heard

Alex say he was letting her up. She was glad Alex was the one who answered the door. She hugged him before looking around the room for the two newcomers.

"You okay?" asked Alex, staring hard at her as her eyes darted around her surroundings.

"Yeah, I'm good." Aoife put a hand on his arm and gave it a squeeze before following the sound of a child laughing from the back bedroom.

There on the bed with their heads bent over a book about trucks were Peter and Roe. Leave it to Peter to have presents for the boy. Aoife stood in the doorway and watched, her heart swelling and aching all at the same time. She had pictured moments like this after Roe was born- all of them together in one place just like in Milan, but she had always pictured Chloe with them. There was a lump in her throat when Peter noticed her and looked up. He gave her a wink and nudged the boy with his elbow.

"Looks like you have a visitor," he said.

Roe's big, green eyes glanced up and he smiled. Chloe was right; he did have Dave's smile. Aoife waved shyly as she stepped into the room and found a seat on the edge of the bed on his other side. With a hand that was suddenly shaking despite her best intentions, Aoife reached up and touched the boy's straight, blonde hair. His smile deepened and Aoife saw the face of her best friend looking up at her.

"Hi, Roe," she breathed out, her heart beating too quickly for her to properly say anything.

"I know who you are," said Roe, his little baby teeth showing as he grinned. "You're the one who was like my mommy right after I was born."

"Oh!" Aoife looked to Peter, but he was too busy staring at Roe.

"Mommy told me. She said you loved me best when I was born."

"That's not true." Aoife shook her head and drew her eyebrows together. "I just helped your mom, she loved you best."

"Mommy said you'd say that," Roe giggled and scrunched a little smaller, as if saying so made him feel bashful. "She said to not believe you. She showed me pictures."

"You're a lot bigger now," said Aoife, allowing the subject to change. She would think about that later.

"I'm six now!"

"I know." Aoife's eyes misted over. "You're all grown up and probably know so many things."

"I know a lot about dinosaurs," said Roe with big eyes. "Daddy reads me books about them all the time."

"Have you ever seen one?"

"Just the ones in the museum." Roe's face grew pensive. "I don't think you can see them in other places."

"Which one is your favorite?"

"The Pterodactyl, of course," the child chirped out, looking from Aoife to Peter and back.

"Of course!" Peter lifted his hands as if the answer was an obvious one.

"They can fly and they ate fish. I like eating fish."

"Maybe we can read a book about Pterodactyls together someday," said Aoife, putting her hand to the back of his head, cradling it for a moment like she used to when he was little. The curve of his skull used to fit so perfectly against her palm, and now he was so big.

"Uncle Peter got me a dinosaur book." Roe pointed to another book sitting by Peter on the bed. "I don't know how to read, so I can only look at the pictures."

"I'll read it to you." Aoife smiled.

"Thanks, Aunt Aoife."

Aoife nodded, her throat too tight to respond. Peter reached behind the child and gave Aoife's shoulder a squeeze before he stood up and walked out of the room.

"I'll go check on your dad," he said as he left.

There was silence in the little bedroom for a minute before Roe looked back up at Aoife. He wasn't smiling, and his eyes were steady on hers, reading her every expression.

"Did you talk to my mommy before she died?" he asked. "She missed you the most. She said she just wanted to talk to you one more time."

"She did." Aoife bit her bottom lip to try to keep it from shaking.

"I prayed that she would see you." Roe looked away.

"Thank you for that," said Aoife quietly. "Your mommy loved you very much."

"I know." Roe sighed. "I wish she didn't have to die. Daddy says it's better now because she's not sick and she can dance again."

"I suppose that is true."

"Aunt Aoife, do I have to dance to be like mommy?"

"No, buddy." Aoife scooted closer to him on the bed. "You are like your mommy just by doing what you love. If you want to dance, you can dance, or if you want to study dinosaurs, you can study dinosaurs."

"Nah." Roe scrunched up his nose as he shook his head. "I don't want to study dinosaurs. I want to fly like pterodactyls."

Aoife smiled down at the boy and slipped her arm around his shoulders. She didn't know how much Chloe and Dave told him about her, but he seemed comfortable with her, as if she were someone he saw regularly, instead of someone he hadn't seen since he was three months old. He leaned against her and sighed.

"Aunt Aoife?"

"Yeah, buddy?"

"Can I hold your hand at the funeral tomorrow?"

Tears trickled down Aoife's cheeks at the child's question. She bent down and pressed a kiss against the top of his head, smelling the fruity aroma of his shampoo.

"Of course you can," she squeezed her words past the lump in her throat.

"Thanks. I know daddy is sad that mommy is gone, but mommy said you loved her best, second after me. I think we should stand together."

"Mmm." Aoife nodded.

Alex came to get them for supper. He saw Aoife's red eyes and Roe's sad face and chuckled lightly as he walked into the room. He sat on Roe's other side and reached his arms around them both in a hug.

"Come on, you two. Let's eat supper. No more long faces today."

"I think Aunt Aoife needs some chocolate." Roe looked up at Alex seriously.

"You think, huh?" Alex's eyes crinkled with his smile. "Who taught you things like this? You're the smartest kid I've ever met in my life."

"Mommy told me about the chocolate."

"That doesn't surprise me." Alex laughed and looked over at Aoife as she wiped her eyes. "Come on, let's get you some chocolate."

Everyone tried to keep the mood light at the meal, mostly focusing on Roe and his incredible ability to hold a conversation with them despite his young age. Dave was a good dad, listening to his son, answering his questions and engaging with him in whatever subject he brought up. Aoife sat quietly, wishing Sam were back already instead of having to wait two more days to have him with her.

After supper, Aoife asked Alex if she could borrow his car. She drove to Sam and Conor's apartment. Conor was there, having come back early from Portugal due to another engagement he couldn't cancel. He was surprised to see Aoife when he answered the door. With a few tears in her eyes she explained how she just needed to borrow one of Sam's jumpers because she didn't have any of his to wear whilst he was away. Conor put an arm around her shoulders to lead her to Sam's room and opened the closet for her. She picked her favorite salmon-colored one and pulled it over her head.

"Would you like some tea?" asked Conor kindly.

"That sounds really nice, actually."

Conor talked about how busy life was, how great it was to be playing that season and about a girl he had been talking to for a while. He wasn't his normal hyper, goofy self, but was calm and friendly which was exactly what Aoife needed right then. When she went to leave, Conor hugged her and told her he was sorry about her friend.

"Thanks, Conor." Aoife remembered that Chloe was gone all over again and had to take a couple deep breaths to steady herself.

Those deep breaths and the small hand of the boy she had taken care of for three months, two weeks and five days were all Aoife had to cling to during Chloe's service. He stood beside her bravely, keeping his eyes straight ahead on the framed picture of Chloe. None of her family came and it ended up just being Dave, Roe, Peter, Alex, herself, and some of the medical staff who had cared for Chloe. Aoife stared at the picture of her and Chloe holding hands— the only piece of evidence she had that she had really seen her best friend just six days earlier.

The ashes were already there for the people Chloe had chosen. There were five of them: Roe, Peter, Alex, Jackie and Aoife. They all knew where their ashes would go and why. It was a somber, serious group that emerged from the room to go their separate ways. Dave and Roe were flying to Italy. The little boy wanted to see where he had been born.

"I want to see where you took care of me, Aunt Aoife," he told her as he hugged her goodbye. "Mommy said I was really special to you."

"You'll always be special to me, Roe. I love you, buddy." Aoife put her hands on his cheeks. "Always. And if you miss me, just look at the sea and know that I think of you when I look at the sea."

"How come?"

"It just reminds me of you. The sea is free and big, just like your heart."

Roe smiled at that. He stood on his tiptoes and pressed a kiss on Aoife's cheek. He waved at her over his shoulder as he jogged over to his dad. Dave was holding the ashes carefully, but Roe reached for them. The child cradled them against his chest as if he was carrying a treasure.

"Do you remember Chloe when she was that age?" asked Peter as he stepped up beside Aoife.

"Mmm." Aoife nodded. "She was always the smartest out of all of us. I knew Roe would be like her."

"I always thought Dave was really smart, but I'm realizing now it was just because he was so much older than us."

"He's a good listener," said Aoife. "And that's important."

"Roe is a good boy. I'm glad he's back in our lives." Peter hugged Aoife.

Three months, two weeks and...

No. Roe was forever now. Again. Still. She would forever carry that little boy in her heart, loving him in the way that only she knew how. Chloe was gone, but her child was still there and Aoife would stay in his life for as long as he let her.

Forever.

Aoife took the train back to Brighton and called Sarah to pick her up from the station. Martin was with Sarah in the car when they arrived. He gave Aoife a big hug and sat with her in the backseat, giving her a shoulder to lean on. They rode in silence, the car squeaking as it went over bumps seeming so loud. Aoife wondered if Martin had closed down his whole shop just to make sure she had her friends if she needed them. She reached over and squeezed his hand at the thought. Once they arrived at her apartment, the two friends went up to make Aoife some tea while Aoife walked across the street to the beach.

There was no one close by as she located a spot to say her final farewell to Chloe. The box of ashes was in her hands, and she tried to focus on what Chloe looked like instead of the fact that her friend was in the box. It wasn't working, and Aoife felt her throat aching and eyes burning. But then...

There was the sea. It was there like an old friend who helped you recover after a long day. The sight of the blue and white waves lapping at the shore was familiar and steady, reminding Aoife that no matter how big pain and life felt, she was so small and it was going to be okay. It was such a calm, sunny day; so opposite of how Aoife felt on the inside.

"Look at the sea, wee one."

A sad smile tugged at the corners of Aoife's lips. Perhaps Chloe didn't know just how much the sea meant to Aoife, or why, but they had spent their summers together on beaches all around the globe. Chloe loved jumping into the waves, coming up out of the water shrieking because it was freezing. She loved seeing how far out she could go and still touch the bottom. That was Chloe: all in.

Aoife took off her shoes and her socks, left her phone with them, and walked into the sea. She waded out until the cold water was up to her waist and the rocks on the bottom were poking into her feet. She paused for a moment. The waves rolled around her, soft and gentle, encouraging her to go deeper. Deeper and deeper she went until a wave crashed over her head. Her feet left the bottom, and she swam forward with one arm, the other holding the box against her body.

"You'll tell the boys for me, won't you, Eef?" Chloe's words echoed through her mind as she swam, her lungs beginning to beg for air. *"That I love them with all my heart."*

"You can tell them tomorrow, Chloe."

The box holding the ashes opened and Aoife felt the ashes float out into the sea. She pushed herself up to the surface and took a deep breath. She looked down in the box as she moved her legs to tread water and saw it was empty.

"You know how much I love you, Eef?"

"Not as much as I love you."

"I know."

If she were Chloe, she would be laughing about something, calling out to anyone close to her to tell them what she was thinking. Aoife realized how lucky she was to have been able to hear so many of Chloe Knight's thoughts during her short life on earth. Chloe was brave, passionate, loyal and smart. She lived life with abandon, feeling things deeply and fighting for what she loved. For a long time she had loved ballet and Aoife and her mom. Then things changed and she loved Dave and the idea of freedom from a cage she didn't realize she had been trapped inside of her whole life.

"Goodbye, Chloe."

Scream it.

"I hate missing you!" Aoife's heart and voice broke as she screamed her words. She slipped back under the water again for a moment, letting it surround her on every side. When she came back up, she gasped for air and spit out the salty taste on her tongue.

The glint of her ring caught her eye and Aoife stared down at it. Chloe had liked it. It had been years since her everyday life was touched by Chloe's words and opinions. A tear slipped down her cheek and Aoife thought about her mom.

In a week she would be flying to Dublin to look at her mother's things that were there. It wouldn't bring her mother back, but it would be nice to see some of the things Rebecca used to own. She twisted the ring on her finger, her feet still kicking to keep her afloat. Life had changed so much since that first day when she looked out the window of the apartment. She felt like a new person, her soul being washed over and over by the waves of life until she was shiny and smooth like the rocks on the beach.

"Miss you, mam," whispered Aoife, her eyes darting up to the blue of the sky.

"Do you know where your name came from?" her second-grade teacher had asked. If only she could go back in time and stand proudly before the class and say that her mother had named her, and that her name was special because it reminded her mother of Ireland. It was special because she was named after her grandmother, a woman who had done many grand and

exciting things. She couldn't, though, just like she couldn't go back and change the fact that she never told her mom that she loved her the last time she saw her in her right mind. Peter always said that Rebecca knew Aoife loved her whether she said it or not. He was probably right.

With the box under her arm, Aoife headed back to shore. Her heart felt heavy, but she knew it was going to be okay. If her time in Brighton had taught her anything, it was that sometimes things came back to you and became a forever in your life again. The salt of the sea dripped on her lips and she tasted it on her tongue. Her feet touched the bottom once more and she walked slowly up the beach, her clothes dripping and stuck against her skin.

She paused once she was out of the reach of the waves and turned to look back out at the water. Even though she would never be sure if her mother knew how she felt about her, she was thankful Chloe had known. It wouldn't be years too late before she heard about Chloe's death from someone who used to treat her as a daughter and now hated her, and Aoife was glad for that.

It wasn't a complete surprise Chloe's family hadn't shown up to the funeral, but Aoife had hoped Therese would prove them all wrong. Maybe it was just for the fact that she had encouraged Chloe to forgive her mother and make peace with the pain that Therese inflicted on her heart. She wondered if Chloe let go of the past before the very end, or if the hurt was still deep until her last breath. Therese had ruined so many things.

Ruined?

Maybe not, thought Aoife with a small smile on her face. She bent over and picked up her shoes and her phone. There she was, in ballet again, dancing on stage alongside Peter and Alex, doing what she had once felt was gone from her forever. Even Roe was back. But besides all of the things she had lost, she had new things, too. She had Martin and Sarah. She had Tansy. She had Sam. She also had her dad.

The sea pounded the rocks behind her, its gentle rhythm following Aoife across the street to her apartment. She was still dripping salty water from her clothes as she walked up the staircase, her bare feet leaving footprints behind her as a testimony of where she had been. Perhaps after Aoife left that place someone new would move in, someone who needed a fresh start, and maybe they would find the salty traces of Aoife's steps there on the stairs. Maybe there would still be a whisper of Aoife's voice murmuring in the room, urging them to look to the sea.

It's all going to be okay, the whisper would say to anyone who stopped to listen. *It doesn't matter how big or hard or painful life may seem, we're going to be okay. The waves of life can wash us clean.*

It's all going to be okay...

The End.

Made in the USA
Lexington, KY
23 January 2017